'Shuah,' he murmure

'Yes, Murray. Oh,

Again she brought

touched, he grasped h

really kissing her no

awake, as the hunge.

that was consuming her. There was no denying the frenzied passion that flared between them. He rolled over, his body half-covering hers, and his hands resumed their caressing and exploring, sensually and with an increasing urgency that brooked no denial—even had she wanted to.

'Shuah?' He said her name again, and there was a questioning note in his voice.

'Yes, Murray. I'm here.'

'Good God!' He sat up abruptly, pushed her away, and stared at her in utter disbelief. His mouth dropped open, only to be closed with a furious snap a moment later. 'I thought I was dreaming!' he exclaimed. 'How the hell did you get here?'

'I came on the train, Murray. And climbed in through the window.'

Olga Daniels was born in Norfolk and still lives there in a Broadland village. Her home is a picturesque flint and thatched farmhouse dating from the fifteenth century which she and her husband renovated from a near-derelict condition. She has been writing for many years—articles, stories, books and has also visualised for children's comics. She has three sons and her interests include English folk dancing, rambling and gardening.

She has written three other Masquerade Historical Romances—*Lord of Leet Castle*, *The Gretna Bride* and *The Bride from Faraway*.

THE UNTAMED BRIDE

Olga Daniels

MILLS & BOON LIMITED
ETON HOUSE   18-24 PARADISE ROAD
RICHMOND   SURREY   TW9 1SR

First published in Great Britain 1988 by Mills & Boon Limited

© Olga Daniels 1988

Australian copyright 1988 Philippine copyright 1988 This edition 1988

ISBN 0 263 76257 2

Set in Times Roman 10 on 10¾ pt. 04-8811-80440 C

Made and printed in Great Britain

FOREWORD

THE HUGE and beautiful island of Borneo lies in the romantic South China Sea and Sarawak is on its northeastern border. The white-fringed blue sea rolls on to its tropical shoreline edged by casuarina trees and nipa palms, while inland is the rich vegetation of tall rainforest. A hundred shades of green blend to form a continuous layer of leafy canopy, slashed by rivers which flow slowly to the sea.

It was to Kuching, the capital of Sarawak, that James Brooke sailed in 1839 to carry thanks from the Governor of Singapore to the raja for help he had given to some shipwrecked British sailors. James Brooke, an Englishman, was born in India and had a deep-rooted love of the east and its people, which stayed with him for the whole of his life. Sarawak was then a province of the Sultan of Brunei but its people were in rebellion against the misrule of the head of the army, and the Sultan's nephew, Raja Muda Hassim, was attempting, without success, to restore order.

Hassim tried to persuade James Brooke to help him. At first he refused, feeling that he had no right to interfere, but a year later Hassim asked him again and promised that if he was successful he should be given the governorship of the country as a reward. He agreed and with only a small force of men was able to crush the revolt very quickly, since most of the rebels were willing to surrender on condition that James Brooke was indeed made their raja.

So began the dynasty of the 'White Rajas', which lasted for over a hundred years. James Brooke enlisted a corps of bright, energetic young men to govern the various districts of his land and introduce law and order to the native tribes. Their first tasks were to wipe out piracy, and to stop both the slave-trade and the practice of head-hunting. James Brooke was fond of his people and, with the assistance of his Resident and District Officers, worked to bring peace and prosperity to the land.

James Brooke never married and he handed over the reins of government to his nephew, Charles, who carried on many of the same traditions, including governing with a council in which there was a native majority. As a young man Charles Brooke had been a District Officer in his uncle's service. He was one of many young men who guarded remote outposts, administering justice and keeping the peace. They went out in their early twenties and could look forward to home leave only once in five years, making the long voyage home via Singapore. The Raja's rules did not permit them to marry until they had completed two terms of service. They lived lonely lives and had great responsibilities, governing vast areas where tribal longhouses could be reached only by boat, and hot, tiring treks through dense jungle.

In just such a remote village Murray Masterson, Resident Officer of the Fourth Division, found Shuah.

CHAPTER ONE

MURRAY MASTERSON, Resident Officer of the Fourth Division, strode along the jungle path, followed by a dozen barefooted soldiers of the Sarawak army. He carried a rifle and had a large sheath-knife and a pistol at his belt. He was almost as sure-footed as the Malays on the rough track over the wet ground, where the roots of huge trees snaked across, the soil worn bare by the feet of people from the kampong. They must be getting near now, after two days' walking from the last village, for he could hear dogs barking and the snorting of pigs.

He had been in the Sarawak Service for ten years, had come straight out after graduating from Cambridge with first class honours in English and history in 1891. Almost a third of his life had been spent away from his own people and culture in the sweating tropical dampness of this alien land, in this interminable jungle that had begun to take hold of his soul. The muddy rank smell of it was all around him now—and silence, except for the occasional cry of a bird and the chattering of monkeys. The natives moved soundlessly, a little apprehensive. Bartulu, this village they were approaching, had not been visited by the white *tuan* recently, and there had been rumours of trouble between its warriors and those of a neighbouring village. The previous Resident from whom Murray Masterson had recently taken over had been, if not neglectful, certainly a trifle careless in his administration. He had given way beneath the strain of loneliness and tension, and Masterson had no intention of allowing such a fate to overtake him. A brilliant red bird streaked from left to right ahead of them and one of the

Malays muttered a few words. Murray held up his hand for silence.

'That was a good omen,' he pronounced, so definitely that they had to believe him. They would have allowed superstition to rule his life as well as their own, if he allowed them.

At last the roofs of houses came into sight and the path was marked by a line of slippery planks leading towards the longhouses, for there were two of them, side by side, almost adjoining. They were built on stilts, standing high on ground that rose from the bank of a stream, brightened by a clump of scarlet cannas. In front was a pool, made by damming the stream just beyond where a wooden footbridge crossed it.

A group of young women were in the pool; the water reached to their thighs, brightly-coloured sarongs clung to their nubile hips, tied close round their waists, above which they were bare. Their breasts, coffee-coloured, shone from immersion in the water, as did the straight black hair that streamed down their shoulders. They were engaged in some sort of frolic, splashing each other and laughing. They did not immediately see Masterson and his men and he slowed his steps, reluctant to disturb the natural spontaneity of the scene. It was pleasing to his eyes, the sight of women's breasts so familiar that it no longer stirred him as it had when he first came to this land where moral values were so very different from those of his own people in Victorian England. He would have regarded the pretty scene as simply a pleasing picture of life in Sarawak—but his eyes lighted on one particular girl, and the sight of her held him riveted to the spot.

Totally different from all her black-haired, black-eyed companions, she stood fully a head taller than any of them, with thick golden-red hair rippling over her shoulders, its rich colour unmistakable even though it was wet. This girl's skin, though tanned, was several shades lighter than that of the others. She was the first of the group to see him, and although they were perhaps twenty yards apart, he could have sworn her eyes were blue—and that there were freckles on her nose!

For a few seconds she stared at him, seeming as mesmerised by his appearance as he was by hers, then she called to the others in their own language, Iban. Startled faces turned towards him, then modestly, self-effacingly, each of them pinched her nose between finger and thumb and sank into the grey-green water. One moment the pool had contained half a dozen laughing young women, the next there was not one, and only the spreading ripples showed where they had been.

Murray Masterson walked on, over the plank bridge and into the village, his mind puzzling the mystery of what he had just seen. He was more shaken then he cared to admit by the sight of what he was sure was an English girl, bare-breasted, cavorting with the natives.

From early childhood, everyone in the village was accustomed to being in the water, playing, diving, swimming. The girls were almost as at home there as on land and could remain under the surface for longer than most people. When Shuah allowed her head to rise above the surface, she saw that the strange-looking, pale-faced man was approaching the longhouse. How tall he was! Even taller than she was—and she not only towered over all the women in the village but was taller than most of the Iban men, too. Her amazement grew as she watched him moving with long strides, seeming unencumbered by his extraordinary clothes, for he was covered from head to foot in white garments, his head crowned with a white helmet—not even his feet were bare!

Yet strange as he seemed, the sight of him brought a stirring of memory, something familiar from her distant past, for she knew she had not always lived here in Bartulu. They said she was aged about five when they brought her here twelve years or more ago. She had been found by the *tuai rumah*, the headman, and some of his warriors when they were on one of their expeditions, a child all alone in a small boat adrift in the South China Sea. Nobody had any idea who she was, but they had treated her kindly—children had a specially privileged place among the Ibans.

They had taken her back up-river with them to their longhouse and the *tuai rumah* had presented her to Kobe, his wife, for their only daughter had died a few months earlier. That Kobe had loved her Shuah had no doubt—she had been cherished and protected, even though she had grown so tall and she was pinkly-pale-looking, so different from the rest of the girls in the tribe.

'You may not be beautiful, Shuah, but you are lovely in your own way,' Kobe had tried to reassure her.

Shuah's heart was heavy as she remembered Kobe, the woman she had called 'Mother', and who had died so suddenly only a short time ago. She missed her so much.

'Come on, Shuah, don't stay there day-dreaming,' called one of the girls. 'We must hang the washing up to dry.'

'There'll be a lot to do, now that we have visitors.'

The other girls were already wading out of the pool as Murray Masterson entered the longhouse. 'Who is that man?' Shuah asked. 'Where does he come from?'

'He's the white *tuan*. He comes from far over the mountains, he'll talk with the chief and the older men and women, stay for two or three nights and go on to visit another village.'

'He's never been here before, has he?'

'Of course he has—or if not him, another man who looks just like him. I can't tell one from the other with these white men,' the girl shrugged.

'The last one who came wasn't so tall—he was fatter, too, and he got drunk on *tuak*,' one of the other girls giggled.

'But why didn't I see him?' exclaimed Shuah.

'For some reason Kobe would never let you out; she used to hide you away when the white man came.'

'We didn't have any warning this time. Besides, it was only Kobe who was worried. I don't suppose it matters.'

'Come on—we must tidy ourselves and prepare to pour out the rice-wine. There'll be a party tonight.'

The girls picked up the clothes they had washed and wrung out and piled on boards beside the stream before they had begun to play about in the water and been disturbed by the sudden appearance of the white man. They carried them to the outer veranda of the longhouse, where they hung them up to dry in the hot sun.

Still Shuah was puzzled—there must have been some reason for her mother to have shielded her from the white man. Did he present some special menace to her? She felt a trifle apprehensive, yet her main feeling was of excited curiosity as she followed her companions into the *ruai*, the long room where all the tribe gathered for communal work, celebrations and discussions. Her gaily-patterned sarong clung wetly to her hips, but was no discomfort in the humid warmth of the day. In the midst of the other girls she began to walk across the main hall of the longhouse, each going to her own *bilek*, the private room of individual families. But Shuah's eyes sought the stranger, and she found herself reluctant to turn away from him.

He was seated very upright, cross-legged, on a newly woven rattan mat in the place of honour by the hearth. It was a place made sacred by the spirits of the shrunken heads that hung in a circle above to ward off evil, old and blackened with smoke, for head-hunting had been banned by the White Raja and mostly the tribes kept to the law. A couple of yards behind the stranger were the Malay warriors and opposite him sat Sabat, the *tuai rumah* of the village, her adoptive father. They had all been served with a half-gourd of rice-wine, and sipped it appreciatively as they talked with friendly animation.

Shuah's first impression of the unusual size of this
man was confirmed as she noticed the broad spread of
his shoulders beneath the finely woven white material of
the high-necked tunic. His back was towards her and he
was bare-headed now, his helmet lying on the floor beside
him, and she could see even in the dim light that his hair
was shiny brown, thick and waving down to the nape of
his neck just above his collar. That too gave her something of a fellow-feeling with him—everyone else she
knew had straight black hair. She had always been the
odd one out with her hair that was copper-coloured and
curly.

She could not see his face, but his voice had a depth
of timbre that was pleasant to listen to. He was discussing the activities of one of the neighbouring tribes
who had been showing signs of hostility recently. When
one of the girls giggled, the stranger looked towards them
and Shuah saw his face; his features, though large, were
attractive. His eyes were shielded by shaggy eyebrows,
and those alone made him look totally different. The
Iban men as well as the women plucked their eyebrows
so that their faces had an open, clear appearance. With
their small snub noses their faces had a flat look compared to that of this stranger, whose features reminded
her of the craggy rocks of the mountains on the edge of
their tribal territory.

'Hurry, Shuah! Your grandmother's beckoning you.'
One of the girls gave her a friendly push.

Shuah hurried along, with a touch of anxiety as she
saw the worried expression on the wrinkled face of old
Uteh, Kobe's mother. Uteh pulled her inside the room
and shut the door firmly. The *bilek* held two large beds
raised about eight inches from the matting-covered floor.
There were ornaments of brassware and pottery intri-
cately patterned. Shuah turned to face Uteh.

'Make haste, Shuah. You're to go out there and meet
him.' Uteh gave a significant nod in the direction of the

door, and went on in a grumbling tone, 'He's been asking who you are. As if we know! I always told Kobe she was wrong to hide you as she did.'

'Why did she hide me?' Shuah asked.

'Only because she loved you. You took the place in her heart of the child who died, and she was always afraid someone would take you away. It's a pity you were out there in the pool today.'

'I was only doing the washing...'

'I know, I know. I can't understand why none of the men saw him coming. I'd have called you inside if I'd known—there's bound to be trouble.'

'What do you think he wants with me?' Shuah asked, her voice betraying the uncertainty she felt.

As they talked, she had changed into a dry sarong, knotting it tightly round her waist. It was her best one, of crimson and black with a richly woven border of golden scrolls. Her grandmother handed her several silver necklaces that she placed over her shoulders to hang over her firm, bare breasts. Bracelets were pushed on to her wrists and her ankles adorned with bangles, then she sat on the floor while her 'grandmother' squatted behind her and began combing her hair, clicking her tongue in exasperation at the near-impossible task of smoothing it and confining it into a tight bun at the back of her head.

'It would have been better if you'd been married,' Uteh said. 'Then not even the white man would dare to take you away. You could stay with us for ever. This is where you belong, isn't it?'

'Yes.' Shuah could not remember any other home, and she had never been more than a day's journey from the village. This white man came from much further away than that, from far beyond the mountains. There was excitement in that thought.

'Your father should have arranged the marriage for you with Dioudi, no matter what you said,' her grandmother grumbled. 'It might have brought us better luck than we've had lately.'

Shuah felt a trifle guilty. Her grandmother had hinted before that if she had married Dioudi, the witch-doctor, Kobe might not have died so suddenly. 'I don't like Dioudi.'

'You would have come to like him, once you were married and you'd borne him a child,' said Uteh. 'You should have been flattered that he offered for you. Not many men would have taken on a woman who was so much bigger than himself.'

Shuah had to admit that was true. It was probably only because Dioudi was the witch-doctor that he had been willing to consider her as a wife, thinking that to possess such an unusual woman would have added to his prestige, which was already considerable. Kobe had been her only ally in her refusal of his offer. She would never allow Shuah to be forced into anything. From that first moment when she had taken the bewildered, hungry, lost little girl into her plump arms she had felt that the child had come to her as a gift from the gods, and her love had had a certain reverence woven into it. Since Kobe had died, Shuah not only mourned her loss, but was daily aware in many ways that her place in the village had changed.

'My father promised he wouldn't make me marry Dioudi,' she said.

'We'll see about that,' snapped Uteh, tight-lipped. She tugged at the thick hair that rebelled against being pulled straight and pegged into a bun with wooden combs. 'I shall advise your father to make the arrangements straight away, before anything worse befalls us.'

Shuah bit her lip, refusing to complain however much the tugging and combing scratched and hurt. She could understand her grandmother's feelings, for Uteh believed that the anger of the gods had been visited upon the family when they had taken Kobe and they would be appeased only when Shuah agreed to bestow her favours on the witch-doctor.

'If it was my fault, I should have been the one to die,' Shuah pointed out.

'The ways of the gods are strange. Now go along and sit quietly beside your father and see what the white *tuan* has to say to you.'

Shuah stood up. Because there was no mirror, she had no idea how she looked—and certainly could not even guess how she would appear to the eyes of the white man. She ducked her head to pass through the low doorway and moved out into the communal *ruai*, where most of the tribe were now gathered. Then she pulled herself up to her full height, and there was pride in her bearing and a sway of natural grace to her hips, tightly encased by the colourful sarong as she walked forward. Her firm young breasts were golden-brown, their beauty enhanced by the shining silver jewellery, which was of good quality as befitted the adopted daughter of the headman. She was dressed very similarly to all the other girls who were now bringing out food and more rice-wine, yet she looked so different with those twists of red-gold hair curling round her English-looking, freckled face.

At her approach, the white *tuan* sprang to his feet with lithe movement, taking her completely by surprise—but confirming her impression that he was indeed even taller than she. He seemed to dominate the longhouse by his very size; the width of his shoulders was emphasised by buttoned straps, his chest showed its breadth beneath the pleated pockets of his jacket, his long legs in the white trousers gave a hint of the power of the muscles rippling beneath the cotton material. Despite his rough journey through the jungle, which must have lasted several days, he had a fresh clean look and she experienced an extraordinary sense of familiarity with him. It was as if she had known him before—or someone very much like him.

His eyes beneath those shaggy brows were brown, and she could see a small scar just below the right one. He regarded her levelly, with an enigmatic expression yet with an intense concentration that suggested he was making a cool assessment of her. His nose had considerable prominence, a strong bone-structure giving his face a commanding air. Though his mouth was full and well-shaped, he held his lips tightly compressed, so that she had no idea what impression she might be making upon him. Everything about him told her that this man was a leader, a chief—strength and stead-fastness were suggested by his upright bearing.

For a long moment they stared at each other, then he said some words in a foreign language that she did not understand, so she shrugged and continued her steady, stately walk towards her father. On reaching his side she smiled at him, sure of her welcome as she dropped down with natural ease to sit close to him on the rattan mat. The *tuai rumah* reached only to her shoulder, but he was a powerful man in the community and Shuah was deeply grateful for the loving care he and Kobe had lavished upon her through the years of her childhood and de-veloping womanhood. Now, however, her attention quickly went back to the stranger, who had resumed his sitting position opposite them.

As their eyes met he spoke to her, and this time he used Iban. 'The *tuai rumah* tells me you are his adopted daughter, and that your name is Shuah.'

'That is true, *tuan*,' she agreed.

'I spoke to you in English when you came in, but you didn't understand what I said, did you?'

'No, *tuan*.'

'I wished you good afternoon and said how surprised I was to see you here.'

'I give you greeting in return, *tuan*.'

'My name is Murray Masterson.'

It sounded strange to her, and she wanted to memorise it, but found it difficult; only one word seemed to stick. 'Mur-ray,' she repeated, watching his face to see if she had said it correctly.

'Good.' His eyes raked over her, disconcerting in their intensity. 'You *must* be English—I would stake my life on it! I wonder where the hell you came from!' He sounded almost angry, as if he thought some information was being deliberately withheld from him. 'Don't you remember?'

'I know very little about myself. I was young when these good people found me and brought me here. I've lived here ever since.'

'So I have just been told! It's an incredible story. I thought I'd heard just about everything in the ten years I have been in Sarawak, but I'm absolutely astounded by finding you here. Have you no name other than Shuah?'

She shrugged. 'Perhaps—but if so, I don't know it. My father says I called myself Shuah when they found me, so I suppose it must be my name.'

'That's true. Shuah—that's what she said,' the *tuai rumah* confirmed.

'Have you nothing that might help to identify you? A locket, perhaps?' Masterson sounded as if he did not quite believe what he had heard, and that he wished it was not true. She had the distinct impression that he looked upon her presence in the village as a problem—one he did not relish in the least.

She could only shrug helplessly. 'I'm just Shuah,' she said, with a smile. 'I've lived here almost all my life, and I've been happy. I have these lovely pieces of jewellery, but they were all given to me by my kind "father" here.'

She held up her arms, arched her hands delicately to show off her silver bracelets and swayed to display the silver necklaces that hung over her breasts. It was a seductive movement from one of the tribal dances that she delighted in performing, but although the *tuan* watched her closely, his face remained impassive. She was disappointed, for she had hoped to please him and she knew her actions had been graceful; the smile from her 'father' told her so. When she turned back to Masterson his expression had changed—he was still unsmiling, but now there was a gleam of desire in his eyes.

It was the look of a man who would like her to entertain him in her *bilek* and her heartbeat quickened, thrilling in primitive response to him. A warm sensation of pleasure flushed over her, which she found both surprising and pleasing, for it had never happened to her before.

She had grown up among the Ibans, who had a very open attitude towards sex. In the longhouse, free love was perfectly acceptable among unmarried people. Shuah was perfectly aware of that, yet she had never felt the least stirring of desire towards the young men of the tribe. The other girls found her attitude difficult to understand and she could not really explain it herself; she had simply shrugged off any advances, and the only one who had persisted was the man she liked least of all—Dioudi, the witch-doctor. Now suddenly she found that Murray Masterson was a man towards whom she could feel a warm response and she lowered her eyes with instinctive shyness.

The velvet cloak of night had fallen over the jungle. Voices were hushed, but the croaking of frogs, the grunting of pigs and the cries of night birds filled the silence. Then Masterson said, 'You're dressed as an Iban, speak their language, live in this longhouse, dance as gracefully as one of their own women—but you are not one of them.' The last words were uttered slowly and with emphasis. 'You are as English as I am, and you should not behave in this uncivilised manner.'

There was a harsh note in his voice that grated on her ears. What did he mean by that? How was she behaving in an uncivilised manner? Was it because of that look which had flashed between them? One thing was certain—he was not pleased with her, and she remained with her eyes downcast.

He then addressed Sabat. 'Tell me again, *tuai rumah*, how it was you found her.'

'Fetch more wine for the *tuan*,' her father instructed.

Obediently Shuah fetched the jug and refilled the gourd, although Masterson had actually drunk very little. She also topped up her father's drink, and then one of the other girls took the jug to attend to the needs of the *tuan*'s soldiers. Shuah returned to her father and squatted on her heels beside him, as he began to recount that story that she had heard many, many times.

'It is true, that from the time she was first found we knew Shuah was not an Iban, but there are many races in this land, some of whom I have never seen. You say she is English...'

'The more I look at her, the more certain I am. But please continue.'

'We'd suffered from bad storms, from fires which had ravaged our rice crop, and a mysterious illness had taken the lives of several of our women and children. Nothing seemed to be going well for the tribe and I led some of our warriors on an expedition to the coast. Not to take heads—you must not think that! We'd collected birds' nests from the caves to trade with the Chinese. Before returning, we put out to sea—only on a peaceful fishing trip of course, *tuan*, and that was when we sighted a small boat drifting apparently empty, and when we came alongside we found the child lying in the bottom. There are tribes who believe in sacrificing a young girl to pro-pitiate the gods. They place her in a canoe and cast it out to sea...'

'I know that only too well, and you know it is forbidden by the White Raja,' said Masterson sternly.

'I do, *tuan*, but not everybody is as law-abiding as my people,' Sabat replied smoothly.

Masterson's eyes flashed their doubt, but he did not interrupt, as the headman continued, 'When we found the child we thought she'd been sacrificed to the gods, and at first we were afraid to touch her. Then she opened her eyes and looked at us. She began to cry, and I offered her a drink of coconut milk and she drank it thirstily and smiled at me with sweet trust, as if I was her friend. Some of my warriors felt we should just push the boat back out to sea and leave the girl to her fate. Others said that perhaps the sea gods had sent her to us for a special purpose and we might anger them if we refused their gift. We talked together for a long time and Shuah began to cry again, and I had a strong feeling, like a sixth sense, that she might have been sent specially to me. You see, my daughter had developed a fever and had been taken by the gods only a few weeks earlier. She was the only child my wife and I had although we had been married for a very long time. In the end it was decided that we should bring Shuah back to the village and consult with all our people about what should be done. We towed the boat up-river with us so that if illfortune befell the tribe, we could take the child back to sea and cast her adrift again. That's how Shuah first came to our village, and from that day on my wife cared for her and loved her as if she was our own. What we did must have been right, for the tribe has prospered in the years she's lived with us.'

The story of the finding of Shuah had become a legend with the tribe, and was recounted whenever there was a gathering. On this occasion, just as usual, it was greeted with words and nods of approval for the happy outcome. Shuah understood very well what a difficult decision the warriors had been obliged to make. Life was full of terrors, disease, storms, crop failures, attacks by enemy tribes, hunting accidents, infant mortality and death in childbirth, barrenness—so many dangers that could be overcome only with the assistance of the gods so that their appeasement was essential to survival.

Masterson nodded gravely. He had lived in Sarawak long enough to understand the power of superstition among the Ibans, and Raja Brooke insisted that local customs must be treated with respect, except for those that were positively evil, like head-hunting and piracy.

'You did well, *tuai rumah*,' he said gravely. 'You have taken good care of this long-lost daughter of the white people. But I believe, now that the gods have led me here to find her, I should take her back with me and present her to the great White Raja, for I am sure she belongs to his tribe.'

Shuah gasped, both excited and alarmed at this astonishing suggestion. She glanced anxiously from the stern face of Murray Masterson to the wrinkled, familiar features of Sabat.

'How can you be so sure of that?' the *tuai rumah* hedged. 'Why would the people of the great White Raja have cast a child adrift if they thought highly of her?'

'They would not have done that deliberately. She must have been travelling with her parents on one of the great boats of the white man when some evil befell them— perhaps they were attacked by pirates, or there was a storm and the ship was lost. I agree with you that the gods took special care of her, and she was fortunate to be carried to you, but I am also sure that now she should be returned to her own people.'

'No!' thundered a great, deep voice from the doorway of the longhouse.

All heads turned to look at the elaborately tattooed Iban who stood there, a small man whose height was enhanced by huge hornbill feathers springing from his head-dress. In one hand he held a hunting-spear and in

the other a long blow-pipe for shooting poisoned darts.
It was Dioudi, the witch-doctor.

A shiver of apprehension shook Shuah's shoulders.
She saw the challenge in the look that flashed between
Masterson and Dioudi, and knew that the witch-doctor
would not readily allow her to leave the village.

CHAPTER TWO

MURRAY MASTERSON gave a polite but cool greeting to the witch-doctor, then turned back to face Sabat, and repeated with an air of command but by no means unreasonably, 'As I was saying, *tuai rumah*, I believe Shuah should now return to her own people.'

In the silence that followed those firm but quietly spoken words, Dioudi walked forward. He moved with the slow majesty of one who knows that others are in awe of him, for he was said to have the power to exorcise evil spirits and even to catch the soul of a dying person and put it back into the body, so that he recovered. Sometimes he used herbs for his magic, but more often he simply uttered mysterious incantations over and over again.

The brilliantly coloured feathers of his head-dress waved gracefully at each step he took. His black hair was cut in a short straight fringe high over his forehead and hung long behind his head, tied in a knot between his shoulderblades, a reminder of the head-hunting past of the Ibans. Dioudi's bare arms and shoulders were heavily tattooed, as he were his sinewy thighs below the yellow and brown patterned loincloth. His ears were pierced at the top, through which panther teeth had been inserted, and he wore silver bands over his knees, ankles and arms.

His bare feet made no sound as he advanced and the longhouse was as quiet as it ever could be, for the snorts of the pigs and the clucking of the hens that lived underneath were seldom stilled, even in the middle of the night. There was a veiled threat in the manner in which he came up behind Murray Masterson, but the white man did not even glance in his direction. Dioudi moved on to sit cross-legged on the rattan mat at Shuah's side, deliberately close, his manner possessive, so that his body touched hers, and she drew away. He awoke only repugnance in her, though she tried desperately to hide it. She escaped by standing up to fetch a gourd and the pitcher of rice-wine with which she served him.

He took the drink and sipped it. Shuah would have remained standing, but Sabat indicated that she should sit down again on the mat, between him and Dioudi. She obeyed, but it was with a strange sense of being held there, of being trapped, although neither of the men laid so much as the lightest restraining finger on her.

Shuah sat up very straight and turned from one to the other of these small dark men, both of whom wished to keep her in the village, each for his own different reasons. Gathered round them were most of the men, women and children of the village and the handful of Malay soldiers in their khaki drill uniforms. She turned her eyes to Masterson, who sat, with almost as much supple ease as the natives, on the opposite side of the hearth, watching her. For quite a long time he regarded her with a level penetrating look as if he was summing up the situation. She wondered if he had assessed her reaction to the entry of Dioudi. He was alert and, she was sure, aware of the tension in the air, but he betrayed no emotion.

The guttural tone of Dioudi's voice held suppressed anger. 'Shuah belongs with us here. She was sent to us by the gods. She has been with us through many difficult years, and life has improved for the tribe.'

'I suggest that the improvement is because the gods have been pleased with the rule of the White Raja,' Masterson said. 'He has put a stop to the raids of the pirates that used to devastate your villages.'

'For that we are grateful,' agreed the *tuai rumah*. 'But it is still necessary that the gods should smile upon our people.'

Murmurs of assent came from around them, and Dioudi continued quickly, 'The gods placed Shuah in our care. If we allow her to go, how do we know you will take good care of her?'

'I give you my word, my promise made on behalf of the White Raja, and you know he deals harshly with those who break his laws.'

'We also know of girls taken from their tribes to live with the white men. They have borne children, and the white man has left them, gone away again over the seas, back to wherever he came from.' Dioudi emphasised his disgust by turning aside and spitting down through one of the wide cracks in the floorboards. The pigs below grunted.

Shuah had herself heard of such cases, and although the Ibans accepted free love among the single people, if there was a child, the father would arrange to support it and it would be part of the wider family of the longhouse. Children were always welcome and much loved—just as she herself had been. It was the custom among the Ibans to remain faithful after marriage, but she was uncertain how such matters were viewed by the tribe to which the great White Raja belonged. She had even heard of races in which a man was permitted to have several wives.

Masterson nodded solemnly and answered the witch-doctor, weighing his words carefully. 'Many of the girls of whom you speak went with the white *tuans* of their own free will, and in most cases the officers make provision for the maintenance of their offspring. I accept that not all my countrymen have behaved well towards your womenfolk, but I assure you it wouldn't be like that for Shuah. She'd be returning to her own people, and they'd welcome her.'

'They cast her adrift in a small boat,' Dioudi said. 'She would have died had our people not been led to find her. That's true, isn't it, my friends?' He appealed to the villagers around him, who chorussed their assent. Dioudi's words were beginning to stir them to concern, to fear and anger. He was quick to realise this and pressed on, emphasising the point. 'Our warriors would risk their lives to defend any of our womenfolk. Shuah is one of us, and every man in this village would rise in anger should you try to carry her away.'

'I have no wish to take Shuah against her will, but let us ask her to tell us what *she* would like.' He addressed her directly. 'Will you come with me to seek your own people, Shuah?'

She sat up straight. 'I—I think I should...' she began. It was as if Murray Masterson had cast a spell upon her, for she felt she could put total trust in him. She would have stood up there and then and followed him out even into the blackness of the jungle night and thought nothing of the evil spirits that lurked there. But she had no chance to voice her opinion.

'No!' Dioudi shouted. 'This matter cannot be left to Shuah, for the fate of all of us is involved. Nor can it be settled by you alone, *tuan*, for we know that the great White Raja has decreed that the wise people of the tribe should be consulted on matters that concern them. You have to ask the headman and the elders.'

'That is so, in most matters...'

'It is the duty of our warriors to protect the wellbeing of the tribe and all its members.' Dioudi spoke with a note of triumph. 'The gods would be angry with our people if any harm were to befall Shuah. She should stay here!'

Growls of agreement from the assembled people re-inforced the witch-doctor's threat. The Malay soldiers glanced anxiously around, and more than one cast his eyes up to the cluster of smoke-blackened, shrunken human heads that hung above the hearth. Masterson must have been very well aware of the hostility that Dioudi was deliberately whipping up among the tribesmen, but he gave no outward sign of apprehension.

'You are quite right to be concerned about Shuah,' he agreed evenly. 'If she were one of your own women, I'd accept all you say, but you know as well as I do that she belongs to the people of the White Raja.'

'Shuah has lived among us for many years; Sabat and Kobe looked after her devotedly. She has been happy here. How do we know she would be happy where you take her?'

'She should live with her own people.'

'She's not a blood-relation of yours, is she?' Dioudi asked with a sneer in his voice.

'No, but I'm sure I'll be able to find those that are. Her parents may be alive, or she may have brothers and sisters. Would you think it right that she never knows them?'

'If that is so, tell them to come here themselves and claim her,' snapped Dioudi.

Several of the elders began to voice their agreement with this suggestion. 'Dioudi speaks wisely,' said one.

'He always counsels us well. If relatives of Shuah's want her back, let them come here.'

'Then we'll know that the gods are pleased.'

Shuah knew their desire to keep her in the village was largely because of fear of the consequences should she leave. A few had an affection for her, but she knew that since Dioudi had expressed his desire to marry her, there were many who had become a little afraid of her.

The witch-doctor, obviously heartened by their support, turned to the chief and spoke directly to him. 'On no account must you allow Shuah to leave your protection, *tuai rumah*, unless it is with someone who can prove he has a rightful claim to her.'

'I believe you are right, Dioudi. Your wisdom has guided us through many problems,' said Sabat. He turned to the elders of the tribe, both men and women. 'But, as is our custom, the final decision is yours.'

Their decision was unanimous.

'Then that is how it shall be,' he announced. 'Shuah remains with us, under my protection, until these relatives you speak about come to fetch her.'

If Masterson was displeased, he gave no sign of it. 'As you wish,' he said. Once the decision had been taken, it was not customary to dispute it.

Shuah felt deep disappointment—unreasonable, perhaps, because a few hours earlier she had been happy in Bartulu, with no thought of leaving it. Her dissatisfaction increased as she saw the smug smile on Dioudi's face, his look of triumph, and an involuntary shiver ran through her. He had power, and he would use it ruthlessly. He could sway the people of the village with his threats; he had roused them now to keep her there, and if she continued to refuse to marry him he might turn against her. Then he could just as easily persuade them to cast her out, to drive her away into the jungle, where she would surely perish.

She turned from Dioudi to the *tuai rumah*, but she could not appeal to him. The decision to keep her had been taken democratically, and he would not be elected to the office of headman again if he overruled them. He was too good a man for her to ask that of him. If she were to go against the will of the tribe, she must act alone and take the consequences. She had always been a little in awe of Dioudi and physically he was repulsive to her, but now that feeling was crystallised into near-terror. Her desperation grew, so that with every passing minute she became more convinced that if she did not go with Murray Masterson when he left, she would never have such an opportunity again.

It was not that she really wished to leave the village, not that she yearned for the company of those people he had said were of her own race, intriguing though such a prospect appeared. It was a much more fundamental conviction that made her decide that she wished to be with him. He seemed to possess a magnetic attraction that she made no effort to resist—to her, he was magnificent. He resembled the shadowy recollection she had of her real father. His large craggy features, his skin which, though healthily tanned, was paler than that of the Ibans, his dark hair that was brown rather than black and fine in texture, and his great size—the fact that he was taller than she, all these things gave her a feeling of compatibility with him.

She wanted to be with him, to find out more about him, and since it was obvious that he would not stay long in the village, somehow or other she must go with him when he left. He was the man with whom she wanted to spend the rest of her life in whatever capacity—as one of his many wives, even as his slave, if he so desired it, anything would be acceptable as long as she was with him. She gave no outward sign of her resolve, and in truth she had no idea how she could get away from the village. Moreover, she knew very well that the men who sat on either side of her would do their utmost to thwart her. She remained motionless, though her mind was feverishly working out ways and means. Her eyes were glued to the face of Masterson—for all her hopes were upon him.

While they talked, night had deepened, torches were lit, their flickering flames making pools of light in the dense darkness. The meeting was over and it was time for relaxing. Some of the younger women had been preparing food, and they now brought in a variety of dishes to set before their chief and his visitors. More *tuak* was poured into the gourds, everyone gathered together to eat, and conversation became more general. Shuah, as befitted her position as daughter of the headman, helped to serve their guest, and she delighted in making sure that the best of everything was offered to Masterson. Yet she had no chance to speak to him other than in the most general way, and he appeared to be almost unaware of her existence as he talked with the *tuai rumah* and the other elders.

The flaming torches cast a wavering light over the dark-skinned people, and there was the occasional whimper of a baby calling its mother, but no child ever cried for long, for there were plenty of people willing to comfort it. After they had eaten, some of the men mended spears ready for the next day's hunting, or repaired old fish-traps or snares. And all the time Shuah's mind wrestled with the problems of how she could persuade Murray Masterson to take her away with him.

It was late when people began to make preparations to retire for the night. The married couples and their families moved from the communal room to the privacy of their own *bilek* to sleep. A vacant room was allocated to Masterson, and Shuah helped to prepare it, placing woven blankets on the low platform bed. The soldiers who had accompanied him would sleep with the bachelors of the village where they had been sitting, simply wrapping blankets round themselves and lying down. At last the torches were snuffed out and the longhouse settled for the night.

Shuah lay awake in the *bilek* she shared with her adoptive father and grandmother. She had no intention of going to sleep; her mind was far too active. When the sounds of heavy breathing told her that both the other occupants of the room were sound asleep, she softly unrolled her naked body from the blanket and slipped into a sarong, knotting it around her waist. Her bare feet carried her soundlessly to the door, and although it creaked slightly as she opened it, that sound was absorbed by others in the never quite silent longhouse.

She glanced up and down the length of the *ruai*, and everyone appeared to be asleep, so she stepped lightly along to Murray Masterson's room. Carefully she opened the door and crept softly inside. She waited on the threshold, listening for the sound of his breathing. The room was strangely, almost uncannily, silent. A rattan mat covered the unglazed window, keeping out the moonlight. Every nerve-ending in her tense body tingled. She had a terrified feeling that she was being watched, and glanced over her shoulder, but there was no movement outside.

Closing the door behind her, she moved slowly towards the bed. She had felt no fear as she set out, yet now terror had a grip on her. Why should the room be so quiet? When her toes touched the edge of the bed, she bent down and put out a hand to feel the rough material of the blanket and moved her fingers forward, seeking the mound of a body beneath. There was no one there!

A sound, a movement, brought a gasp to her lips. Then with a suddenness that took her completely off guard, her hand was grasped and she was pulled forward so that she was lying helplessly stretched over the bed. A knee was placed in the small of her back, holding her there.

'Who are you, and what are you doing in here?' Masterson's voice was low but distinct, carrying that note of command that was so evident in all that he did.

'It's Shuah, *tuan*,' she whispered urgently. 'I want only to talk to you. Please don't wake up the rest of the longhouse!'

'Are you alone?' he asked, and she detected the doubt in his voice.

'Yes. Please don't be angry, *tuan*!'

'What do you want?' His voice was gruff, but the pressure of his knee was removed from her back and he released his hold on her wrist.

'*Tuan*—I must go away with you.'

'So you shall, but not this time.' His voice was even, as if he was humouring a child. It increased her determination.

'Yes,' she said fiercely, 'this time. Don't leave me here.'

'The *tuai rumah* has made conditions, and quite rightly. I have to respect his wishes and so should you.'

'I always have done, until now. I have great love and respect for my father, but...'

'I am glad to hear it. I can see how devoted he is; that is why I am content to leave you here a while longer. I can't take you with me without their consent. If I did that, it might start an uprising—people could be killed. I can't risk that. Just be patient, child.'

'I'm not a child! If I were, there'd be no problem. I *want* to go with you, *tuan.*' She rolled over and pulled herself up into a sitting position, lifted one hand and lightly touched his cheek.

The effect on Murray Masterson was as though he had felt the sting of a viper. He leapt to his feet, drew back and stood glowering down at her. 'You don't know what you're asking!' he snapped. He turned and walked towards the window, pulled away the rattan covering, letting in a glimmer of moonlight and the sounds of croaking frogs, pattering rain and a soughing wind in the forest trees. Then abruptly he marched back. He wore only a short cotton sarong that covered him from the waist to halfway down his muscular thighs. When he spoke again, his voice had a gruff, throaty note. 'The condition the *tuai rumah* made was reasonable enough. He has your welfare at heart.'

'I know that...'

'Then leave the matter as it is. I'll be back very soon, and then I'll take you to find your own people.'

'If I don't go with you now, I may never be able to.' She knelt on the low bed and gazed up at him with pleading eyes.

'Don't be ridiculous, Shuah! I cannot force these people to let you go. I've only a handful of men with me. When I return, I'll bring more troops. And, to safeguard your reputation, I'll bring along another white man.'

It infuriated her, the way he kept making obstacles. And what was this new problem he was worrying about? 'What does that mean?' she asked. 'What is—my reputation?'

He seemed to find difficulty in answering, but at last he said, 'You'll have a lot to learn about the ways of white people, Shuah. For now, just take my word that it would not be right for you to leave here and spend several days and nights alone in my company.'

'Why?' she asked curiously.

He sighed. 'Because there are rules, conventions, and everyone has to conform to them. It would be considered quite wrong for me, as an unmarried man, to spend time alone in the company of a young lady, especially if she is young and beautiful.'

She seized upon his words, sprang to her feet and reached out to rest her hands upon his broad, bare shoulders. His skin felt deliciously silky beneath her touch. 'Am I beautiful?' she asked. There was no hint of coquetry in her voice, but she awaited his reply with intense interest.

'Yes,' he replied in a stiff sort of voice. She found him very difficult to understand—not because he was in any way deficient in his use of the Iban language, but because she sensed that he did not say all that he meant, and that was not the way with the tribespeople.

'Truly? I mean, could you say it to my "father"?'

'But of course.'

'I think you are magnificent.' She smiled, and leaned forward and felt his breath fan over her face, as if he was struggling to control himself. Then his arms closed around her, he drew her tightly to him, and her bare breasts were flattened against the hard barrel of his chest. She lifted her face. 'Could you ask to marry me?'

'No!' he thundered. 'That I certainly will not do.'

'But you said I am beautiful—that must mean you would like to marry me.'

'It may mean so in Iban, but I assure you it does not mean the same in the language of our people, yours and mine. You are English; you must always remember that.'

'I don't see why being English should change me so much.'

'But it will,' he said, and there was a note of regret in his voice that puzzled her. He heaved a great sigh and was silent for several seconds, yet he still held her close against him and she felt immensely comforted. 'You have so much to learn,' he muttered throatily. 'You just don't know what you're talking about.'

'Yes, I do, *tuan*. And I know that if you go away without me, Dioudi will insist on marrying me before you come back.'

'You must not agree to that.'

'I don't want to, and so far my father has not insisted, but my grandmother is putting pressure on me to accept, so I may be forced to.'

'You mustn't—you can't!'

'There's only one way to prevent it. You must marry me yourself, *tuan*.'

A rough cry from the doorway of the *bilek* made her swing round. Dioudi stood there, and the moonlight caught the sharp curved blade of the parang he held threateningly in his hand. Shuah screamed. Dioudi took a step forward, but almost immediately he was grasped from behind and the knife fell from his hand as his wrist was twisted. He choked as another arm caught him violently round the throat. Two of the Malay soldiers who had accompanied Masterson held the witch-doctor in a hold from which he could not escape.

In the commotion that followed, the whole longhouse woke up. Men, women and children, partly clothed or quite naked, came out of their *bileks*, wiping the sleep from their eyes, chattering excitedly, anxious to discover what the drama was about.

'What's going on?'

'There was a terrific din. My wife thought we were being attacked by pirates, as in the old days!'

'They say Dioudi threatened the *tuan* with a knife because Shuah was with him.'

'He'll bring the fury of the White Raja down on us!'

'It's all because of Shuah.'

Shuah kept well back in the darkness of the room, standing tall and proud, even though her heart was beating so fast it felt as if it must burst. The threats that had boomed from the lips of Dioudi were there also in the voices of the people as they crowded round the doorway, straining to look inside. They were angry and upset, the warriors were poised to fight, and they heavily outnumbered the soldiers who had forced Dioudi to his knees.

'Release him,' Masterson said.

'But, *tuan*, he threatened you with a knife,' objected the sergeant.

'I'm aware of that.' Masterson picked up the knife that had clattered to the floor and held it in his hands, as though assessing its weight—and its danger.

'Silence!' The voice of the *tuai rumah* rang out clearly, and at once a space was made for him to pass through. He looked from Dioudi to Masterson, and then his shrewd eyes moved over and rested on Shuah.

He did not ask what she was doing there, in the room of the white man. It was as if he already knew, and there was a touch of sadness in his eyes that squeezed at her heart. He thought she was rejecting him, perhaps felt that she no longer loved him—and that was far from the truth. She took a step forward, almost unable to prevent herself from running into his arms, as she had done so often when she was a child, yet she knew she could not do that. She had brought trouble on the tribe and on herself, and she must take the consequences. She stood humbly with her hands clasped in front of her.

Sabat turned away, raised one arm, and said, 'Let us sit by the hearth and hear from Dioudi and the *tuan* what this is all about.'

At first, no one moved. Curiosity, excitement, barely suppressed anger flickered in the eyes that darted from one to the other of those inside the room. Throughout the disturbance, Masterson remained as calm as if threats to his life occurred every day, and now he moved towards the headman.

'I shall gladly speak to you,' he said. 'But before I do, with your permission, there's something about which I would like to consult Shuah—alone.' His words made it a request, but the tone in which he spoke was authoritative.

There was a brief silence before the *tuai rumah* answered, 'Very well. We shall await you.'

His quiet dignity helped to calm the situation. He was the people's elected leader and they knew they could trust him. They began to move back around the hearth, where the embers of the fire still glowed, sitting cross-legged beneath the blackened shrunken heads. There the drama of the evening's events would be talked through.

Shuah wondered what Masterson wished to speak to her about, for he had rejected her suggestion that he should marry her. She felt humiliated and helpless, but her pride would not allow her to let him see how deeply she had been hurt, and she waited in silence.

CHAPTER THREE

MURRAY MASTERSON did not shut the door to the room. He obviously wished this interview to appear open, to arouse no suspicion of treachery. They could be seen by any of the villagers who chose to peer in, which they did with natural curiosity. With a sweep of his arm he indicated to Shuah that she should step back a little, and he walked with her to stand by the far wall, close to the open window, out of earshot.

They faced each other, not touching, Shuah's hands hanging by her sides as she waited to hear what he had to say. He did not seem to find it easy. 'Circumstances force me to change my mind, Shuah,' he said grimly. 'I see no way out of this impasse other than that which you suggest.'

'You mean...?' She felt quite bewildered.

'I shall speak to the *tuai rumah* and tell him that I wish to marry you.'

It was what she had wanted, yet his acceptance brought no joy to her heart. She searched his face for some sign that there would be pleasure for him in the marriage, but his features remained cold and hard. It all seemed unreal, so different from the way she had pictured it when she came to his room. It *would* have been different but for Dioudi's intervention, she was sure, for she had felt the throb of passion in Murray when he held her in his arms. Now she was so confused by his attitude that she could only stand meekly before him.

'If that is your wish, *tuan*,' she said.

'It is not my wish,' he answered harshly. 'It is simply that I can't see any other solution. But I want you to understand that, since it will be an Iban ceremony, it will not be a true and binding marriage.'

'What—what do you mean?' Her eyes swept over his craggy face.

'Exactly what I say! I'll ask the *tuai rumah* for permission to marry you, and if he agrees...'

'I'm sure he will. I'll tell him it's what I want, too,' she interrupted eagerly.

'Listen to me carefully, Shuah.' He spoke slowly. 'I can see that you would be under threat from Dioudi if I left without you, and therefore you must come away with me. We'll go through this wedding ceremony, but it will be only a marriage of convenience. However, as you will then to all intents and purposes be my wife, you will be able to leave the village with me. It will, as you suggested, solve everything.'

She scanned his face anxiously. Some of what he said made sense, but not all. 'I shall be under your protection, won't I? You'll help me and look after me, *tuan*?'

'Of course. I give you my word on that. What I'm trying to explain is that this ritual we shall go through will be meaningless—it can have no validity whatever under English law.'

'Oh.' She was still far from understanding what he meant, but she knew that different tribes had different rules and she was in no position to argue. 'Does it matter?'

'It most certainly does! I'll explain later—but rest assured that you've nothing to fear from me, Shuah. Our marriage will be in name only.'

Every word he spoke made her more puzzled. How could you marry someone and not feel you were bound to them? What did he mean by a marriage in name only? Nothing he was saying made much sense, except that he intended to ask Sabat to entrust her to him as his bride. Murray had said he would explain it to her later, and she was willing to wait, trusting that he would make everything clear as she lay in his arms that night. Happiness welled up in her, her face beamed in a huge smile.

He remained solemn. 'You are agreeable to my proposition, Shuah?'

'Yes, *tuan*.' She nodded vigorously.

'Good. Then wait here while I think what to do about Dioudi, and speak to the *tuai rumah*.'

Shuah would have been proud to walk out to the *ruai* holding hands with Murray, but he moved quickly, bending from the waist to negotiate the low doorway. The chattering voices were silenced. She followed as far as the door and stood watching as he strode over to take the place that awaited him, opposite her father.

Dioudi sat between two of the Malay soldiers, with another two close behind, silent now, but his face was contorted with rage. He had been ready to kill, and he had been thwarted. If he was put to death, he would accept it; the worst thing that could happen would be to lose face, to be ridiculed. If he had had the power to kill with a look, the Resident would have dropped dead on the spot. The soldiers grasped Dioudi's arms as if they feared he might even yet spring to the attack, but Masterson signalled to them to release their hold.

'*Tuai rumah*, there's been a misunderstanding,' he said loudly and clearly. 'Dioudi is not to blame for what happened. He thought I was a threat to Shuah, and therefore that I was a danger to the whole of your village. Believe me, it is not like that at all. I came with messages of goodwill from the Great White Raja, and I assure you and all your people that I have only your wellbeing at heart.'

Sabat nodded gravely. 'You may tell the Great White Raja that we are his loyal subjects.'

'I'll most certainly do that,' said Masterson. 'I shall also tell him how well you have looked after Shuah. Last night, quite rightly, you agreed that she should leave your care only if she was in the charge of someone who had proved himself capable of looking after her properly.'

'That is so.'

'Now, however, that I have seen how beautiful Shuah is, I come to you with a request: I wish to marry her, and humbly beg you to give your permission.' He paused. A gasp of surprise breathed over the room, followed by a portentous hush. He continued, 'I promise to cherish and protect her, as you have done, to see that she is well provided for, and that in every way I shall do my best to ensure her future happiness.' Shuah listened with shining eyes—surely he could not say those words and not mean them? But he had not yet finished. 'I shall send presents to your village—tools and spears for hunting, blankets, brass gongs and tobacco-boxes and many other things.'

There were murmurs of pleasure from the assembled people, but the headman held up his hand for silence as Masterson continued.

'That is my proposal, *tuai rumah*. I await your decision most humbly. Will you accept me as your son-in-law?'

Shuah held her breath, waiting for her father to answer. He seemed to be weighing the proposition up in his mind. 'Shuah has not known you very long, *tuan*. Is she willing to accept you as a husband?'

'She has stated so to me.'

Dioudi wriggled uncomfortably. 'Shuah should stay here. She belongs to the tribe,' he said.

'I believed that, too,' said Sabat, and there was a note of sorrow in his voice. 'But the events of this evening have caused me to think otherwise.'

'You are right to doubt and to question,' said Masterson. 'I know it was because Dioudi had the good of the tribe at heart that he came to my room and challenged me. I bear him no ill-will for that, and to prove it I am willing to give him six Chinese porcelain jars, as is the custom in your peace-making ceremony.'

It was a generous offer, Shuah knew that, and it showed understanding of the ways of the Ibans. Such jars were expensive and very important to the prestige of the tribe, and she felt flattered that Murray Masterson was willing to make such a generous offering on her behalf. Surely it must mean that he thought highly of her? She could see that Dioudi was tempted, for the handing over of the tall, beautifully decorated jars was full of meaning and customarily ended great feuds, thereby satisfying the honour of both sides.

'Dioudi, if you'll accept my offer to make peace, I shall send the jars to you here in Bartulu within a month.'

Dioudi's head lifted as Masterson addressed him. The jars would be kept in the longhouse and would enhance his esteem in the eyes of the tribe. He did not, however, look at or speak to the Resident directly, but addressed his reply to the *tuai rumah*. 'Is it your will that I make peace with this man?'

'It is.'

'Then so be it. I accept your offer, and relinquish my claim to Shuah.'

'Good. Then, *tuai rumah*, I repeat my request that I may be allowed to marry your adopted daughter. I know it is not an easy decision for you, to allow Shuah to leave your longhouse when you have looked after her and loved her for so long. But I promise to take good care of her.'

The *tuai rumah* looked round at the elders, those same men and women who had decided before that Shuah should stay in the village until she was claimed by a genuine relative. It would be their decision, not his alone.

Would they accept this new proposition? Shuah's eyes darted anxiously from one face to another. Their mood had changed, that was obvious—they had been shaken by the events of the evening—by her going to the *bilek* of the *tuan*, and by Dioudi's intervention. They feared there would be continual trouble if she remained. Although she could not hear what was being said, Shuah knew them well enough to guess. There were enough dangers in the jungle to worry without quarrelling over women, and now that Dioudi had been mollified, there was less reason for them to object.

At last one of the elders lifted his hand. He was to act as spokesman. 'The decision about whom your daughter should marry must rest with you, *tuai rumah*,' he said. 'But if you are in agreement that she should wed the white man and go away to live with his people, we shall not oppose it.'

'Then it shall be so.' The headman looked directly at Murray Masterson. 'You have my permission to marry Shuah—if that is what she wishes. Where is she?'

All faces then turned in her direction, and Shuah felt suddenly shy as she walked to where her father sat. He was clad only in his loincloth, his brown skin marked with tattoos which told the story of his life, of his success in battles fought long since, of the heads he had taken from the enemy. His perceptive eyes moved lovingly over her face, and she dropped down close beside him and leaned her head on his bony shoulder with genuine affection. He was a little man compared with her, wizened with years spent in the jungle, his face wrinkled although he was only about fifty years of age, but he had taken the place of that big white father who had been lost in the shipwreck. He had shown her only love and kindness during the years she had been part of his family, and he was showing that same loving care now.

'Is it true, Shuah?' he asked. 'Do you wish to be married to this man?'

'Yes, Father,' she replied solemnly.

'Then I give my consent.'

'Thank you, *tuai rumah*,' Masterson said. 'May I also request that the ceremony shall take place very soon, for I must return as quickly as possible to the Residency.'

'It shall be arranged for the day after tomorrow,' said the *tuai rumah*. 'Now let us retire again to our beds, sleep, and be ready to make preparations for the feast.'

Shuah glanced at Murray, a trifle shyly, still puzzled by the strange things he had said. He had risen to his feet when she entered the *ruai* and now stood looking enormously tall among the small brown Ibans, and although the decision that had been taken appeared to have been arrived at by the will of the villagers and their headman, she was under no illusion. It was Murray who had dominated the proceedings. He had been magnanimous towards Dioudi, but that had only been because the witch-doctor presented no actual threat to him; neither man had lost face in the arrangement.

Murray's air of assurance was obvious in the way he now returned her look; his eyes still held the cool, enigmatic expression that told her little about him. She hoped she would be able to fulfil whatever he required of her as a wife—for as far as she was concerned when they went through the Iban ceremony, it would bind her to him, totally and for ever. Solemnly she bade him goodnight, then walked towards the headman's *bilek*, assuming an appearance of calm it was not easy to maintain.

Shuah was awake early, and although a thick mist had risen outside, making the air chilly, she set off for the customary early morning bathe, easily negotiating the notched pole that led to the river bank. She had slept only intermittently, and thought no one else in the longhouse was awake, but as she approached the pool, someone was there before her.

Murray Masterson was a strong swimmer. She noticed how his arms flashed with muscular regularity, his face beneath the water cutting through it at speed. The bathing-pool was fenced off from the river to prevent crocodiles from entering it, and by damming, it had been broadened and deepened to make a sizeable lake. Shuah waved a greeting and ran down into the water to join him.

'Good morning, *tuan*,' she called.

He swam over to her and stood up, and droplets of water cascaded from his broad shoulders and down his strong, sun-tanned arms.

'You're up early,' he remarked. 'Did you sleep well?'

'Not really,' she said, with sweet candour. 'My mind would not settle to rest.' She wondered if it had been the same for him, and remarked, 'You're up early too.'

'I always get up early,' he replied non-committally. 'Can't stand lying late in bed. This custom of your people to have an early morning bathe suits me very well.'

He sounded as if it was not usual in his country, which puzzled her—she could not imagine starting the day without a dip in the coolish water of the pool. There was no time to ask him more, as other people were beginning to make their way down the well-trodden path between the huge scarlet canna flowers. If they stayed where they were they would soon be surrounded, and Shuah wanted to have Murray's company alone just a little longer.

'I'll race you to the other side,' she suggested.

'Done. You call the start.'

'Let's go.'

Shuah had learned to swim soon after she came to Bartulu and swam hard now, trying to beat Murray, but he was far too strong and she was aware that he did not even exert himself to the full to keep pace with her.

On the opposite side of the river, she pulled herself up to sit on a branch-like root that thrust out invitingly. There was space for Murray beside her, but he stood up in the water, folding his arms, seeming somehow remote although he was so close. All round them came the croaking of hundreds of frogs.

'Look!' he exclaimed. She glanced to where he pointed and saw a frog carrying a baby on its back. 'The Malays have a legend about that. They say the mother frog takes the babies down to the water's edge to listen to the father frogs so that they can learn to croak.'

Shuah smiled. 'He certainly teaches them some weird sounds! It always surprises me that so much noise can come from such a small creature.'

She watched the frogs for some time, and when she looked at Murray again, he was regarding her with an intense and wondering expression.

'Shuah, have you no idea who you really are?' he asked. 'Have you ever tried to think back to the past? Is there no recollection that might give a clue to your identity?'

She shook her head. Until he had arrived, it had not been a subject that concerned her very much. She had been part of the whole and complete family in the longhouse, and like everyone else, she had lived only for the day. 'I remember my father a little. I believe he looked like you. I know he was big and tall. I can't recall much about my mother, except that I have an idea she was ill. I seem to see her lying down in the cabin of a big boat. I wish I could remember more.' He gave a sigh, as if it was a great problem, and she added apologetically, 'I'm sorry, *tuan*.'

'Not your fault,' he said abruptly. 'And there's no need for you to call me *tuan*. Do you not remember my name, Murray?'

She repeated 'Mur-ray' slowly, and said it again. 'Mur-ray. Do you like my name?'

'Shuah? It's not your real name.' He dismissed it almost contemptuously. 'Shall we go back?'

She could have stayed there happily for much longer, but since he seemed to wish to leave, she agreed. When they were married, they would have plenty of time together. He held up his arms to help her from her perch on the tree, and the touch of his hands as he grasped her bare waist sent a tingle of excitement through her, but he simply dropped her into the pool and released his hold immediately. Before she could quite recover from the speed of that movement he had turned and was swimming strongly away. She followed at a more leisurely pace. When he had almost reached the bank, he stood up and waded out of the water, gave a friendly nod to the Ibans on either side and strode away up the path. The short sarong knotted round his waist sheathed his narrow hips and, being wet, clung to his muscular thighs as he moved briskly along and disappeared inside the longhouse.

Shuah joined the other girls, splashing and frolicking with them as she had always done in the past, but already it seemed she had become different. They all wanted to talk about her forthcoming wedding and gathered round, chattering excitedly. That she was to marry the white man and leave the village with him was an amazing event filled with drama. Some were frankly envious that she would see some of the wonders of the outside world, stories of which filtered through into the depths of the jungle. Many said they would be too scared even to think of leaving family and friends to go away with a stranger. One thing they all had in common was a great excitement at the prospect of the wedding feast that would take place the next day.

For the rest of that day everybody worked hard, making preparations. Decorations of palm-leaves and flowers were brought in and hung up in the inner and outer rooms of the longhouse. Pigs and chickens were killed, and the men went off hunting, some hoping to shoot monkeys and birds with poisoned darts from their blow-pipes, while others went up-river to catch fish. The women set to work, vigorously cleaning the whole of the

longhouse or cooking huge piles of rice-cakes, while
others plucked and dressed the fowls and cut up the pigs.
Shuah worked with the cooks, for she had been well
trained in domestic duties by Kobe, and although there
was so much to be done, it was tackled willingly with
happy talk and laughter, and she had little time to think
about this big step she was about to undertake.

It seemed unbelievable that in the morning of the previous day she had not known Murray Masterson. Now
she was contracted to marry him tomorrow, and the day
after that she would leave the village and all that had
been familiar to her. What sort of life would he take her
to? What had he meant by saying that the ceremony
would not be binding? How could all that was being
prepared today in their honour and all that would happen
tomorrow be meaningless? She could not understand,
no matter how much she puzzled over it—and she could
not bring herself to ask him again. Certainly she did not
wish at this stage to risk any complications that might
make him change his mind. She could not bear it if he
went away and left her here, as he had originally
intended.

Shuah's wedding day dawned fair and bright and
began as usual with a morning bathe in the pool.
Although she was again early, there was no sign of
Murray, but someone told her he had already been for
his dip. No breakfast was prepared, but those who were
hungry ate up the leftovers from the previous evening's
meal, for the women had to get the fires roaring as
quickly as they could to cook the wedding feast. Soon
portions of meat were dropped into pots to boil with
herbs and vegetables, or speared on sticks to roast over
the flames.

Some guests from a neighbouring village arrived,
having made the journey up-river in long narrow proas
paddled by a dozen or so oarsmen. Ceremonial garments were brought out and brushed or mended. Shuah

was helped to dress by her grandmother and two young girls in a beautiful cotton sarong she had woven herself much earlier, never dreaming that she would be wearing it on such an occasion, and she was glad now that she had taken so much care with the delicate pattern. Her hair was drawn back from her face and fastened in a neat bun at the back, but tendrils of its luxuriant gleaming copper soon escaped and curled round her face. She was encased in a tight corselet of silver rings threaded on coils of rattan, which held her rigid. Dozens of silver bangles were put on her arms, her wrists, and round her knees and ankles.

When she was ready, she was taken out to where Murray Masterson awaited her. He had resisted all efforts to persuade him to don Iban ceremonial dress and wore a clean white uniform, with a cotton jacket buttoned high at the neck and long trousers. His eyes regarded her seriously, betraying no emotion, and she had the impression that he was enduring rather than enjoying, the occasion.

A gong boomed, and out of the forest came Dioudi. Murray's generous gift had evidently reconciled him to losing Shuah, and he had not needed much persuasion to play the important role that fell to him as witch-doctor to the tribe. He was clad in a magnificent bead-encrusted garment, and he carried his war-parang in one hand and a staff decorated with ornamental grasses and feathers in the other. He went to the door of each room to perform a short ceremony and chant incantations to exorcise evil spirits.

Then they all moved to the outer veranda where an orchestra of gongs and drums played the traditional rhythms. Suddenly, with a blood-curdling yell, a young man leaped forward and began to dance, swaying with supple grace. The hornbill feathers of his head-dress waved as his lithe body bent and twisted and silver bracelets jangled on his wrists and ankles.

Later everyone moved in procession around the longhouse and down to the pool, casting blessings on all those things that were so important to them. Finally Shuah and Murray returned to the longhouse to stand before the *tuai rumah*, who solemnly took their right hands and held them between his own. Shuah felt the firm pressure of Murray's fingers over hers as her father pronounced the words that in the tradition of the Ibans declared them man and wife.

The formal part of the ceremony being completed, everybody was ready for the joyous celebrations to begin. Food and wine was brought out, there was more music and dancing, singing and story-telling. Again the legend of how Shuah had been found adrift in the small boat was recounted, and there was special emphasis on each word as they were about to lose her.

Murray listened intently, still trying to find some clue to her identify, questioning her father and the other men who had found her, probing their memories for additional information, but everything they knew had already been woven into the tale. They had absolutely no idea who she was or where she had come from; even the boat in which she had been found had rotted away in the jungle damp.

At last, the evening came to an end. Shuah, as was expected of her now that she was his wife, took Murray's hand and led him to the room that had been allocated to him on his arrival and which she was to share with him on this their wedding night.

As soon as the door was closed behind them, she turned to him with a warm smile ready to lift up her arms and entwine them about his neck, awaiting his kiss. He however took a step back, avoiding her touch, as deliberately as if she had some terrible plague, and the smile died on her face.

'I told you this was to be a marriage in name only,' he said. His voice was harsh.

She stared at him, but it was difficult to make out his features, for the kerosene lamp cast only a faint yellow glow. 'I don't understand. You promised you would explain.'

'I mean that I shall not sleep with you, Shuah.' His reply shocked and horrified her so that she involuntarily took a step backwards.

'But why not? Don't you like me, Mur-ray?'

'We went through this ceremony only so that you could leave the village with me in safety. I intend to return you to your family, if I can find them, as soon as possible. Until then, although we shall have to pass a great deal of time in each other's company, we shall treat each other as if we were brother and sister, and not live as man and wife.'

She shook her head. 'But do you really think that's possible? Do you think I might be your sister?'

'No!' he exclaimed. 'I know damn well you're not. I haven't got a sister! Now go and lie down on the bed. I shall sleep on the floor over by the window.'

He sounded so angry that tears started into Shuah's eyes. She began to wonder if she had done the right thing in marrying this great man who was so unreasonable. She walked obediently over to the bed and began to remove all her jewellery, the finery she had been decked out in for her wedding. She unpinned her hair and shook it so that it streamed in a mass of copper waves over her shoulders and halfway down her back. She reached behind her waist to try and unfasten the silver corselet, but it was hooked up so tightly that it was impossible for her to do it herself. Murray was standing by the window with his back turned to her.

'Mur-ray,' she said softly. 'Please will you help me?'

'What do you want?'

'I can't undo my corselet.' He made no reply, and she thought he was going to refuse. 'I can't ask anyone else— they would think it most strange, as my husband is here.'

He turned and strode over to where she stood, walked behind her and inserted his fingers inside the top of the rigid adornment.

'Please be careful,' she implored. 'It's a family heirloom.'

He seemed to know exactly how it was fastened and began immediately to unhook it. She felt the warmth of his fingers, and they trembled slightly as they encountered the bare flesh of the small of her back. His breath stirred her flowing hair as she stood very still, waiting until he had unlaced the rattan almost to the bottom. Then abruptly he stepped back and withdrew his hands.

'You'll be able to manage now,' he said. 'Hurry up and get to bed. We've a long journey tomorrow, and I want to set out as early as possible.'

He returned to his self-allotted position by the window and lay down on the floor with his back very firmly turned towards her.

Shuah felt as if all the happiness of the day had dried to a cracked shell. Miserably she chewed at her knuckles to prevent herself from weeping openly. Mur-ray did not like her; he did not even want to make love to her—and what was the point of being married if he felt like that? The ways of the white man were exceedingly odd—were they all like Mur-ray Masterson? Maybe that was why she had never seen one before—because very few ever managed to get born! No doubt she would find out as time went on. If that was how he wanted their life to be, she must somehow make the most of it and try to please him in other ways, and perhaps eventually he would come to like her—just a little.

CHAPTER FOUR

WHEN SHUAH awoke in the morning she was alone in the *bilek*. The blanket beneath which Murray had slept was neatly folded, and on top of it was the kitbag packed with his personal things. His clean uniform, which one of the soldiers had laundered the previous day, was hung up, immaculate and fresh. She guessed where he was and at once jumped from her bed, stepped into her sarong, twisted it round her slender waist and hurried down the sloping path to the river, eager to join him.

Although she was not so early as usual, several others were equally tardy, the celebrations of the previous day having gone on late, and the *tuak* had flowed freely. Some of the women gave her laughing greetings, pointedly referring to her as a new bride, and with no inhibitions teased her about her changed status. She smiled back and shrugged off their remarks, for not for the world would she lower her prestige by admitting how disappointing her wedding night had been.

Her eyes sought Murray. He had again swum across the pool and was close to the bank where they had watched the frogs, but he was not alone. With him were his soldiers and some of the Iban men, and they were engaged in some sort of game, divided into teams throwing a ball and tackling each other, with a great deal of shouting and laughter. There was no place for a woman in that mêlée and her hope of a repetition of the previous pleasant interlude vanished. She stayed well away from them, bathed quickly and walked back to the longhouse.

Murray had said they were to leave as early as possible and she still had to gather together a few things to take with her. There was little enough: the silver bangles, bracelets and necklaces that Sabat had given her, including some that had once been Kobe's and which therefore had a special significance. She must take the four sarongs she had made from the cotton that was grown near the village. She had spun the thread, dyed it and woven it into a prettily patterned rectangle, then sewn the single seam to make a sarong. It was the simplest of garments, a wide tube—one had only to step into it, wrap it tightly round the waist, pleat the spare material at one side and tuck it firmly in at the top.

When she returned to the longhouse she lingered by one of the looms, running her fingers over the simple structure, remembering wistfully the many hours she had spent contentedly working there. Kobe had taught her to weave on that very loom, sitting on a rattan mat, using her body to keep the material taut and straight as she plied the shuttle. She wondered if she would ever use it again.

Murray Masterson came into the longhouse damp from his bathe, wearing only a calf-lenth sarong—her husband, yet still a stranger whose ways and moods were unknown.

'Are you ready?' he asked abruptly. 'We must set off as soon as we've had breakfast.'

She moved away from the loom, deeply conscious that she was about to leave behind all that was familiar and go away with this big autocratic man. She was doing so willingly. It was what she had chosen, but had she made a wise decision? If her life became less happy, she had only herself to blame.

'Yes,' she said. 'Shall I pack food for the journey?'

'There's no need. My soldiers have seen to that, so all you need is to pack your own things.'

'I have very little. I'll soon be ready.'

'Good. Then I'll get dressed.'

He moved on and entered their room. She followed him. He had taken off his wet sarong and was stepping into the long white trousers. She noticed with astonishment how very white his bottom was, but in seconds he had pulled up the trousers and, standing with his back to her, fastened the buttons down the front. When she had removed her own wet sarong, fascinated by the sight of him, she tried to look round at her own backside to see if it was equally white.

'Murray, is my bottom as white as yours?' she asked.

He uttered a sound that was rather like a laugh being choked and spun round sharply—she had her naked back to him, but was looking over her shoulder, smiling as she awaited his verdict. There was no sign of merriment in his face, however, and his voice was sharp.

'Shuah, you must not ask questions like that! Young ladies are not supposed to notice such things.'

'But I could not help seeing . . .'

'That's enough. Get dressed at once.'

Crestfallen, unable to understand why he had become so enraged at her simple question, she turned away and obediently reached for the clean sarong she had decided to wear for the journey. She packed her few possessions in a woven bag, then made her way to her father's room. Sabat looked up as she entered and gave her a brief smile, then returned to his task of making darts for his blow-pipe. Shuah gave a greeting to him and to her grandmother, who was setting out cold rice-cakes and portions of cooked fish for breakfast. Murray joined them, dominating the room with his great size, and was soon engaged in some last-minute exchanges of information with the *tuai rumah*.

It had been arranged that Shuah and Murray and his squad of soldiers should be rowed down-river to its confluence with the Rejang, where Murray had left his own boat. Everyone from the village gathered by the riverside to see them embark, to touch them and wish them good luck. Now that the moment of parting had come, she felt quite emotional and there were tears behind her eyes; even her grandmother hugged her tightly and seemed reluctant to say the words of farewell.

'It's not for ever,' Shuah cried. 'I'll come back and visit you.'

'I am old, my dear. I shan't be here, even if you do,' said Uteh.

'Oh, you will—you must be! I can come back soon, can't I, Murray?'

'I can't promise,' he said. 'It's a long, long journey to England, far across the sea. You'll have to go there to find your relatives and it may not be easy for you to return.'

'But not impossible,' she pleaded. 'You've come from this faraway land you call England—so does the White Raja and his ranee.'

'True,' admitted Murray, and his mouth softened in a smile that suggested he was tolerating a foolishness. 'But in all honesty I have to say I think it unlikely.'

'Will you not visit Bartulu again?' she asked.

'Most probably I shall next year.'

She clapped her hands. 'Then that's it, Uteh! I'll come here whenever my husband does. A year will soon pass, and then I'll be back to visit you all. I couldn't bear to think I'd never sit here and talk with you ever again.'

She felt as if her heart had lifted. She ignored the frown that came on to Murray's face and threw her arms round the *tuai rumah*'s neck and hugged him.

'You'll always be welcome, Shuah,' he said. 'And you can be sure of one thing—we'll never forget you. Even after you have gone we shall tell the legend of how we found you and also, now, it will include the tale of how the white man came and married you and took you away to search for your own people.'

'I'll think of you all—often. And I shall be back, Father, I'm quite determined on that!'

With that she walked down the rough steps cut into the bank on to some tree-trunks that served as a landing-stage and stepped on to one of the several proas that were drawn up there. They were narrow boats about thirty feet long, hewn out of tree-trunks and built up at the sides with planks. Shuah took her seat in the middle and Murray stepped in and sat behind her. Two of his soldiers came into the same boat and also about two dozen Ibans, and with shouts of farewell they began to paddle away with strong but leisurely strokes. Other proas followed, forming a procession of about five boats in each of which were some of the soldiers and a dozen Ibans. Very quickly Bartulu was left behind as the river wound through the jungle.

They made such an early start that the sun had barely risen and there was a thick fog, but soon that began to lift and then she could see the huge trees, festooned with creepers growing thickly and hanging down over the peaty-brown, smooth-flowing river. The Ibans did not talk much as they plied their paddles, but occasionally one would point out a troop of monkeys, or a special kind of fish or bird, or a wild pig. Whenever they saw such things Murray drew Shuah's attention, and after mentioning the Iban name by which she knew them he told her the English word and insisted that she repeat it several times.

'You must start learning to speak your own language,' he said. 'For instance, this is my hand—and this is my foot—now you say those words.'

She tried to remember the words he told her and at first she did quite well, but there were so many of them and they were so strange that she began to flounder and she could tell that Murray was beginning to get exasperated. So she concentrated harder because she was anxious to please him, and tried to shape her mouth round the extraordinary sounds that he expected her to repeat. One thing became quite clear—she had a great deal to learn about this strange race of people to which, he insisted, she belonged.

'Perhaps I am not English,' she objected, beginning to think she hated the very sounds they made. 'Perhaps I am really an Iban, although I am rather big and pale...'

Then suddenly he began to laugh and his face softened, and she felt a warm pleasure. She had liked his face when it looked craggy and rock-like but now, when he smiled, it was as if sunshine lit and softened its contours. There were little crinkly lines round his eyes, endearingly human, and she almost dared to hope that he liked her.

'You won't feel like that when you get among other English women,' he said. 'Then you'll realise that you're a beautiful English rose.'

'What is this—an English rose?'

'It's a flower.'

'Is it a pretty flower?' she asked, still feeling doubtful.

'Oh yes, one of the loveliest.'

That took her breath away momentarily, for it did not tie in with his attitude of the previous night. She shook her head. 'I don't understand you.'

'You don't need to. I have no part in your life beyond taking you away from that village.' He kept his voice to a whisper so that the others in the boat could not overhear, but the harsh note was back and it strangled the joy that had leapt into her heart. 'Think of me only as your escort.'

'I can't do that,' she objected. 'You're my husband.'

'You know the position, Shuah. Don't make it too hard for me,' he growled. 'I assure you, when we reach England, you'll come to realise that I'm right.'

She threw him an enquiring glance, but he turned away with his face set back in those stern lines that she had come to associate with him. Already she knew better than to challenge him when he looked like that—yet she found fascination even in that forbidding expression.

They travelled on for some time in silence until a change in the surroundings indicated that they were about to approach another village. The jungle trees opened out to reveal clearings where the land had been burned and hill rice planted, and there were coconut and sago palms.

People came to the river's edge and waved and shouted, and some of the men set out in their boats to accompany them for a short time on their journey. They knew Masterson, for he had called at that village earlier on his tour of the district, and now he shouted greetings and, in response to their curiosity, readily told them he was returning to his own boat but that he or one of his officers would visit them again before long. The Ibans ceased their rowing while these pleasantries were exchanged, and were eager and proud to tell the villagers that the Resident had married a woman from their village. Then Shuah, too, had to wave to them, and some of the men in the other boats came up so close that she could lean over and touch their fingertips with her own, a gesture of goodwill that had been introduced by the first White Raja.

After midday they came to groves of bananas, with long leaves tinted in brilliant emerald green, and then a new sound came to her ears, a roar that grew louder and louder, coming from ahead. She glanced anxiously at Murray.

'What's that?'

'We're coming to the rapids,' he answered. 'It's all right—these fellows are skilled boatsmen. They'll get us over.'

Shuah's heart was in her throat as the speed of the boat quickened, being drawn to where the water flashed white, dashing over rocks, huge jagged rocks that threatened to break the frail craft to pieces. The Ibans evidently knew this stretch of water well, for they entered it with wild whoops of excitement, relishing the challenge as they steered between the threatening rocks with ease and skill. She grasped the narrow seat on which she was perched as they were tossed from one direction to another, the paddlers using all their strength but only just managing to keep the boat on course. When an enormous rock loomed ahead, she was sure they would crash into it, that the boat must overturn and they would all be thrown into the frothing water.

Murray leaned forward and covered her hand with his. 'It's all right,' he said with a calmness that was comforting. 'These men know what they're doing. Relax, and you'll find it exhilarating.'

Shuah could not quite do that, but the feel of Murray's hand clasping hers with warmth and strength gave her confidence. His assurance was so positive she had to believe him and she began to feel something of the thrill he spoke about as she watched how skilfully the men kept the boat going. Almost as abruptly as they had entered the rapids, they came clear of them and floated safely into smooth water, although they were still moving fast. Suddenly all tension was dispelled, the men's faces relaxed and they began to laugh and talk again. She was almost sorry the danger was over as Murray released her hand, making her feel alone again.

It was early evening by the time they reached the village where he had left his boat. Because of the lack of tracks through the jungle, almost all travel was made by river. Half a dozen Malay soldiers had remained there to guard the Resident's large proa, and they now lined up to greet the returning party. Murray stepped out of the boat and turned back to hold out a helping hand for Shuah, which she found surprising but pleasant. He indicated that she should precede him up the notched pole that led to the longhouse, and offered a hand for that too. She had no need of help, but took it, for it gave her a happy sense of belonging.

That feeling was soon dashed. They were greeted by the *penghulu*, the chief of several villages in the area, who was quite old by Iban standards, probably close on sixty. His black hair was slightly tinged with grey, and his skin wrinkled, giving the tattoos—of which he had a great many—a strangely distorted look. In his youth he must have been a great warrior, for each tattoo marked a victory over his enemies, and indicated that he had taken many heads. He walked towards Murray with his hand extended in greeting, and they touched fingertips.

'Welcome back, *tuan*,' he said. 'I trust you have had a safe journey to Bartulu and the other villages?'

'I return your greetings, *penghulu*,' Masterson replied, his face stern. He reached out and grasped Shuah's hand, drawing her forward. 'Did you know that this young English woman was living in Bartulu?'

The chief's face remained impassive. 'She's the woman who was found as a child cast adrift in a boat, isn't she?' he asked.

'Exactly. Why have you never told any of the officers about her?'

The *penghulu* shrugged. 'Why should I, *tuan*? I understood you were not interested in our women?'

Masterson's lips tightened. The chief was being presumptuous, but it was necessary to keep things on a calm level. 'Shuah is not one of your women,' he said. 'She is English.'

'English?' he repeated. 'I don't know what an English woman or child looks like, so how could I tell? Why are you taking her away?'

'We are married,' he said. 'I am taking her to Kuching, to place her in the care of the White Raja.'

A wide smile broke over the chief's face. His earlier remarks had been uttered defensively, but now he concluded confidently, 'That will make a very happy ending to the story!'

'It would have been better if she had been returned to her own people soon after she was found,' Masterson rebuked him sternly. 'Finding her now will cause great problems.'

Shuah felt desolate to hear Murray talking in this way. She stood with her eyes downcast, wondering why he was making such a fuss—she had thought that, after they were married, all would be well. The *penghulu* was not at all repentant.

'She has been well looked after—see how tall she is. Would she look as she does if my people had neglected her? You would not have married her if you didn't think she'd make a fine wife, would you?'

Shuah held her breath as she waited for Murray to answer that question. She was disconcerted when he simply avoided it and said, 'She has to be educated in western ways. Life won't be easy for her in England after growing up in Sarawak.'

'She's young. She'll soon learn your ways. Come, *tuan*, sit and allow my grand-daughter to bring rice-wine, and we'll celebrate your arrival.'

'Very well,' he said. 'But first we'd like to bathe and change. We have had a long day's journey in the proa, and I feel hot and sticky.'

The pool was similar to that at Bartulu, and Shuah revelled in the cool refreshing water, where it seemed that almost all the people of the village decided to join them. After their dip, they were shown to a *bilek* that was to be theirs for the night, and there for the first time since morning she was alone with Murray.

'We'll have to share the room, I'm afraid,' he said. 'Must keep up the pretence of being married for one more night, while the men from Bartulu are still with us. I'll sleep on the floor over there.' He nodded his head in the direction of the wall furthest away from the bed.

Her heart plummeted. It was to be the same as before; he did not wish to come to her bed. She stood in her wet sarong, feeling suddenly tired and dispirited. She had never heard of such a strange marriage, but she could only accept it. 'As you wish, *tuan*.'

A sound like a growl was wrenched from his mouth. 'Yes,' he thundered, 'it is as I wish. And I told you not to call me that! My name is Murray!'

'Yes, Murray.'

How lonely you could feel, sharing a room with someone who so deliberately rejected you! For her, it was the second miserable night of her marriage.

In the morning, after their bathe, Murray hurried up to their *bilek* ahead of her; when she entered, he was already dressed in his clean white drill suit. He handed her one of his shirts.

'I want you to wear this,' he said.

Her face wreathed with smiles as she held up the white cotton garment. It was the first present he had given her, something to wear, something that had belonged to him. 'Thank you! Thank you, Murray,' she exclaimed, and threw her arms round his neck and lifted her lips to kiss him.

She felt the warm pressure of his lips upon hers, experienced again that thrill that raced through her blood as her body, damp from the swim, made contact with his. He kissed her back—she was sure of it, and her eyes were as warm and smiling as her mouth as she gazed at him, but a moment later he grasped her upper arms and pushed her away.

'Good heavens, child, don't make such a fuss! It's only one of my shirts to cover your...yourself. I can't have you arriving at the Fort looking like one of the natives. Put it on, and get ready for the journey.'

Hurt and angry, she was about to throw the garment to the floor, but he took it from her and held it up. 'Turn round,' he said, and this time there was a more gentle note in his voice. 'I'll help you. Put your arms in the sleeves.'

She obeyed, and then he turned her round and fastened the first two buttons down the front to show her how to do them. His fingers fumbled, and she heard him breathing quite heavily, considering it was such a simple task. The shirt was big on her shoulders, and he suggested she should roll up the sleeves to shorten them, then stood back to appraise her appearance. She awaited his verdict with some anxiety—she was so eager to please.

'Put your clean sarong over the top,' he instructed. He turned while she unfastened and stepped out of the damp one and twisted a dry one round her waist.

'Like this?' she asked.

He turned and regarded her critically, then nodded. 'I can't honestly say it does anything for you, but at least it's more modest.'

'What does that mean, Murray? What is "modest"?'

'What indeed?' he said, as if he too was wondering, then he spoke quite sharply. 'Don't ask me to explain now; it would take too long, and I want to get away.'

They were waved off in the friendliest fashion by the *penghulu* and his people. Shuah and Murray now travelled in the Resident's personal proa, which was especially large and roofed amidships with palm-leaf thatch to give protection from the hot sun. Different teams of Ibans took over the work of paddling that and the other boats in which the soldiers travelled.

It was late afternoon when they arrived at Simgga Fort, a square stockade about twenty feet high built of ironwood with watch-towers at the corners. On each side was a wide veranda with an overhanging roof from which the heavy tropical rain could cascade into open drains. It had been built several years before, when there had been rebellious tribes to subdue, and was the home of the Resident for that division. A crowd of Malays and Ibans gathered to greet them, and almost immediately two young white men hurried over, putting on their sola topis as they emerged from the fort. The long thin features of the taller man and the round reddish face of the other expressed scarcely hidden surprise, shock even, as they stared at Shuah.

'Welcome back, sir,' said the shorter, plumper young man.

Murray stepped out of the boat, turned back and politely offered a hand to assist Shuah to disembark. 'Shuah,' he said, speaking in Iban, 'these are my two District Officers—George Jarrett...' He indicated the taller of the two young men, who promptly lifted his topi to reveal hair of a pale yellowy colour that she had never seen before. He was lankily tall, with narrow shoulders and thin bony wrists, and an unhappy expression that did not change in the least as he stepped forward and held out his hand. She touched his fingertips lightly, which seemed to surprise him.

'And this is Harry Lumsden,' Murray continued. Lumsden had already swept his topi from his curly ginger head, reached out and grasped her hand tightly within his and shook it up and down in what Shuah felt was a most extraordinary fashion. He had a merry grin on his round face.

'Welcome to Simgga, Miss Shuah,' he said.

'Thank you,' Shuah responded.

'I say, wherever did you learn to speak such good Iban?' His astonishment made his face look rounder and redder than ever.

'That's a long story,' said Murray. 'And it will have to wait until later. Come, Shuah, I'll take you up to the Fort.'

Within the forbidding walls was quite spacious accommodation, and on the further side, with a view out to sea, a very pleasant veranda. Murray clapped his hands, and a Chinese boy came running.

'Shuah, this is Koi,' he introduced him. 'He'll see to anything you need. His parents do my cooking and general cleaning.' Turning to Koi, he instructed him to make tea for the memsahib. Then he indicated with a sweep of his arm that she could precede him into a room at the back. It contained a single bed draped with white net mosquito curtains, which Shuah thought rather pretty. He came only as far as the doorway, and glanced quickly around to check that it was in good order.

'It's very nice,' she said.

'It's normally my room. I'll have my things moved out later. Now I have to leave you, to catch up on the work that's come in while I've been away. You'll hear the gong when it's time for dinner. I suggest you rest here until then.' He turned to go, but paused in the doorway and turned back with that authoritative air that was part of his great attraction. 'I'll tell the officers the main facts of your story—but I shan't mention that wedding ceremony we went through. It meant nothing, and it's best forgotten—agreed?' He left without giving her time to reply.

He did not see the slow, gentle way she shook her head as she stood for a moment staring at the door he had closed behind him. She pouted a little—strange, fascinating creature, would she ever understand him? She had no intention of resting; she was far too interested in her new surroundings, especially the view of the sea. On the western side of the Fort, a large double doorway stood wide open. She waited until Murray's footsteps had faded, then opened it, glanced round the empty room, hurried across and walked outside. She did not linger on the veranda, but, delighting in her freedom after two days of being cooped up on the boat, ran down some steps and over the grass. She passed through a grove of casuarina trees and came to where soft brownish sand edged the blue water that gently washed in with white-capped wavelets.

The hot afternoon sun beat down, making the sand hot for her bare feet. She stood for quite a long time at the water's edge, just allowing the ripples to cool her toes, drinking in her very first glimpse of the sea. The South China Sea—she had obviously seen it when she was a child, for she had been found somewhere out there, on that vast expanse. She gazed and marvelled, and the water was so inviting that she stripped off the shirt Murray had given her, tossed it aside and waded in. She swam happily for some time, then, feeling refreshed, returned to the beach. The sun had set in a spectacular flare of red, purple and gold while she had been swimming, and darkness was about to fall with its usual dramatic suddenness. She picked up the shirt, but did not bother to put it on because that would make it wet, and although she was conscious of the honour Murray had bestowed on her with the gift, she felt more comfortable without it.

Happily she wandered back in the direction of the Fort. Lamps had been lit on the veranda, and in their light she could see Murray and the two English officers, together with three Malayan officials, all sipping long cool drinks. They did not at first see her, for she was hidden by the darkness and the brown trunks of the casuarinas. She noticed that they were not sitting on rattan mats on the floor but on bamboo chairs. The men were all concentrating on something Murray was telling them, and somehow she guessed he was explaining how he had found her.

She approached slowly, reluctant to disturb them, until the sound of the gong rang out. Then she ran, still holding the shirt in her hand, anxious not to keep Murray waiting. Harry Lumsden was the first to see her and choked into his drink, brought his feet off the rail of the veranda and crashed his chair back with a bang. She ran on. Murray leapt to his feet, vaulted over the rail and rushed towards her.

'Put that shirt on, Shuah!' He grasped it roughly, and standing deliberately to shield her from the view of the men on the veranda, he held it up for her to put on. 'You can't walk around here half-naked!'

'But I didn't want to get it wet!'

'You've got to start behaving like a white woman, whether you want to or not,' he said.

She did not really understand what she had done wrong, but evidently in his eyes it was important that she should cover the upper part of her body. She slipped her arms into the sleeves and did up the buttons.

'Tomorrow I'll have to send you to the bazaar to get some more suitable clothes made,' he said, and his voice was more kindly. 'Now, let's go in for dinner.'

CHAPTER FIVE

MURRAY LED her back to the veranda, where the two young Englishmen were on their feet.

'I say, sir, may I escort the young lady in to dinner?' Harry Lumsden asked boldly.

'If you wish,' Murray agreed with an air of indifference.

Lumsden beamed all over his round red face as he held out his crooked arm so deliberately that Shuah could not fail to understand she was supposed to place her hand within it. 'Murray's been telling us how he found you—it's an incredible story! I went to Bartulu a few months ago and I didn't see you. I wish I had!'

Shuah could not help smiling as she remembered how one of the girls had described the last officer who visited the longhouse, saying he had got drunk on *tuak*. Harry Lumsden was nice, so friendly and open in his admiration of her that she could not help liking him—but she was glad it had been Murray Masterson who found her.

The table, covered with a long white cloth, had been set for dinner in the main room. A black-haired, dark-skinned boy sat by the wall rhythmically moving a sheet of cloth suspended from the ceiling by means of a cord attached to his big toe, to waft the air around and cool it. Two Chinese servants stood by the door to the kitchen quarters, waiting for the Resident's party to take their places. Lumsden led Shuah to one of the cane chairs and pulled it from the table, inviting her to take her seat there. She had never sat at a table before, hesitated for a moment, and seeing that the three men remained standing, felt obliged to stand also until he leaned forward and whispered to her, 'Please sit down, Shuah.'

As soon as she was seated, the men drew out their chairs and sat down also. Murray was at the head of the table, on her immediate left, while Lumsden sat on the other side of her and the lugubrious-looking George Jarrett was opposite. The meal was well cooked, and although the dishes were prepared in the Chinese style, the ingredients, rice, fish, chicken and local vegetables, were all familiar to her and she ate with relish. Mosquito nets had been fixed at the windows and doors, the boy continued to work the 'fan', and the Chinese servants came and went almost silently, bringing fresh dishes and removing empty plates.

'Will you be staying here long?' asked Harry.

She glanced at Murray, for only he knew the answer to that, and she, too, had wondered what plans he had for her.

'I'll send a letter off in the morning to the Raja in Kuching, asking for his advice. It'll take at least a week to get a reply, but I imagine he'll wish Shuah to be taken there as soon as possible. I'll request him to send the steamship.'

'Quite right. A lady can't possibly travel in one of those Iban war boats,' said Harry. 'I'd be happy to escort Shuah to Kuching, if you can't spare the time yourself, sir.'

'I'm sure you would,' Murray said drily, 'but I consider it my duty to take Shuah to meet the Raja and try to root out some information about who she is, and make plans for her future.'

Shuah was pleased—even though Murray had spoken of accompanying her as a duty, but Harry looked so crestfallen that she wanted to say something to cheer him up.

'Is it very nice, this place called Kuching?'

'Not really—not like home!' he sighed.

'What is home?'

'England! It's just over two years since I came out here, and I've got another three to serve before I'll get home leave.'

'Is England so very nice?'

'Best place in the world,' said Harry.

'Depends where you live.' George broke into the conversation. 'It's not much fun for the poor people who live in the big cities.'

They argued on, and Shuah felt somewhat confused, then she lost track of the conversation altogether because they lapsed into English, until Murray reminded them that she could not understand.

Harry was at once contrite. 'Sorry, Miss Shuah. Just wasn't thinking. George makes such a misery of everything, he makes me quite angry at times.'

'Will you go back to England?' Shuah asked, addressing Murray.

'I'm due for home leave in about seven months,' he told her.

'Going to get married this leave, aren't you, Murray? I wonder what your wife'll think about living out here in the wilderness.'

'I've told her what it's like. She's a sensible girl,' Murray said.

Shuah felt a small constriction in the pit of her stomach. Was this why Murray kept away from her? He had specially asked her not to mention their wedding, and because of that she held back the questions she would have liked to ask and instead turned to Harry. 'Do you have a wife?'

'No, I shan't get permission to marry till after my second tour.'

'Don't see why that should worry you; you've got a pretty Kayan girl to comfort you meanwhile,' said George.

Harry looked uncomfortable, pretended he had not heard and quickly changed the subject. 'Miss Shuah will need something more feminine to wear when she goes to Kuching,' he said. 'You can't take her there in one of your old shirts.'

'Quite right, Harry. Perhaps you'll escort her to the bazaar tomorrow and see about getting something made up for her,' Murray answered easily.

'I'll be delighted!' Harry agreed. 'But I don't suppose they can make European clothes.'

'Something Malay or Chinese will be more comfortable in this climate. I also think that each of you should spend an hour or so a day teaching Shuah to speak English. She won't be here long, but we can make a start. I'll also give her some lessons myself.'

'Gosh, yes—delighted!' Harry beamed again.

Even George nodded with reasonable grace. 'Good idea, sir.'

The meal ended, and as the servants cleared the table a group of Ibans appeared at the open doorway. They were from a different tribe from those of Bartulu and their dress had slight variations, bright scarlet loincloths, black and silver calf and arm bangles, and very elaborate tattooing. Murray invited them in, and sitting on rattan mats, they were given little tots of gin which they drank neat, smacking their lips in appreciation. They looked curiously at Shuah, for she was the first white woman who had ever been to that outstation, but unsure of the etiquette on such an occasion, she remained quietly in the background.

They had come to talk of their troubles and worries to the Resident, and Murray listened and gave advice and reassurance, and Harry poured out a second tot of gin for each man. Shuah guessed that the drink was almost as important a part of the visit as the talk, and said so to George.

'They certainly enjoy a drop of gin, but there's more to it than that. It establishes contact with the local people, keeps us well informed about what's going on in the area, and that makes for good government. The Raja encourages it,' he added, as if that ended any criticism.

Shuah retired early to her own room, before the Ibans had gone, but she heard them leaving soon afterwards. Then from away in the jungle she heard the sound of drums, rhythmical and penetrating, and smiled, knowing that in some longhouse a party was going on—perhaps it was a wedding celebration. That thought was comforting, for it reminded her of the marriage ceremony she had gone through with Murray. She was his wife, whatever he might say. She wished he was not committed to marrying this other girl—this sensible girl— but if it was so, she would rather share him than lose him. She too would try to be a sensible girl, then, some time, surely he would come to her? With that thought she fell asleep.

Next day she slipped away early to bathe in the river, and when she returned, remembered to lift her sarong high and tie the knot above her breasts. After breakfast, which she ate alone, for Murray had left the Fort before daybreak, Harry called on her to escort her to the bazaar. She was delighted with the selection of pretty fabrics on sale, and encouraged by Harry, who told her that Murray wanted her to have the best, she chose three very pretty ones, to be made into jackets that she could wear with her sarongs. She was reluctant to spend too much, for although she had no real idea of money, she recognised that such garments must cost something.

Harry was good company, and he often made her laugh, for to her ears he spoke a sort of broken dialect, not always being able to get the right pronunciation. When they returned from the bazaar, he stayed on in the bungalow and began to teach her the English words for various objects in the room. Then it was his turn to laugh at the mistakes she made. In the early afternoon George came along and, as instructed by Murray, sat with her for an hour or so, teaching her more words.

He was less fun, but even so there was something pleasantly solid in his companionship. When she was with Harry she was never quite sure if she could trust him, but it was not like that at all with George.

After George had left, she wandered idly around the bungalow, looking at various things that were strange to her. She could speak to the boy who was pulling the fan because he too spoke Iban, but she could not communicate with the Chinese family, who spoke only Cantonese and some broken English. She wandered away and down to the sea.

The wavelets rippled in to the shore and she walked along ankle deep, kicking at the water, feeling lonely. She cast her eyes ahead, surveying the curving shoreline, then looked up to see a Brahminy kite soaring high over the casuarina trees. That was a good omen—the king of birds! She could hardly believe it when, within a few moments, a voice called her name.

'Shuah, coming for a swim?'

Murray was running down the beach towards her. He was wearing only a short sarong and the upper part of his powerful torso was naked, the muscles rippling under the firm, tanned skin. Her heart lifted with pleasure at his invitation; she needed no second bidding, and without another thought unbuttoned the shirt she found so restrictive, threw it aside, and followed him into the water.

He plunged under immediately and joyously she did the same, delighting in the refreshing feel of the water. As she swam towards him, he looked back; he was watching her, waiting for her, and she smiled and teasingly dived under. She could see him beneath the water but twisted round him, making a game of it, using the suppleness of her body to evade him, for she knew he was chasing her. Then sharply she surfaced, coming up abruptly immediately in front of him, with her face only a few feet away from his. She smiled, his craggy face seemed relaxed, but he reacted to the challenge she had thrown at him—he crashed towards her, heaving himself half out of the water as he lunged, but reading the threat in his eyes, she had already spun away to evade his outstretched hands.

She saw him glance round through the splash he had made, and immediately dived beneath the surface again. She swam a short distance under water, then popped up, expecting to see him behind her, but only ripples showed where he had ducked under. As she swam in a small circle, suddenly she felt his hand grasp her ankle and she yelled out in surprise, kicked out with her other foot, tried to escape, but he held on and she was helpless. She jack-knifed, so that she could grasp his shoulders, and then he released his hold.

With a twist she turned, still holding on to his shoulder, and their faces were so close that they almost touched beneath the water, bubbles from his mouth playing around hers. Then together they rose, and as they came to the surface, her body came into contact with his and she felt a tremor run through him. His skin beneath the water had a quality of silk, which stirred a tingling yearning in her breasts. Her long hair floated around them both as if it would enmesh them.

'You're like a mermaid,' he murmured huskily.

She was not sure what he meant, but she smiled because she was so close to him and because he looked happy. She lifted her face and rubbed it against his, and both were wet. He moved his face. Water trickled over their lips as they met. He kissed her hungrily and she clung to him, delighting in the sensations that poured from his strongly masculine body. She was almost out of her depth and had to hold on to him, but the water was warm and buoyant and he obviously found it no effort to support her.

She ran her hands over the back of his head, feeling the contours of it, the rounded bone beneath his scalp, twining her fingers into the wetness of his hair. And all the time his lips moved over hers, sensually, demandingly, as if they could never have enough. Irrationally she longed to stay there for ever, locked in his arms, with his kisses raining over her—but suddenly, as abruptly as his lips had found hers, he drew back.

'This is madness!' he said. 'I've no right...'

She was bewildered by his withdrawal, as if she had lost a vital support, for she had been transported to a world of absolute delight by the delicious sensations that coursed through her.

'We belong together,' she murmured.

'No! Never!' The words were spoken with such staccato venom that she released the hold she had kept on him. His head was lifted high, his eyes apparently fixed on some distant object away on the horizon. He was not even looking at her.

'Why?' she breathed.

'I'll explain—but allow me a moment to pull myself together. I won't take advantage of your innocence.'

With a gentle but firm touch he lifted her hands from his shoulders and pushed her from him. She floated easily away, and at once he plunged forward and struck out for the shore, swam a few yards, then stood up and waded out. She rolled over in the water and followed him, keeping her pace slow, accepting that he wished to be on his own for some reason best known to himself, but that acceptance did nothing to assuage the hollowness within her. He had rejected the love she had offered, and for her the beauty had gone out of the day.

Her eyes followed him as he emerged from the sea and walked a little way up the beach. His wet sarong clung to his strong thighs, moulded itself to his lean hips as he bent and picked up the shirt she had discarded. He remained with his back to her as she walked over to join him, but obviously he was aware of where she was, even though her footsteps made little sound. He held out the shirt, still without turning.

'Put it on,' he ordered.

She took it from him, pushed her wet arms into the sleeves, fastened the buttons and waited. A few moments later he turned round, glanced at her, and sat down on the beach. He was perfectly calm, totally in control, and only the grimly set lines of his face hinted at the struggle he had waged with himself.

'Sit down, Shuah. You deserve an explanation, and I'll attempt to give you one.'

Sensing that he would not wish her to be too close to him, she dropped gracefully on to the sand and sat cross-legged as she was accustomed to do in the longhouse. His eyes were shielded by those shaggy eyebrows, and she could not see his expression; his full well-shaped lips, that had so recently been pressed passionately to hers, were compressed into a tight, level line.

'First of all, Shuah, I am not a free man.' He paused as if to make sure that she had heard and understood. He was speaking in Iban, using carefully chosen words. His eyes flickered questioningly over her face, and for some reason a lump came into her throat. She swallowed and nodded.

'I'm engaged to be married to a lady in England. Her name is Dorothy Mortimer,' he continued slowly and with great emphasis on each word as if determined to make her understand. 'It's six years since I proposed to her and she accepted me. We both knew it would be a long time before we could marry, but she promised to wait—and she has waited. After my next leave she'll come here with me as my wife. She's willing to accept the rigours of life in this outstation, to be exiled here for my sake, and not all women would do that. I admire and respect her. Our future together is mapped out, so you see why I can never really be your husband, Shuah.'

She waited a minute, then because the bruising of his kisses was still on her lips, she ventured to say, tentatively, 'But you do like me, don't you?'

'Of course I like you, Shuah.' There was a note of impatience in his voice now. 'You're a sweet child, but that's all you are.'

'I'm not a child, Murray! I'm a grown woman—I could have been a mother twice over by now...'

'Many girls of your age are still at finishing school in England,' he replied.

'What does that mean?'

'It means that you still have a lot to learn, Shuah. You've no idea what it's like to be a civilised western woman. Believe me, your attachment to me developed only because I'm the first white man you've ever seen. When you meet other men, young men who are nearer your own age, then you'll understand.'

'I've met Harry and George...'

He gave a light laugh. 'So you have, and they're both absolutely bowled over by you! I can see it, even though George doesn't wear his heart on his sleeve like Harry does. But in any event it wouldn't be advisable for you to fall in love with either of them, because they won't get permission from the Raja to marry for a very long time. He expects all his officers in Sarawak to do ten years in the service before he'll even think of increasing their salary so that they can support a wife. Now you know exactly what the position is, Shuah.'

She sat very still and quiet, thinking over what he had said, and really it made very little difference to her, as far as she could see. She was Murray Masterson's wife—and even if he married this other woman, this Dorothy he spoke about, then she, Shuah, would still be his Number One wife. As for falling in love with other young men, that idea she treated with disdain. She would be faithful, as was expected of all responsible, adult Ibans.

'Yes, Murray.'

'Good.' He heaved a sigh, as if he was mightily relieved, but his gaze lingered on her face. 'You're a lovely child, Shuah, and I hope you'll always think of

me as a friend. I promise I'll look after you, protect
your interests and do everything I can to help you to
find your relatives. You can trust me; you know that,
don't you?'

'Yes.' She breathed the word like a sigh. She did trust
him, utterly and completely—in fact she rather wished
he was a bit less honourable, because evidently it was
that side of his character that kept him away from her.
Has he any idea of the thoughts and yearnings that
pulsate so strongly within me? she wondered. Suddenly
he leapt to his feet and reached down to grab her hand
and draw her up beside him. He kept hold of her fingers,
just lightly, and together they walked back to the
bungalow.

The following day the dressmaker called at the Fort,
bringing the finished garments. Shuah was delighted and
excited as she looked in a mirror that hung on one of
the walls, although she could see only her head and
shoulders in it. Two of the little jackets were of fine
cotton, but there was one very special one, of dark blue
satin, which showed her red-gold hair to advantage and
intensified the blueness of her eyes. It fastened down the
front with little golden balls that twisted through golden
loops, and was similarly decorated down the sides of the
slashed cuffs of the narrow sleeves. Harry had also suggested that she should have a couple of pretty silk scarves
to wrap over her head, or round her shoulders. It was
all new and exciting, and she spent a happy morning
trying on the various combinations of sarongs and tunics
until Harry called to give her some more tuition in
English.

'I say, you do look pretty!' he exclaimed enthusiastically. 'I think we made the right choice there.' Then,
with a mischievous twinkle in his eye, he added softly,
'But I thought you looked really beautiful when you
came up to the bungalow from the beach that first
evening you were here, Shuah.'

She glanced at him warily, unwilling to encourage such compliments, wishing she could tell him she was Murray's wife. As it was, she could only try to turn his thoughts into a different direction by saying, 'Shall we start the lesson? I have so much to learn.'

Harry happily complied with Murray's instructions to teach her some English in the mornings, and George arrived punctually in the middle of the afternoon to carry on with the lesson. She worked hard, determined to learn as much and as quickly as she could. George always carried on relentlessly for more than the agreed hour, seeming never to want to finish, and when at last he left she usually felt her head was reeling with the effort. If it was not raining, she went again to the beach in the late afternoon and waited there hopefully. But Murray never again joined her, and she always ended by swimming alone, then returning to the bungalow before the gong rang for dinner.

Just as Murray had predicted, it took over a week for word to come back from the Raja, Charles Brooke. He sent his steamship, HHS *Aline*, under the command of its Malay captain, bearing a letter that Murray translated into Iban and read out to her.

'The Raja sends his greetings, and hopes to have the pleasure of meeting you in the Astana—that's his residence in Kuching. He'll be interested to hear your story from your own lips.'

'Sounds as though the old devil doesn't quite believe it!' remarked Harry.

Murray ignored the interruption and continued to translate. 'He sends his yacht, HHS *Aline*, and trusts you'll have a pleasant journey.'

'He—he doesn't say if he knows who I am?' Shuah asked hesitantly.

Murray shook his head. 'It's too early to hope for that, but when the Raja's heard your story in full, he should be able to trace something. There must be some record if a ship was lost off this coast twelve or so years ago. Don't worry, Shuah, I'm sure there'll be positive news once we get to Kuching.' He glanced at the letter again. 'The rest of it is about the usual matters concerning the governing of the division.'

'You're not planning to send me there alone, are you?' Shuah exclaimed. 'I shan't know anybody, and everything will be strange?'

'If the Raja expects you to stay here, sir, I'll make the trip,' Harry offered eagerly.

Murray withered him with a look. 'I shall escort Shuah to Kuching.'

'Don't think he'll like that, you know,' Harry said. 'Won't expect someone as senior as you to leave the division...'

'I make my own decisions,' Murray's tone was icy. 'We'll leave tomorrow. You and George have managed well enough while I've been up-river—you can carry on for another week or two.'

Harry twisted a face behind Murray's back like a thwarted schoolboy, making Shuah smile, but she was relieved that she would not be parted from Murray.

The yacht was a wooden gunboat, steam-driven but of shallow draft, so that on the high tide it could just negotiate the bar of sand that lay submerged beyond the mouth of every river in Sarawak. The voyage would take about three days, and Shuah was given a small cabin furnished with a bed, dressing-table and narrow wardrobe.

Cane chairs were placed on deck and she enjoyed sitting there, especially as Murray often joined her. He insisted that she studied English for several hours every day, but he also pointed out places of interest and showed her how to use the binoculars, which she found quite amazing. Breakfast was brought to her cabin by a dark-skinned boy, who was probably about twelve years old. He had a wide friendly smile, but since he did not understand any Iban, Shuah could talk to him only by using the few words of English she had learned, and she was pleased that they managed to communicate a little.

Early on the morning of the third day Shuah woke up to realise that they were sailing in calmer waters. The yacht had crossed the bar on the high tide and was now entering a broad, winding river. The pale brown water reached right to the edges of the forest trees, while beyond, half hidden by mist, the Santubong mountain rose like a great green cliff. Along the shoreline were groves of casuarina trees with long reddish-brown trunks and feathery leaves moving continuously in the light breeze. Murray came to the rail and stood beside her.

'We've just entered the Sarawak River, which leads to Kuching,' he said. 'We'll be there in about two and a half hours.'

In some ways the scenery was familiar, but the closeness to the sea and the fact that this river was a busy highway made it different. Mangroves grew in the mud that was revealed as the tide dropped, and among their roots she recognised crocodiles that entered the water with a sickening flop. Behind them, troops of monkeys were swinging in the branches of the trees. They sailed past small houses built on stilts, and naked brown children played in and out of the water. Already some women were washing clothes and others were filling long bamboo jars that they carried on their heads. Shuah noticed that they wore their sarongs tied just under the armpits, not at their waists as she had always done.

She felt she was beginning to learn western ways, but that did nothing to diminish her anxiety about this meeting with the great White Raja that lay ahead. In particular there was the ever-nagging question: would she discover from him anything about who she was or who were her parents? Or why she had been adrift in that empty boat? Was it possible that some of her family had also been saved and were living in Kuching? All her hopes were centred on this all-powerful ruler of Sarawak.

'Is the Raja a kind man?' she asked Murray.

'I don't think that's a description many men would use about him,' said Murray, 'but he'll deal very courteously with you. He can't resist a pretty woman, even though he's well into his seventies! He's a remarkable man in many ways. They say he was very handsome in his youth, but he's disfigured now by having a glass eye—he lost the other in a hunting accident in England. Rode into the branch of a tree.'

'He sounds quite unpleasant, yet you speak as if you admire him.'

'I do. There's no doubt he's a formidable character, and he's carried on the good work that was started by his uncle, the first White Raja. Between them they've made the country a safer and more prosperous place. The one thing even their worst enemies have to admit is that both men have been entirely devoted to Sarawak. Charles would sacrifice himself and everyone else if he thought it would be good for the place. He won't exploit its people, nor will he allow anyone else to do so. Yes, I do admire him. I wouldn't have stayed on in his service if I hadn't.'

Other smaller craft passed by, boats of all sorts and sizes, from sampans to larger houseboats where whole Malay families lived. As they neared the town itself, Chinese chop-houses and godowns clustered on their port side, while to starboard, Murray pointed out the Astana.

'That's the home of the Raja,' he said. 'We'll go there as soon as the ship's docked, but you won't be able to stay there, because the Ranee is probably in England. I may as well tell you that there's not much love in that marriage, and the Raja doesn't make his wife very welcome when she visits Sarawak, but his eldest two sons are here. They work as District Officers, and he drives them every bit as hard as he does the rest of us.'

'You'll stay with me, won't you?' Shuah pleaded. Everything he said about this formidable man, the White Raja, made her more and more anxious.

'I'll be about for a few days,' Murray said. Then he looked down at her and smiled. 'Don't worry. You'll make a great impression. Everyone will love you!'

There was little comfort in that. She did not want everybody to love her, only Murray—and he was positively eager to hand her over to these strangers and leave her there. It was in a mood of near panic that she disembarked from the *Aline* into the proa and was paddled to the landing-stage of the Raja's palace.

CHAPTER SIX

THE PROA was brought skilfully in beside the stone steps that led up to a tall narrow gatehouse. Murray stepped out first and offered a hand to help Shuah, and she walked with him towards the Astana. It was set on a low green hill amid tall bamboos and betel-nut palms and borders of exotic flowers that filled the air with sweet perfume. To the right was a square grey tower where a sentry stood on guard, and attached to this but slightly behind, built on high brick pillars, was a large white-walled dwelling. Three people came out to stand on the wide veranda of the first floor, watching their approach.

One was an elderly man, tall, straight-backed and with an air of immense authority, dressed in a uniform of white drill similar to that worn by Murray Masterson, but decorated with a row of coloured ribbons. Obviously it was the Raja himself, and beside him were two ladies, both wearing white sola topis, and dressed in white gowns that covered them from their necks to their feet. One was as tall as Shuah, but the other was shorter and plump. The expressions on the faces of those ladies was both forbidding and puzzled, which Shuah found disconcerting.

'That's the Raja. The ladies are the wives of his chief officers,' Murray whispered to her.

Nervous though she was, Shuah would not show it and held her head high, moving easily in her sarong and a short scoop-necked jacket of apple green. Her thick golden-red hair was caught back, twisted into a knot at the back of her head, but strands escaped to curl softly around her face. Steadily she and Murray walked on and

soon they were close enough for her to make out the
hawklike features of the Raja. Her feelings were very
mixed, for she could not help being in awe of him—this
man who ruled Sarawak with a rod of iron, yet had a
reputation for justice, of whom many tales of valour
and ferocity were told in the longhouses. His age commanded her respect, yet also made him vulnerable. He
fixed her with an arrogant stare from his one good eye,
while the false one glittered glassily, but although his
expression was unsmiling, she felt he was not entirely
displeased with her appearance. He lifted a gnarled-
knuckled hand and tugged at his bristly white moustache.

'Ha, Masterson! What's this, then?' he growled in
greeting. 'Didn't expect to see you here today.'

'Sir, I promised my protection to this young lady and
therefore felt it necessary to accompany her until I could
place her safely into your care.'

'Hmmph! No trouble in your division, I take it?'

'None at all, sir,' Murray replied confidently. He
turned to Shuah, and taking her hand, led her up a wide
flight of steps until she was standing immediately in front
of the formidable old man. Then he introduced her,
speaking in Iban. 'Shuah—this is His Highness the Raja
of Sarawak.' She bowed her head slightly and held out
her hand to touch the Raja's fingertips. The single
penetrating eye flickered over her face and the lips
beneath the thick white moustache almost smiled.

'Strange story, what! Could hardly believe it when I
got your letter, Masterson—but I see what you mean.
Girl certainly looks English.' He turned to the two ladies
beside him. 'What do you think?'

'It's quite incredible, I agree, Raja. The girl's certainly far too tall to be an Iban, and that hair! Freckles,
too! And blue eyes! What did you say her name was,
Mr Masterson?'

'Shuah. Allow me to introduce you to Mrs Crossley.'

Shuah held out her hand to touch Mrs Crossley's lightly with her fingertips and was surprised when that lady grasped it firmly and pumped it up and down vigorously. The same thing happened when Murray introduced her to the other lady, Mrs Bell, though much more gently.

'Shuah can't be her real name,' protested Mrs Crossley.

'It's what she was called in Bartulu. She knows of no other.'

'Never heard anything so outrageous!' said the second lady. 'Do you speak English, Shuah?'

'I have learn little,' Shuah replied carefully.

'Better than nothing, I suppose.'

'Come inside,' commanded the Raja.

He led the way across the veranda into a very large room that stretched the whole length of the bungalow. Its ceiling was heavily carved with dragons and beautiful flowers, in the very best Chinese style. The Raja seated himself in a comfortable old chair with a sagging seat.

'Come and sit beside me, Shuah. Tell me all about yourself.' This time he addressed her directly and in excellent Iban.

She had become accustomed to sitting on chairs in the few days she had been at the Fort and on the boat, and settled herself gracefully on a low stool close to the old man.

'I know very little about myself—only what I've been told—because I was so young when the *tuai rumah* and his men found me,' she began.

The Raja listened attentively until she had finished relating the story just as she had heard it so often. Then he looked sharply at Murray. 'Why wasn't she noticed before? That's what I'd like to know. It seems she's been in Bartulu for twelve years. I know you've been appointed Resident only recently, Masterson, but I can't think why none of my officers discovered her long before this!'

'I didn't realise it, but my adoptive mother used to hide me,' Shuah said. 'I think she was afraid I would be taken away, and she loved me very much. She was so good to me, but she died a short time ago. I loved her, too.'

The Raja pulled at his moustache again. He appeared to be thinking deeply. 'Could you find no clues to her identity?' he asked Murray, still speaking in Iban.

'Unfortunately no, sir. The men had no idea how or why the child came to be adrift in an open boat. I questioned them closely, because I suspected that they might have been on a piratical raid, that they might even have engineered the disaster—but they were unshakable in their story. The child was there, in the boat, alone, and they saw no other vessel that day. They say they brought back the boat in which she was found, but it has rotted away since then. I could find nothing that could help to identify either the ship or the child.'

Hopefully Shuah gazed into the hawk-like face of the Raja. 'I should so much like to know who I am.'

'Of course you would! So would we all! I've been racking my brains and making enquiries, but so far I haven't discovered anything positive.'

Somehow Shuah had not anticipated such difficulty; she had assumed that somewhere in the legends of this white tribe there would be a story that would link her to them. Her disappointment must have shown in her face, for the Raja spoke again, more kindly.

'Twelve years ago would make it around 1893. Now at the back of my mind I've a dim recollection of a ship being lost at about that time. I've sent to Singapore. Most vessels call there, so they may find some clue. It's difficult though, especially when we have no factual details, not even the ship's name. We'll just have to wait and see if their records show anything.'

Shuah looked from the Raja to Murray, but his handsome face was as non-committal as ever. He nodded, and said, 'It seems very possible that there is a connection between that shipwreck and Shuah being found adrift in what I assume was a lifeboat. At least it's a start.'

'Don't want to raise false hopes,' barked the Raja, fixing Shuah with his one good eye. 'Must have some confirmation first. Meantime, I've arranged for Mrs Crossley and Mrs Bell to look after you.'

'But—can't I stay with Murray, please?'

The Raja appeared not to hear and spoke to the two ladies in English, and almost immediately Mrs Crossley rose from the sofa. She marched purposefully to where Shuah sat very still and quiet, took hold of her arm, made motions for her to get up, and as soon as she was on her feet began positively dragging her towards the door.

'Murray, what am I to do?' Shuah pleaded.

'Just go with Mrs Crossley like a good girl, Shuah.' He spoke as if to a child. 'It's for your own good.'

'But when will I see you again?'

'I'll walk over this evening. Then I'll explain everything to you.'

The stern set of his craggy features told her that further argument would be useless, though his words were some comfort. She felt as if a prop had been wrenched from under her, but she had no alternative but to accompany Mrs Crossley and Mrs Bell out of the Astana.

'Where's your sola topi?' demanded Mrs Crossley, as they descended the steps and walked out into the hot sunshine. 'You'll get sunstroke.' She tapped the white helmet on her head to indicate what she meant.

Shuah looked at the helmet perched high above Mrs Crossley's tight bun, and struggled with her English. 'It's pretty,' she said.

A chortle of laughter burst from Mrs Bell. 'That's the last thing I'd call a topi! We wear them only because they say you'll die of sunstroke if you don't. We must find one for her tomorrow, Mrs Crossley.'

'We must indeed! I don't know how she's survived so long in this dreadful climate without one.' Mrs Crossley nodded her head emphatically.

The laughter had made the ladies seem much more friendly, although Shuah had no idea what she had said to cause it. Nor could she follow their quick conversation as they walked one on either side of her across a wide lawn and then through gardens where palm trees, bananas and pineapples rioted in half-cultivated disarray. Both ladies lived in bungalows that stood only a short distance from each other, and which were built in almost identical styles, similar but smaller than that of the Raja, but without the ornamentation that gave character and dignity to his residence. It had been decided, apparently on precedence, that Shuah should stay with Mrs Crossley, and Mrs Bell parted from them at the door.

'I'll show you your room,' Mrs Crossley said, and guided her through the spacious airy bungalow.

Shuah's room was dominated by a large bed hung round with mosquito netting. Opposite was a reading table and lamp and two rattan chairs. Hanging baskets with orchids in full flower decorated one wall, which was lined with glowing golden-brown wood and there were wide windows, netted to keep out insects. It was a pretty room with pictures of strange-looking landscapes. Mrs Crossley pointed to a watercolour of a village green with a tall church tower rising over some spreading trees and a line of cottages whose dormer windows overlooked the street. Then, seeing the puzzled expression on Shuah's face, she spoke slowly and clearly pointed to one particular house, then to herself, and then mimed cradling and rocking a child. 'That's the house where I was born.'

Suddenly Shuah understood, and she smiled and nodded vigorously, and Mrs Crossley smiled back and her large-boned face came to life. Its warmth made Shuah think that perhaps there might be more to this lady than she had seen so far. A man's voice called from the outer room.

'My husband,' said Mrs Crossley. 'Come and meet him.'

He was plump and pleasant and obviously uncomfortably hot, but he looked up with a smile as his wife introduced Shuah. She reached out to touch his fingertips, but just as his wife had done, he clasped her hand between his and pumped it up and down. 'Welcome to Kuching,' he said.

A Malay servant entered, carrying a tall glass of some beverage on a small tray. Mr Crossley took it and sank down beneath a fan, mopping the sweat from his round red face. He spoke good Iban, but he was a quiet man and seemed content to listen to his wife talking; since she spoke in English, Shuah understood little. She would have liked to sit on the floor in comfort, but obeyed Mrs Crossley and seated herself on one of the rattan chairs. She was waiting for Murray, confident that he would keep his word, though time dragged interminably.

It was long after dinner when at last the servant showed him in, and Shuah sat bolt upright, her hands tightening on the arms of the chair, her eyes riveted on his face. Mrs Crossley had been playing light classical pieces on a rather tinkly piano, while her husband sat back, sipping whisky and water, his eyelids drooping sleepily, occasionally emitting a snore that would jerk him back to a momentary wakefulness.

'Ah, Mr Masterson.' Mrs Crossley greeted him without leaving her piano stool. 'Come and sing something for me.'

'Willingly—in a moment,' he replied, and walked across to Shuah, regarding her quizzically with his perceptive brown eyes. In the dim light of the oil-lamps his features were sharpened, his shaggy eyebrows and that

small scar just below his right eye darkened by deep
shadows. He was dressed as immaculately as usual,
holding himself upright, authoritative even there among
friends.

'You've settled in all right?' He spoke in Iban, and it
was more a demand than a question.

'Yes, thank you. Mr and Mrs Crossley are very kind.'
What else could she say? She assumed that later she
would have the opportunity to speak to Murray alone.

He nodded, and his face relaxed. 'They're good
people,' he told her. 'I know you'll be safe with them.
You see, Shuah, I don't think you really understand what
a very great deal you have to learn before you can take
your proper place in English society. The people who
live in Sarawak, like myself, the Raja and the Crossleys,
we understand the sort of upbringing you've had in
Bartulu, and, believe me, Shuah, it's very different from
what it would have been in England. You have to be
taught, not only how to speak English, but all sorts of
things about behaviour and customs, and you'll learn
all that from Mrs Crossley and Mrs Bell. So you see why
it's important for you to stay with them until the time
you actually go to England?'

'I'm not sure I want to go to England. I don't know
if I'll like it there.' She pouted a little, but her doubts
were genuine.

'Of course you'll like it,' he commanded. 'You want
to know who you really are, don't you? And to meet
other members of your family?'

She did—but whoever these people were, however
loving and kind, they could never take precedence over
her husband. 'Well—yes, of course—but...'

'Good,' he interrupted. 'That's settled, then.'

She wanted to say to him—no, it's not good. I don't
want to stay here without you, but that would have been
ungracious, especially as Mr Crossley was wide awake
now and had been listening to their conversation.

'You'll be all right with us, Shuah,' he said. She could tell he meant it. 'My wife'll enjoy having you around—it's pretty lonely for the womenfolk out here.'

'Exactly. Excellent for everyone,' Murray said, quite brusquely.

He appeared to think that was the end of the matter, and accepted a whisky and soda from Mr Crossley and walked over to the piano to consult with Mrs Crossley about a suitable song. She set up the music, played a few trills on the piano and Murray began to sing an aria from a light opera in a clear, rich baritone. Shuah listened enraptured. After that he sang another piece, and then he and Mrs Crossley sang a duet. Shuah experienced a tinge of jealousy and the feeling grew in her that Murray was casting her aside, that he had finished with her. She forced herself to wait patiently for an opportunity to speak to him alone, but when he left the piano he joined Mr Crossley for a long conversation that she could not follow. At last he stood up, and came towards her, holding out his hand.

'You've already learned our European custom of shaking hands, I believe.' He reached out, clasped hers, and held it. 'I have to leave now, and tomorrow I must return to my station.'

'You can stay here,' she interrupted him quickly. 'I have nice *bilek*.'

Murray looked quite shocked, and so did Mr Crossley, who glanced anxiously at his wife, glad that she had never learned Iban, only Malay, and just enough of that to deal with the servants and shop in the bazaar.

But when Murray spoke, his voice was quite gentle, as if he was humouring a child. 'No, Shuah. I'm staying at the Astana tonight. Mr and Mrs Crossley will take good care of you.'

'When will I see you again?' she asked.

He gave a wry smile and shrugged his shoulders. 'Who knows? For now at any rate, it has to be goodbye.'

She was devastated. He was leaving her—and spoke as if he might never see her again. Bewildered, she simply stood stock-still as he dropped her hand and moved away. She watched in shocked silence as he said goodnight to Mr and Mrs Crossley, and without another glance in her direction walked out of the room. She took a few steps towards the door, but Mrs Crossley was there before her, turning a key in the lock, making it clear that Shuah was not to be allowed to follow him.

'I think it's time we all went to bed,' Mrs Crossley said.

With a pretence of meekness, Shuah said goodnight and walked to the room that was to be hers. She closed the door behind her and hurried over to the wide windows—it was the work of a moment to open them and clamber out. The warm night air was filled with the sound of cicadas and the scent of sweet-smelling flowers. She moved as quietly as she could across the veranda, swung over the rail, leapt to the springy grass, and then she ran. Murray was not to be seen, but she remembered the direction of the Astana and there was enough light from the moon to guide her. He was almost back at the palace when she caught sight of him.

'Murray!' she called. He did not hear her at first, but he was not walking very fast and as she ran on she began to catch up with him. He was about to put a foot on the first of the steps leading to the veranda when she called out a second time.

He turned sharply. 'What the...!' He broke off, sounding anything but pleased.

'Don't leave me here—I can't bear it.' She hurtled herself into his arms and felt them close round her, drawing her tightly against his warm strong body, and she was comforted. He would not hold her like that if he meant to abandon her, surely? She raised her face towards his, yearning for his kiss—but it did not come.

'Shuah.' His voice was harsh. 'This is nonsense! You must understand that I have no further part in your life. You're safe here, you'll be well looked after, and soon you'll go to England.'

'I won't go anywhere without you!' she protested. 'If you may not sleep in my room at the Crossley's, then let me stay with you here.'

'No, Shuah.'

'Murray, you're my husband! We should be together, always.'

A sound like a snort of anger came from the veranda close by, followed by a scraping sound of a chair being moved hastily back. She felt the stiffening of Murray's body, and she clung to him more closely as they both turned to face whatever or whoever was there.

'What's that you say?' roared the voice of the Raja. He had obviously been sitting on the veranda in the dark and had overheard her remark. 'Did I hear it right? Did that girl say you were her husband, Masterson?' he bellowed.

Murray quickly recovered his composure. 'It's a misunderstanding, sir. I can explain.'

'You'd better! Come up here, both of you.'

The Raja was seated on a cane chair, leaning forward with his hands folded over the top of a walking-stick. Shuah was glad that Murray kept one arm reassuringly round her waist as he guided her to stand before the all-powerful ruler.

'So? What's this, then? I'm listening.'

'I had to bring Shuah away from Bartulu, but the people were anxious about her—to them, she had been a sort of talisman sent by the gods. If I had simply marched off with her, it could have caused an uprising. The witch-doctor was whipping them up...' In a quiet voice Murray recounted his version of the circumstances under which they had gone through the marriage ceremony.

'It's outrageous!' snapped the Raja. 'To think that one of my officers could go through such a charade! I've a good mind to dismiss you on the spot, Masterson.'

'I'm sorry you feel like that, sir,' said Murray stiffly. 'I did what I felt was best, not only for Shuah but also in the interests of keeping law and order in your country. I made it clear to her that it could never be a real marriage between us, that it would not be binding.'

The Raja turned to Shuah. 'What do you have to say?'

'Murray did what was necessary, Raja. Otherwise I should have been forced into marriage with Dioudi, and I did not want that.'

'But you called Masterson "husband" just now. Have you been living as man and wife, eh?'

Murray's voice rang out, loud and clear. 'No, sir. Certainly not! I promised Shuah before we went through the wedding ceremony that it would be in name only, and I've kept my word.'

Shuah hung her head, for she felt ashamed that Murray had so consistently rejected her.

'Is that true, Shuah?' The Raja insisted that she should answer.

'Yes, Raja...'

The sound of heavy footsteps crashing towards them, accompanied by heavy breathing, made them pause and look beyond the veranda. 'Phew! That you, Raja? Have you—seen—Shuah? Girl's gone...' The words were gasped out breathlessly as Mr Crossley hurried towards them.

'She's here,' replied Murray.

'Thank goodness for that! Wife was devastated! Went to—her room—to see if she was settled—and she'd gone! Window open—couldn't think what had happened.'

'She's all right—there's nothing to worry about. Just a bit of a misunderstanding,' Murray said evenly.

'You'd better tell Crossley the background,' said the Raja, and Murray again recounted the story of his marriage to Shuah.

'Good God!' exclaimed Mr Crossley when he had finished. 'But I thought you were engaged to a lady back home, Masterson?'

'I was about to mention that commitment,' said the Raja. 'I take it you still wish to honour the arrangement?'

'Sir, do you doubt my integrity? I've been engaged to Dorothy Mortimer for six years, and I must remind you, Raja, that I already have your consent to bring her out with me as my wife when I return.'

'Then so be it. I can see you made this extraordinary decision with the best of intentions, and since the marriage has not been consummated and Shuah was in no way deceived by your actions, I accept that it was not a valid marriage under English law. I'll take no further action over it. You're one of my most trusted officers, Masterson. See that this story goes no further. May I have your word of honour that no one else shall hear of it, gentlemen?'

Both Murray and Mr Crossley gave their assurances to the Raja, and then he turned to Shuah.

'You see, my dear, you are free. You've never been truly married to Murray Masterson. You may not fully understand at this moment, but, believe me, it has all happened for the best. When you return to England and find your relatives, no doubt they'll assist you to find some young man whom you'll wish to marry.'

'But suppose I have no relations?' she protested.

'Nonsense! Everyone has relations. Too many, usually!' snapped the Raja.

'But even if I have, they may not want me. Oh, Murray!' she grasped his arm. 'Please don't send me away?'

He placed his hand, warm and comforting, over hers. 'Shuah, you're worrying unnecessarily. Everything will work out well for you, if you just do as you're told. Go now with Mr Crossley and stay with him and his wife. Learn as much as you can from them, and as soon as news comes of your relatives, you'll be able to go to England and take your proper place there. I have to return to my division tomorrow.'

'Take me with you!'

'Impossible!' decreed the Raja. 'No women there. Enough of this nonsense. Take her back to your wife, Crossley.'

Mr Crossley said, gently, 'You'll be all right with us, my dear.'

'No—no! I go with you, Murray!' She was near to tears.

He was still holding her hand, which she had placed pleadingly on his arm, and gave her fingers a gentle squeeze. 'Shuah, you must do as we say. I wouldn't leave you if I thought for one moment you wouldn't be happy here. The Crossleys are good, kind people, and staying with them will be a wonderful opportunity for you. Learn all you can from them—will you do that?' She nodded reluctantly. 'Promise me?' he persisted, looking down at her earnestly, and she wanted so much to please him.

'Yes, Murray. I will try.'

'Good. Now go.' He moved away from her as he spoke, allowing her hand to fall from his, and his voice was so stern that she could only obey.

Sadly she allowed Mr Crossley to lead her back to the bungalow. She was both hurt and puzzled by some of the things that had been said. Murray intended to marry this other lady, that was quite clear—nothing she could say or do would alter that. But, equally, nothing Murray or the Raja or anyone else said would make her change her mind on the simple, indisputable face that she had made a vow to take Murray Masterson as her husband.

Mrs Crossley was pacing up and down the living-room in a state of considerable agitation, and when Shuah entered she rushed over to her, but it was with relief, not anger. 'Oh, my dear, wherever have you been? Are you all right?'

Although she spoke in English, her concern was so sincere that Shuah understood and was touched by it. She had not intended to cause any worry, and was sorry that she had done so. She apologised in Iban, and Mr Crossley had to translate, explaining that Shuah had been alarmed at being separated from Murray Masterson because she had not understood why she was staying with them. He had given his word to the Raja to make no mention of the marriage, and kept it to the letter, not even telling his wife. If Mrs Crossley suspected that there was more to it than she had been told, she was too wise to question her husband. As soon as she was assured that Shuah would stay quietly in her room, and make no further attempt to leave it until the morning, she suggested wisely that they should all go to bed.

The following day, however, Mrs Crossley kept a close watch over Shuah, never leaving her alone for a moment. They all took tea and fruit together on the veranda at six o'clock in the cool of the morning, and shortly after that Mr Crossley left for his office. Mrs Crossley, who had been wearing a loose cotton negligée, showed Shuah the bathroom that was to be hers. It had no windows, the only light coming through narrow chinks between the boards close to the ceiling. The floor was tiled, with little channels for the water to run away, and in one corner stood a huge stoneware jar filled with cool water. There were stone slabs beside the jar, and above it hung a basket of woven palm leaves.

'It's for washing yourself,' she explained to Shuah.

Shuah looked at it in amazement. 'Why not go to the river?'

'The river's dirty,' said Mrs Crossley, adding emphasis by twisting her face into an expression of distaste. 'You wash here.'

When she had left, Shuah looked at the huge jar in amazement. She walked all round it, then stripped off her clothes, climbed up the steps and just managed to slip into the jar. The water was certainly cool, and she shivered slightly, splashing it over herself. It seemed a very uncomfortable way of washing—and when she was ready to get out, that proved to be exceedingly difficult. She wondered how Mr Crossley could ever get into such a jar, and the very thought made her chuckle, for he was so very much larger than she. When she tried to pull herself up, there was not sufficient space to lift her arms, and when at last she did, she could not get a firm enough hold.

'Shuah, are you still in there?' Mrs Crossley called from outside the door with a note of panic in her voice.

'I—I cannot move!' Shuah managed to call back.

The door opened, and Mrs Crossley peeped round it. 'Forgive me...' She broke off, seeing Shuah's head sticking up from inside the jar, stood stock still in amazement, then burst out laughing. Momentarily she was helpless with mirth, then she hurried over. 'Oh, my dear, I should have explained! You're not supposed to get into the jar. But never mind—let me help you.' She climbed up the steps so that she could grasp Shuah's hands, and with that help and Shuah's natural agility she was soon extricated and wrapped in a towel.

She felt rather foolish, but Mrs Crossley was only amused and began to explain. 'You should dip this into the water——' she reached up for the woven basket '—and pour it over yourself.'

Shuah dressed in a fresh sarong and another of the little jackets Murray had bought for her, then wandered back to the veranda. The lawn stretched from the bungalow to the edge of the busy river, where a wide variety of craft moved to and fro, mostly native proas, but also sampans, junks and small steamboats. Across the water lay the town of Kuching, looking neat and fresh in the clear morning light. She heard Mrs Crossley speaking to the cook and guessed she was giving orders for the day's meals, and a little later Mrs Bell walked over.

The ladies had planned to take Shuah on a shopping expedition, for they were far from satisfied with her clothes and were determined to get her some European-style garments. There was some difficulty because she had no money, and although they were willing to be generous, their husbands were not so highly paid that they could spare much. They talked of asking the Raja, but he was notoriously mean. When his children were young, he had not even given his wife enough money to clothe them properly and they had often been dressed in their father's old suits cut down. The Ranee had pawned a famous diamond called the 'Star of Sarawak' to pay for their education.

However, Mrs Crossley and Mrs Bell were determined that Shuah should have some high-necked lace-trimmed white cotton gowns that would be in keeping with her status as an English lady. She must now wear shoes and, most importantly, a sola topi. There were several of these hanging up in the Crossley's bungalow, and they found one that almost fitted and had it cleaned immediately.

With that thrust uncomfortably over Shuah's luxuriant auburn hair, they took her by boat across the wide river and walked up into the bazaar. There were traders of many nationalities, and a wide assortment of goods both local and from distant lands—luscious fruits and vegetables, fish both dried and fresh, sacks of rice and beans, meat, tea, coffee, porcelain and stoneware, rattan baskets and mats, jumbled in picturesque confusion on stalls and on mats on the pavements. Shuah was fascinated by the colourful array. She would have loved a gown made from some of the exquisite silk that was on display, but accepted with gratitude the fine white cotton that Mrs Crossley and Mrs Bell declared to be suitable. She stood meekly when they took her to the dressmaker's and instructed the woman to make a gown in a style similar to those they themselves wore. Shoes were difficult, for she had no recollection of wearing anything on her feet, and could not imagine that they would ever be comfortable, but she was measured, and two pairs of shoes, one white and one black, were ordered for her. Mrs Crossley and Mrs Bell were determined that Shuah should look entirely English from now on.

CHAPTER SEVEN

DAYS PASSED in which Shuah tried to come to terms with her new self, to learn English, to read and write and to behave as did Mrs Crossley and Mrs Bell. It was that in particular that she found difficult. They were horrified when they found her sitting cross-legged on the floor—and equally so when she sat thus on the sofa! She would have given up trying had she not made that promise to Murray. She longed to go for a bathe in the river, to swim, to splash, luxuriate in the feel of the water all about her—scooping it from the jar to pour over herself was but a poor substitute. She missed being physically occupied, gathering plants from the jungle, planting rice, and even pounding and grinding it, hard work though that was.

But she struggled to conform, convinced that only by becoming completely Anglicised could she hope to win a place in Murray's heart. His attitude suggested that he still remembered her as he had first seen her, frolicking in the river with the other girls, living the life of an Iban—and he expected his wife to be one of his own kind. She fought to repress much of the natural liveliness of her nature, to model herself on those two middle-aged English women who devoted themselves to teaching her and to whom she was a substitute for their own children at boarding school in England and not seen for years on end.

Mrs Crossley decreed that Shuah must have a personal maid, and allocated to her a girl whose name was Madu, which meant 'honey'. Madu was Malay, a little younger than Shuah, a happy, good-natured girl with a ready smile, the daughter of the Raja's butler and his

Number Three wife. Because both her parents had always been in service with English people Madu spoke that language quite well, and Shuah had made enough progress to communicate with her.

As she came to know Madu better, Shuah learned a little of what it was like to live in a household where the husband had three wives, and she tried to reconcile herself to how it would be when she was reunited with Murray. His resolution to marry this woman called Dorothy when he returned to England was matched by her own determination never to give him up. If she could not be his only wife, she would be his Number One wife and make the best of it.

Madu's father Subu was a high-ranking servant of the Raja, the one whose duty it was to hold the yellow umbrella above His Highness's head on state occasions. No one else was allowed beneath the shade of that huge yellow umbrella, and Subu was proud to be its bearer. On those occasions when they attended these ceremonies, all three of Subu's wives would appear, walking in strict order of precedence, and if either Number Two or Number Three wife wished to make a remark, they always asked permission of Number One wife before venturing to do so. Shuah noted that with some satisfaction—she would do the same when this Dorothy woman became Murray's Number Two wife!

One morning, about ten days after Shuah had arrived in Kuching, Mrs Crossley hurried out to where she sat on the veranda, carefully copying letters into an exercise book. 'I've just received a message from the Raja—he wishes to see you,' she said.

Shuah looked up, and her heart gave a little leap of excitement. 'Perhaps he has news—of my father and mother?'

'He doesn't say, but the steamer from Singapore docked yesterday, so it's very possible. We're to call upon him at four o'clock this afternoon.'

Both Mrs Crossley and Mrs Bell decided they should accompany Shuah to the Astana, where Subu ushered them into the Raja's presence. He was seated behind an enormous desk as they entered but stood up and advanced with his hand outstretched in greeting, a custom Shuah now accepted easily. She watched his expression hopefully, but could tell nothing from his face, and even his one good eye seemed to glitter as glassily as his false one. He saw that they were seated comfortably, and enquired after their health, and the ladies responded with some remarks about the amount of rain they had suffered recently, and Shuah felt that they would never get to the real point, but at last he began.

'I have received news from Singapore about the ship that was lost in 1893. She was called the *Lady Brenda*, and was mainly a cargo vessel manned by a mixed Malay and European crew. However, she had accommodation for half a dozen passengers, and among them were a man with his wife and a small girl. The couple were listed as Mr and Mrs Edward Sutherland.'

Shuah sat bolt upright, listening eagerly, and as Charles Brooke spoke slowly and very clearly, she was able to understand most of what he said.

'And the child? Was she named?' Mrs Crossley asked.

'No. The information came only from the port authorities, since the ship's papers obviously went down with her. There's no information as to how or why she was lost, but it was presumed that she foundered during a storm. It would appear that the ship was on its way to the Dutch East Indies, and it was not until she was overdue that any enquiries were made, and by then, of course, it was far too late.'

'How very sad!' exclaimed Mrs Bell. 'I wonder what happened?'

'That's something we'll probably never know,' the Raja replied brusquely.

'But you think that the child must have been Shuah?' Mrs Crossley asked.

The Raja nodded and gave one of his rare smiles, and Shuah's heart warmed to him. 'Not many English people travel in these waters with small children even nowadays, and there were fewer twelve years ago. I think the co-incidence is too great for there not to be a connection. I'm quite convinced——' He turned to Shuah, waved a hand in her direction with stiff old-fashioned gallantry, and announced, 'that this is Miss Sutherland.'

'Miss Sutherland,' Shuah repeated with a kind of breathless wonder, for having another name gave her a strange feeling that she had become a different person.

'Miss Sutherland!' exclaimed Mrs Crossley, with a nod of approval.

'What a charming name!' declared Mrs Bell.

'Did the authorities in Singapore have a home address for the Sutherlands?' Mrs Crossley asked.

'Regretfully not. But Mr Sutherland was listed as a plant-hunter, so I've sent a message to London, to Kew Gardens, to see if anyone there can throw any light on the matter. Most botanists have connections with Kew, so it's possible that we may find out something through them.' The Raja stood up in his usual abrupt manner, indicating that the interview was at an end. 'I'll inform you as soon as I receive a reply. Meantime, keep on with your studies, Miss Sutherland.'

'I will, Raja, and thank you.'

As she walked back to the Crossleys' bungalow, Shuah asked anxiously, 'How long do you think it will be before the Raja receives news from England?'

'Letters take about six weeks each way,' Mrs Crossley explained, 'so it'll be at least three months before we can expect a reply.'

Weeks and months passed, and Shuah increased her vocabulary and her knowledge of English manners and customs. She spent her very first Christmas, found it a delightful occasion, and wondered if Murray was celebrating in the similar style far away at Simgga Fort. Never a day passed but she thought of him, even though she heard no news. His face would flash into her mind's eye, so vividly sometimes that her heart would beat faster and she would glance around, half expecting to see him. Then an intense sadness would come over her, almost despair, and sometimes when she was alone in her room she could not help crying a little. It never occurred to her to send him a letter, though she was now able to read and write reasonably well, and she received no communication from him.

Eventually she received another summons to visit the Raja in his office. She had now met him on several occasions and had lost some of her awe of him, although she always kept her distance. He had a reputation for flirting with all the young ladies, and it was said that more than one child in Kuching bore a strong resemblance to Charles Brooke. Shuah was glad that again both Mrs Crossley and Mrs Bell were to accompany her. They were received as before, shown in by Subu, and Shuah waited expectantly as the customary pleasantries were exchanged by the older ladies.

'I've received a letter from Kew, with reference to Mr Edward Sutherland,' the Raja said at last. 'It seems they know of him, and they speak of him in glowing terms. They had been informed that he and his wife were presumed drowned, some time in 1893, and very much regretted this tragic loss. Evidently he was greatly respected for his work as a botanist, and they mention they have a screw pine he collected in Malaya. They also have an orchid called "Sweet Suzanne" that they say he developed.'

'Fascinating!' exclaimed Mrs Bell. ' "Sweet Suzanne"—I wonder if that was his wife's name?'

'Don't know about that. Didn't get any details about his wife,' said the Raja. 'But apparently he was a man of some distinction in the field of botany. I collect orchids myself, but I haven't heard of that one.'

'Have they given a home address for Mr Sutherland? Or the names of any living relatives?' asked Mrs Crossley.

'Nothing. They searched through their records, and the only address they had was a rented house in London. This the Sutherlands left when they set sail for the Far East, and they gave no forwarding address.'

'What a pity! Is there anywhere else we could make enquiries?'

'It's damned difficult from so far away. Best thing would be for Shuah to make her own enquiries when she gets back. These people at Kew say they'll be delighted to meet the daughter of Edward Sutherland upon her return to England. Meantime, they'll make further enquiries. Don't know if they'll come up with anything. Miss Sutherland ready to take her place in England yet, Mrs Crossley? What d'you think, eh?'

'I really don't know. She's very immature in many ways. I don't see how we can let her go there alone, not knowing anything about her relatives.'

'I go when Murray goes,' Shuah said firmly.

The other three stared at her, for she had not mentioned him in all the months she had been with them.

'Masterson, eh!' commented the Raja. 'I suppose that might be the answer. He's due for leave in a month's time. Suppose I book Miss Sutherland on to the same boat, then he could keep an eye on her and help her to find out more about her parents?'

'I should like that,' said Shuah.

'Shouldn't she have a chaperon?' suggested Mrs Bell, hesitantly.

'She came up-river alone with him, from Bartulu. Masterson's a man of honour—I can rely on him. Besides he's going to get married on this leave,' the Raja pointed out.

'Yes,' Mrs Crossley admitted, albeit reluctantly. 'It's not strictly proper, but I don't see what else we can do.'

'Quite!' barked the Raja. 'I'll make the arrangements, and let Masterson know when I next see him.'

Three more weeks passed, and Shuah's excitement and apprehension mounted. The thought of being reunited with Murray Masterson brought a flood of joy—but it was tempered by doubts. Would he be impressed by the great effort she had made to learn English and to speak it with the precise accent that Mrs Crossley insisted upon? She could now read a simple book or a newspaper—Mr Crossley had the London *Times* sent out from England, and although the news was six weeks old, it helped to give Shuah some idea of life there. She knew how to behave at table, to eat with a knife and fork, and which cutlery was for which course. She had attended several of the dinners and receptions given by the Raja for Europeans in Kuching, and had even begun to master the social art of making small talk. She had been given instruction in dancing, with Mrs Bell taking the man's part while Mrs Crossley played the piano. She was a skilled musician and Shuah loved to listen to her play, especially as it always conjured up memories of the evening Murray had visited them and had sung in his rich vibrant voice.

Less entertaining, but compulsory for all the Raja's officials and their families, was the weekly event known as Band Day, when everyone was expected to dress in their best clothes and congregate on one of the lawns by the Astana to listen to his official silver band. As the Raja himself was very deaf, he had no idea how well or badly the music sounded—to most of the audience it was awful, but no one dared to say so. Shuah found it much less attractive than the gongs and drums she had been accustomed to all her life, and had it not been for Mrs Crossley's expertise on the piano, she would have formed a very poor impression of western music.

It was on a Band Day that she saw Murray Masterson again. She had known he was expected soon, and that she was to leave Kuching with him, but travel was so dependent on tides and weather than no one could be certain when boats would arrive. The band was grinding out its usual loud music, the Raja, with two pretty women seated on either side of him, tapped his walking-stick to the rhythm, while the rest of the crowd shuffled on their cane chairs and looked around. No one was allowed to leave before the end of the concert. Shuah's eyes strayed to the river, and she saw a large war-proa coming in. It was a seagoing craft paddled by thirty men, with awnings of palm leaf covering the centre part of it, but what caused her to leap up from her chair was the sight of Murray. He was poised on the prow of the boat and stepped off the moment it touched the landing-stage.

'Murray!' she called, forgetting all injunctions that no one must leave or interrupt before the playing of the Sarawak National Anthem. She was about to run across to greet him, but Mrs Crossley was swifter—grasping her arm with a strong hand, she pulled her back into her chair.

'Sit still,' she commanded in a hissing tone that was positively threatening. 'Do you want to disgrace me? After all the time I've spent teaching you manners?'

Shuah dropped back into her seat, momentarily shamed. Mrs Crossley and Mrs Bell had both been so kind to her; the last thing she wanted was to displease them. But although she forced herself to sit still, her head seemed to turn of its own volition in the direction of the tall, imposing figure of the man she thought of as her husband.

He was moving with an unhurried stride towards the group around the bandstand, his white uniform immaculate as ever, his sola topi adding to his already considerable height. Joy flooded her heart as she watched him approach and come smartly to a halt behind the

Raja's chair. Her eyes feasted on the sight of his rugged face, his positive features, his tanned skin and even lingered lovingly on that small scar by the side of his eye. The Raja seemed to be unaware that he was there, until those very attractive young ladies who sat beside him glanced up with a fluttering movement to smile at Murray, then he looked round and nodded a welcome. The two men exchanged brief greetings and, that formally attended to, Murray stood up very straight and scanned the assembled company.

He inclined his head in greeting to several of the people, including Mrs Crossley and Mrs Bell. From beneath the shade of her topi, Shuah watched him, waited for his gaze to rest on her, and her lips parted in eager anticipation—but his eyes skimmed past her and straight on to someone else to whom he bowed a smiling acknowledgment. She felt hurt and bewildered. Why had he no smile for her?

The rest of the concert was even more unbearable than the first part, and it was a relief when at last the Sarawak National Anthem was played and everyone stood stiffly to attention. Shuah's natural inclination would have been to rush across to Murray the moment its last note died away, but now she felt unsure of her welcome. That cold glance she had received from him restrained her. Besides, Mrs Crossley moved her large-boned body in front of Shuah so that she would have had to dodge round in a most unladylike manner. Her attitude reminded Shuah that Murray himself wanted her to learn English ways, and she must obey implicitly, or she would wreck what little chance she had of winning his love. So she stood in an unnaturally meek and subdued attitude. Her hands were clasped before her, her flaming hair pulled tightly back beneath the topi, her body encased in a white cotton long-sleeved gown that covered her from her chin to the tips of her toes. Only her eyes darted constantly over to

Murray who, after shaking hands with several people, fell into step with the Raja moving back to the Astana.

'Come along, Shuah,' Mrs Crossley said brusquely. 'We can return to the bungalow now.'

'May I not speak to Murray?'

'Mr Masterson—and I must ask you to drop this familiar way of speech you have when referring to him, Shuah—Mr Masterson will be in conference with the Raja. If he wishes to speak to you he will, I am sure, visit us in the bungalow.'

'But he hasn't even looked at me!' protested Shuah.

'That, my dear, is all the more reason why you must not take it upon yourself to be too familiar. It would be most unladylike for you to make advances to him. A lady must have her pride, and leave it to the man to approach her. Come, child.' She took a firm grip on Shuah's arm and steered her firmly away.

Shuah glanced back once, trying to catch Murray's eye, but he continued to ignore her. All the happiness she had felt on seeing him again crumbled. Did she really have to refer to him as 'Mr Masterson'? She put the query to Mrs Crossley, adding, 'He himself told me to call him "Murray".'

'That may well be, but then you could not speak English and no doubt he thought it would be easier for you. I assure you that no self-respecting English girl would call a young man who was not closely related to her by anything other than his title and surname. Now that you have been trained in etiquette, he'll expect you to conform and call him "Mr Masterson".'

All evening Shuah waited and hoped that Murray would come to the bungalow. She said no more about it to Mrs Crossley, but every slight sound from outside made her glance up expectantly, only to be disappointed. Mrs Crossley as usual played the piano for an hour or so, and Shuah wondered if she too wished that Murray—Mr Masterson—would walk in, as he had on that previous occasion, to sing to her accompaniment, but if so, they were both disappointed. It was customary for everyone to go to bed early, since the day started at dawn before the heat became too intense, and by nine-thirty Shuah knew she would have to give up hope for that day.

The Straits steamship from Singapore arrived in the harbour early the following morning—a major event, because it carried not only passengers and much-needed goods but mail and newspapers, keeping contact with the outside world. It would leave the next day, with Shuah and Murray Masterson among the passengers. She could hardly believe it and felt a mixture of apprehension and excitement. If only she knew why Murray seemed to be avoiding her, if only he had shown some pleasure in seeing her again, but that quick cold glance was all she had received.

It was not until the following morning, when Mr and Mrs Crossley and Mrs Bell walked to the ship with her, that she saw Murray again. On this occasion they all moved towards him, and Mrs Crossley did not reprimand Shuah when she stepped forward a little before the others, holding out her hand decorously, as she had been instructed. She wore the same white dress as on Band Day, freshly laundered ready for the journey, and that compulsory topi sat uncomfortably on her head, for she was never allowed out of doors without it.

'Good morning, Mr Masterson,' Shuah said, slowly and clearly. 'I trust I see you well?'

His head jerked up, an expression of surprise came over his face, and he leaned forward to peer beneath the topi into her face. 'Shuah! You're still here!'

He sounded so astonished, and pleased too, that her heart gave a little leap. 'Of course! Didn't you see me the other day?' she asked breathlessly.

'When?' he asked.

'When you arrived... At the band concert.'

He shook his head. 'Were you there?' Then a broad smile broke over his craggy features. 'It's that damned topi! You're quite lost under it!'

'I don't know why I have to wear it,' she protested. 'I managed all my life without one and never got sunstroke...'

'We're not going into all that again,' Mrs Crossley interrupted. 'Everyone has to conform.' Then she wagged her finger in Murray's direction. 'And you mind your language, young man.'

Murray ignored the interruption and continued to regard Shuah, but the spontaneous pleasure that had lighted his face when she first spoke to him was masked now. His scrutiny was thorough, and she wondered if her struggle to achieve the standards set by Mrs Crossley had been sufficient to meet with his approval.

'You look so different!' he commented, then added, 'I thought you had left for England long ago.'

It was her turn to raise her eyebrows. 'But it's been arranged all along! I'm leaving today—with you.'

'Surely you knew that, Mr Masterson?' Mrs Crossley said. 'The Raja booked Miss Sutherland on the same boat as you from Singapore to Marseilles so that she could travel in your care. I admit I thought it a little unorthodox, but there was no alternative, and we all know you to be a man of honour and integrity. We're trusting you to take good care of Miss Sutherland.'

'Why wasn't I told?' Murray asked.

'We assumed the Raja had notified you, old boy,' said Mr Crossley. 'Can't think why he didn't. A bit forgetful these days—at least on things that don't directly concern Sarawak. Anyway, it's a pleasant enough duty. There's many a young man would envy you!'

'Miss Sutherland, I believe you said?'

'It's my new name—do you like it?' Shuah asked eagerly.

Murray glanced from her to Mr Crossley. 'Does this mean that some information has come through?'

'A little. The ship was probably the *Lady Brenda*, and there was an English plant-hunter on board with his wife and small daughter. It foundered on its way to the Dutch East Indies. Shuah has the facts in writing, but they're checking their records at Kew, and no doubt by the time you get there, they'll have something more to hand.'

'I hope so,' Murray said.

She wished he had shown more pleasure in her news. His response was non-committal, as if he did not relish the prospect of being responsible for her again, but that did not entirely dampen the joy she felt at being with him. They all moved on and boarded the ship, and Mrs Crossley and Mrs Bell saw her to her cabin, which was clean and comfortable. They sat around talking for a time, until the call came for those not sailing to leave the ship. Shuah went up on deck, and Murray stood quietly behind her as together they watched the final preparations for departure, and she waved as they sailed out of Kuching. She experienced a pang of regret, for the place and the people had become familiar.

'Are you happy to be going back to England, Mr Masterson?' she asked.

He did not reply immediately, and when she turned to him, his face was held in taut, grim lines. He did not look especially happy, then meeting her questioning eyes, he relaxed into an amused sardonic smile. 'Naturally, but it's a strange thing. When I'm here, I dream of the things I'd be doing in England, but when I'm there, I find they never quite match my expectations. I think I've spent so long in Sarawak now that I'll never really settle back home until it's time for me to retire. But what about you, Shuah?'

'I don't know. I—I think I'm a little frightened. I'm glad you'll be with me.'

He placed one hand comfortingly over hers where it rested on the rail. 'You've nothing to worry about. Just relax and enjoy the trip. I'll find you a chair. Come this way.'

He indicated one of a pair of comfortable cane chairs, and she smiled up at him as she settled into it, expecting him to join her there, but almost immediately he left, saying he had received some letters he wished to read. She was so disappointed that she had to struggle to keep tears from welling into her eyes. The farewells and seeing Kuching fade away into the distance made her feel emotional and vulnerable. The prospect of going to this foreign land called England and meeting relatives who would be complete strangers to her was daunting. More especially she was hurt that Murray had given so little thought to her, had assumed that she had already left Kuching—and, worse, would not have been sorry if she had!

It boded ill for her future, and the premonition that he intended to hand her over to strangers at the first opportunity was more frightening than she cared to admit. Then she reminded herself that Murray had told her she had nothing to worry about. She tried—but did not quite believe him. However, since she could do nothing about it at this stage, she made herself sit back and watch as they made their slow way out of the wide mouth of the river, over the bar and out to sea. A light lunch was served at mid-day, when she met some of the other passengers, mostly Chinese and Malays travelling on business, all of whom spoke English. Murray chatted to them with an easy friendliness that Shuah envied. The afternoon passed uneventfully, and she complied with the accepted practice of taking a siesta.

At dinner that evening, although Murray sat beside her and was affable enough, he was also in great demand by other travellers, who sought his opinion on various topics related to Sarawak. After the meal, feeling far from sleepy, Shuah slipped away from the dining-saloon and made her way up to the deck to stand by the rail gazing out over the starlit sea. The sound and feel of the engines throbbed, the dark mysterious sea was glassily calm and the ship left a shining white wake behind.

She had put up her hair in the manner Mrs Crossley had taught her, but now, standing with the light breeze blowing into her face, she pulled out the restrictive pins and allowed it to fall over her shoulders in a cascade of red-gold. She tucked the pins carefully into the little black velvet handbag embroidered with sequins that Mrs Bell had made and given her as a parting gift. She had been there a few minutes when she heard footsteps, and turning, saw Murray walking towards her. He halted at her side and leaned on the rail.

'Watching the waves?'

'I was trying to make myself remember when I was at sea before,' she said.

'And can you?'

She shook her head. 'It's frustrating. I feel I should remember something, even if it's only being frightened, or wet, or whether it was dark or light—but I just have no recollection at all.'

'That's not surprising, because you were so young. You mustn't upset yourself about it.'

'I can't help it, because it makes my future seem so uncertain, and I keep thinking—suppose I don't find these relatives in England?' She turned her wide blue eyes to him appealingly.

'You already know your name, and that your father has a connection with Kew Gardens. I'm sure that will lead us to find your family. Come, Shuah, it's not like you to worry about things!'

'But that's part of the trouble, don't you see, Mur—
...Mr Masterson? I don't know who I am, or what I am!'

'You're Shuah. Just Shuah. Remember, you said that to me once? That's the all-important thing, being yourself.'

'But it's not enough, is it? Background is important—I've realised that since I've been staying with Mrs Crossley.'

'It's important—but it's not everything. You've got looks and personality, and you'll be all right in England, believe me!'

She was pleased that he seemed to approve of her again, even though she feared that in a moment he might change his tone. Tentatively she asked, 'When we go to England, can I stay with you?'

'Yes, of course. I'll take you to Father's house, and you can stay there until I've worked out your future. Now cheer up.'

She smiled. At least he was not seeking to abandon her at the first opportunity.

'That's better,' he approved. 'That's how I remember you. You'll have a marvellous time in Singapore and on the voyage.' He straightened up as he spoke and stood tall and gazed down at her, and his voice was a sort of growl. 'You'll have all the young men falling in love with you.'

'But, Mr Masterson...'

'Why do you persist in calling me "Mr Masterson"? It used always to be "Murray".'

'Mrs Crossley said I should—I thought you'd prefer it.'

'Well, I don't. I want you to call me "Murray", just as you always have.' There was an oddly gruff note in his voice. He lifted a strand of her hair lightly between his fingers as if testing its weight. She held her breath to catch his softly-spoken words. 'You have beautiful hair, Shuah. You should always wear it this way, streaming over your shoulders in the moonlight, not tucked away under that hideous topi!'

'The topi is awful, isn't it?' she chuckled. 'It didn't even fit!'

He laughed with her. 'It never occurred to me that Mrs Crossley would take your transformation so totally and literally as to make you wear a topi, after all the years you've been in Sarawak without one!'

It warmed her heart to see him look so happy. It was even worth the discomfort of the topi, she thought as she smiled up at him, and the long lonely weeks when they had been apart seemed to peel away and she felt as close to him as ever she had been. She stood with her face lifted to his, and being with him was the most natural and lovely thing in the world. She leaned towards him, vibrant with the joy of being so close.

Then the laughter faded from his face, his eyes raked over her in the moonlight, and the look in them sent a thrill tingling down her spine so exquisite that she caught her breath. Suddenly his arms were round her, drawing her so tightly to him that her lips parted and immediately he began to rain kisses, hungry searing kisses, upon her. She clung to him, all fear of the future disappeared. When he kissed her like that, she knew where she belonged; she had no need of anyone else in the whole world. She belonged to him and to him alone—she was his Number One wife! His body was stirred by hers—she felt it, knew it, and was overjoyed by the pleasure of that sensation.

Time might have stood still while she was held in his embrace. But even in that moment when she believed there was total accord between them she felt him draw away. He opened his arms, which had drawn her so rapturously and tightly to him, releasing her, though she had no wish to go. He lifted his face from hers, leaving her lips swollen with longing, his hands were on her shoulders—but only to hold her from him.

'This is madness,' he muttered, and his voice was hoarse. 'I'm your guardian. Heaven help me, it's my duty to protect you!'

'But when we love so much...'

'No!' He gave a dry laugh. 'This passion isn't love! You're not so naïve as to believe that!'

'It is to me...'

'No,' he repeated, but more gently this time. 'You don't know enough about life in the west to understand. Believe me, I know. This feeling you have for me will fade soon enough when you meet more young men of your own age and race.' He squared his shoulders stiffly and took a step back. 'Enough of this nonsense. Go to your cabin, Shuah. We have a long journey ahead of us, so let's make up our minds to enjoy it, and no complications.'

CHAPTER EIGHT

FORTY-EIGHT hours after leaving Kuching they sailed into Singapore Harbour, and docked among the medley of Malay fishing-boats, Chinese junks and sampans, huge European liners, cargo ships from all over the world and British naval vessels. Porters handled their luggage while Shuah and Murray were whisked by rickshaw to Raffles Hotel, their runner making his way nimbly through the traffic, ringing his bell, his bare feet pattering on the road. She gazed in astonishment at the crowded city, its huge buildings lining streets thronged with Tamils, Chinese, Malays, Armenians, Jews, Bengalis and Europeans.

In Raffles Hotel, which prided itself on being patronised by 'Royalty, Nobility and Distinguished Personages', suites had been booked for them in advance and Shuah was delighted to find that her room over-looked the harbour. She stood by the window of her sitting-room for a long time, dreamily watching the wealth of life that was evident outside, but she could find only a superficial pleasure in the scene. She had been so happy that first evening on the ship. When he had kissed her, the first touch of his lips had awoken a flood of yearning of almost frightening intensity. It had been like a stab wound to her heart when he had pushed her away, telling her to go below to her cabin—alone.

Every time she saw him she scanned his face anxiously, hoping for some sign of warmth, but he might as well have hidden behind a mask as far as she was concerned. She could make no real contact with him. It had been he who had wished her to acquire a European image, and she had tried her best, gathered meticulously every piece of information she could from Mrs Crossley, but she began to feel it had all been a wasted effort. She might just as well have remained as she was.

Murray was attracted to her—that had been evident when he had held her in his arms and kissed her so ardently, but it seemed that, no matter how hard she tried, he did not quite approve of her. He did not want to be her husband—so she might as well admit defeat. The only way to please him would be by distancing herself from him. That would not be easy, especially as they were travelling together, but if that was what he wanted, then so be it. She would not grovel for his affection. Having been brought up as the daughter of a village headman, she knew that she was every bit as good as he. If only she did not love him so much! But enough of that nonsense. She would, if she could, find other friends, just as he always wished.

With that decision firmly made she squared her shoulders, straightened her back, swung away from the window and began to explore her suite. The sitting-room was opulently furnished: there was a circular table covered with a lace-edged cloth and flanked by dark, polished chairs; a well-stuffed, chintz-covered sofa stood along one wall and a writing-table by another. Beyond that was the bedroom, where the large four-poster was draped with mosquito curtains. A soft carpet woven with delicate colours covered the floor except for about eighteen inches around the edges where the dark floorboards were highly polished. From the ceiling of each room fans whirred gently, wafting cool air about— though Shuah was mystified as to the whereabouts of the 'punkah-wallah' who must be operating it.

Another door opened off the bedroom, leading to a small dressing-room and that in turn led to the bathroom, rather like the one she had used in Kuching with a huge jar filled with cool water and a tin cup to splash it over herself. She bathed, and when she emerged, wrapped in a huge towel, a smiling Malay amah had arrived and had unpacked and smoothed out those demure gowns Mrs Crossley had chosen as being suitable for her on the journey. None was in the height of fashion, though she knew nothing of that, and she decided to wear an evening gown of very fine cotton in palest blue, with a low scooped neckline fringed with lace and small puffed sleeves which showed her gracefully rounded arms to perfection.

The amah helped to put up her rich golden-red hair, not too tightly, tweaking several softly curling strands forward round her face. The whole effect was prettily feminine, and Shuah was glad the freckles did not seem too prominent. She added several of her collection of gold bracelets and necklaces and then, as the amah left, returned to her sitting-room. Darkness fell, lights came on all over the city, and Shuah looked around for a lamp, but although there were several they had no oil or wicks and she did not know how to light them. She shrugged, and waited, quietly and patiently. Soon there was a knock on her door. She guessed it was Murray, and called 'Come in.'

'Sitting in the dark?' he remarked, and a moment later the room was filled with light.

She blinked. 'How did you do that?'

'It's electric lighting. You just push this switch up or down—see?'

She ran across to him and tried it for herself, switching the light on and off several times. 'It's magic!' she exclaimed in awe.

'Nonsense! It's science! The fans are worked by electricity, too. You'll get used to it.'

Would she? And would she get used to the effect he had on her as she looked at him dressed formally for dinner? His starched white shirt with little stand-up wings to the collar showed up his healthy tanned skin; the smooth fit of his black dinner-jacket emphasised his broad shoulders. Was it only hunger that gave her that weak feeling in the pit of her stomach or was it something to do with his handsome face and commanding figure?

'Ready to come down for dinner?' he asked coolly, distantly, in that attitude he had adopted since that first evening on the boat when he had held her in his arms—but she must not think of that!

The spacious marble-floored dining-room was already quite well filled when they entered, and voices and laughter lightly bubbled all around. Murray guided her, following a waiter, and as they crossed the floor a hush settled over the room. Shuah glanced from one side to the other and became uncomfortably aware that they were the centre of attention. It was as if every face in the room was turned towards them and she could not help noticing that while the eyes of the men lingered upon her, the women almost immediately turned their attention to Murray.

The waiter indicated a table immaculately set with shining cutlery upon a snowy cloth and a delightful arrangement of orchids in the centre. Murray held her chair, all his concentration was upon her. If he were aware of the looks they received he gave no sign of it, but seated himself opposite her and spoke to the waiter, who handed a large menu to each of them. Shuah looked at it with interest and anticipation but was disappointed to find she was unable to make sense of it. She glanced across to Murray, remembering some advice Mrs Crossley had given her.

'I cannot make up my mind,' she said. 'I'd be grateful if you could choose for me.'

'You mean you can't read it!' he replied perceptively.

She tossed her head, miffed that he had hit upon the truth, but before she could make any retort he grinned at her, and added, 'But that's not surprising, because it's mostly in French. They rather pride themselves on their French cuisine in this place.'

She smiled back at him—it was a relief to feel that she was not simply stupid! 'It'll all be strange to me anyway.'

'Of course,' he said, and he sounded so understanding that she relaxed, ready to enjoy the evening.

'Murray Masterson! Good to see you, old boy!' boomed a loud voice. A short, rather overweight, red-faced man was hurrying over to their table, his hand outstretched in greeting. Murray was on his feet in an instant, pumping the other man's hand up and down enthusiastically.

'Chubby Palmer! What are you doing in Singapore?'

'Just back from leave, curse it! I'll be back up-country tomorrow. By the way, do you know Peter, now Lord Barrington?' Chubby turned and beckoned forward a younger man, tall and slender and fair-haired. Murray shook hands with him, then turned towards Shuah.

'Allow me to present an old friend, Mr Palmer— Robert Palmer, though he's been known as "Chubby" since we were at school together. Miss Sutherland.'

She held out her hand and was aware of the intense scrutiny she received from Chubby Palmer. 'I'm delighted to meet you, Miss Sutherland.'

Then Lord Barrington was introduced and she found herself staring into a bold pair of eyes of an intense blue set in a good-looking lightly tanned face.

'I say, this is a stroke of luck bumping into you two! I'm on my way back to England on the next boat, so we'll be travelling companions.'

'How did you know Miss Sutherland and I were leaving?' Murray asked.

'Good heavens, old boy, the whole colony has been agog with the story! This is the young lady you found hidden away in an Iban longhouse, isn't it? You lucky devil—you didn't think you could keep her all to yourself, did you?'

'I hadn't realised that the story was generally known.'

'There have been messages coming and going between the old Raja and the shipping office and Government House—it's been the sensation of the year, I can tell you! I heard last night that you'd be coming in on the Straits steamer.'

'That accounts for the curiosity as we came in,' Murray said drily.

'That's putting it mildly!' said Lord Barrington. 'But it wasn't just that that made people stare, you know. I, for one, never expected that the young lady would be so beautiful.'

He clicked his heels and gave her a gallant bow as he said those last words, and the expression in his eyes emphasised that he meant what he said.

Murray regarded him sombrely and changed the subject. 'You're going home on leave, I take it?'

'Going home for good, old boy! Finished out here— and I never want to see another rubber tree as long as I live! Six years of my life I've spent buried in the jungle, and wouldn't have been due for leave for donkey's years, but I've inherited the baronetcy and the estates from my uncle. Came right out of the blue. I was never even in line for it, but both he and his son were drowned in a sailing accident. A tragedy, of course.'

'But good luck for you, Peter!' said Chubby Palmer, giving him a friendly slap on the back.

'True.' He lifted his shoulders in a significant shrug.

'I say, Murray, it's great seeing you again!' Chubby Palmer said. 'We were about to eat. Mind if we join you?'

For some reason Shuah could not understand, since he had seemed so pleased to see his old friend again, Murray did not appear to be enthusiastic at the suggestion, but he nodded his head. 'Certainly. I'll ask the waiter to set two more places.'

Lord Barrington sat on Shuah's right and Chubby Palmer on her left, and neither of them made any attempt to hide their interest in her and their pleasure at being in her company.

'I'll be able to dine out on this for months!' Chubby Palmer grinned. 'You must tell us all about it. What was it like to grow up in the jungle with the Ibans?'

'I was never aware of anything strange about it—it was all I knew,' she answered candidly. 'I was quite young when I was rescued from the sea by the *tuai rumah* and his warriors. He and his wife loved me as if I'd been their own daughter, and I had a very happy childhood.'

'I can believe that. I've heard that Iban children are allowed to run wild, and are thoroughly spoilt by European standards!'

'What does that mean—spoilt?' Shuah asked.

'No lessons, no discipline, just playing about, staying up till all hours of the night,' he explained.

'And it was not like that for you, Lord Barrington?'

'Gosh no! I had to mind my P's and Q's or I'd get sent to bed with no supper. I had an absolute dragon of a Nanny when I was little, and it was worse when I went to school. There was plenty of discipline for me. I'll bet there was for you too, wasn't there, Murray?'

'Murray was always getting into trouble,' Chubby Palmer laughed. 'He was the ring-leader in all our pranks. He thought up some corkers, too! He was a law unto himself.'

'There were some stupid rules and so-called traditions in that establishment. They deserved to be challenged,' Murray remarked.

Chubby Palmer nodded his head emphatically. 'Never knew a fellow to upset the masters the way you did, Murray. I always thought they knew you were too clever for them. You'd have got away with it quite often, but they'd appeal for the culprit to step forward—and you always did!'

'They'd have thrashed some poor innocent creature if I hadn't.'

'But why?' asked Shuah in growing amazement.

'Schooldays weren't the happiest in my life,' Murray said shortly, and snapped his lips shut in a way that prevented the subject being pursued.

'Nor mine, old boy,' agreed Lord Barrington. 'That was why I almost envied Shuah growing up in an Iban village.'

'Except that she now has to learn all those things that we've learned over many years,' Murray said, and Shuah felt she detected a note of criticism in his voice.

Lord Barrington turned to her with a grin. 'I'll be happy to be your devoted teacher during the voyage.'

'I shall conduct Miss Sutherland's studies myself,' Murray said in a tone that brooked no argument. 'I have all the necessary books, and I know exactly what stage she's reached.'

'I wasn't thinking only of her academic studies,' Lord Barrington said. He deliberately turned back to Shuah. 'There's more to life than that! Don't let him work you too hard.'

She caught an undercurrent of tension between the two men, and glancing anxiously at Murray, saw the tight set of his lips.

'Miss Sutherland is in my charge during this trip, and will remain so until I hand her over to her relatives in England,' he said.

'I heard that no one knows who they are,' Chubby Palmer remarked.

'We've one or two clues.'

'It's such a fascinating story. Do you remember nothing at all of your parents, Miss Sutherland?'

She told them what little she knew and they plied her with questions, all of which she answered as freely as she was able, and the atmosphere lightened, especially as some of her statements made her companions laugh. The food was delicious, and it seemed to Shuah that it would have been a very happy occasion had Murray not been so quiet—almost withdrawn.

They were lingering over coffee when Chubby Palmer said, 'I saw Dorothy Mortimer when I was at home. She tells me you're getting married this leave. She's looking forward to coming out with you, I believe. I can't think why!'

Shuah sat bolt upright at the mention of that name. An uneasy tension made her widen her eyes, keenly observing the three men. Murray remained relaxed and cool.

'That's right. We've been engaged for nearly six years.'

'You're a lucky man, Murray. Can't imagine any woman waiting even half that long for me!' said Lord Barrington.

'She'd be mad if she did!' snorted Chubby.

'Dorothy's one of the best. Quite an exceptional young lady, and I am indeed a lucky man,' Murray said gravely.

'Absolutely!' agreed Chubby Palmer. 'She was looking very well, I thought. I'd have popped the question myself if you hadn't beaten me to it.'

Murray gave him a disbelieving smile. He was quite sure of himself over this Dorothy of his, thought Shuah bitterly. She clenched her hands into tight little fists and wished Chubby Palmer *had* carried her off! But that was a ridiculous thought—no woman could possibly prefer him to Murray Masterson!

'Anyway, I was with my parents, and we met your father after morning service.'

'You saw my father, too?' Murray interrupted. 'How was the old man?'

'He's fine, just fine—and why wouldn't he be, with Dorothy fussing around him like a daughter already?'

Shuah was listening with intense interest, jealously anxious to learn all she could about Dorothy Mortimer and about Murray's father, too. But soon their conversation moved on to other people and she gave up trying to follow it. Lord Barrington took hold of her hand as it lay on the table. The touch startled her. She had almost forgotten he was there.

'Would you like to dance, Miss Sutherland?' he asked.

She smiled, and remembered the formula Mrs Crossley had instilled into her. 'Thank you, Lord Barrington. I would like that very much.'

In the spacious ballroom an orchestra was playing, set amid tall potted palms and tubs of bush orchids; fans circled overhead between the elegant chandeliers, and the windows were opened wide to the sultry night, leading to the veranda and gardens. Lord Barrington escorted her on to the floor, placed his hand carefully on her waist, waited for the beat, then swung her into the dance. She felt a little stiff and awkward at first for she had never before danced in the arms of a man, but Mrs Bell had been a good teacher and Shuah found she could follow her partner's lead easily. Then she relaxed to the pleasure of the movement, and he smiled down at her.

'Where did you learn to dance? Certainly not in the longhouse!'

'There were two very kind English ladies in Kuching, and they undertook to teach me, Lord Barrington.'

'I wish you'd call me Peter,' he said. 'I haven't got used to this "Lord Barrington" stuff yet.'

'As long as you call me Shuah,' she responded.

'I'd be delighted to have that honour,' he smiled. He tightened the hold of his arm round her waist and executed a deft spin as the music finished. She began to move back in the direction of the dining-room, but Peter caught hold of her arm. 'Let's stay here and dance again,' he suggested. 'I'm sure those two have plenty to talk about, reminiscing on their schooldays and old friends. Can I get you a drink?'

'No, thank you, Peter. But another dance would be very pleasant.'

They danced again, and again, and with each dance Peter seemed to hold her closer, which she found a little surprising. It was quite different from the way Mrs Bell had danced, but since some of the other couples did the same, she supposed it was all correct.

Then suddenly, Murray was there, touching Peter's shoulder. 'This has gone on long enough. Break it up, Barrington.'

Murray Masterson's features were set in harsh lines, his lips compressed in a controlled anger which surprised Shuah. At first she thought Peter was going to refuse. He stood with one arm tightly round her waist. She felt the tension in the air and drew back a little, and then Peter released her, lifted her hand to his lips and kissed it.

'We'll dance again on the voyage,' he promised. 'Thank you for a delightful evening, Shuah.'

Even before Peter had walked away, Murray moved into place as her partner, grasped her right hand in his left, and encircled her waist with such a positive grip that she was drawn against his body and held close for a few seconds whilst he stood poised to move into the dance. Then he whisked her away at such speed and with so much vigour that she felt as if she was being carried on air around the ballroom. His sense of rhythm was perfect, her feet seemed scarcely to touch the ground, and her pleasure was so intense that it rendered her breathless.

Not until the music ended and he spun her round— faster, much faster, even then Peter had done—did he speak to her. Then his voice was as cold as his expression. 'Now, if you've had enough dancing for one evening, I'll escort you to your room.'

She felt disappointed and deflated. 'Do we have to leave?'

'Yes, unless you're determined to ruin your reputation even before we leave Singapore,' he barked.

'Peter said you wished to talk to Mr Palmer...'

'He should have known better. He allowed his pleasure in your company to get the better of him.'

'I'm sorry. I've still so much to learn.'

'True. Come, I'll see you to your rooms.'

His cool attitude persisted throughout their stay at Raffles Hotel, and remained after the liner sailed a couple of days later. It dampened her enjoyment of the bustling, colourful scene as they left the docks at Singapore accompanied by blasts from the ship's siren. He had distanced himself from her, not too ostensibly, yet she was conscious of the rift when, every morning after breakfast, Murray with the utmost politeness began to conduct her lessons. Although in the main he concentrated on English, reading and writing, he broadened their scope to include simple arithmetic, geography, British and European history, bible study, and a little botany.

The first morning he took her up to the deck where they found some cane chairs and a table on which she could work, but there was no peace. Shuah and her strange story were too well known—all their fellow-passengers showed some curiosity about her. Sometimes it was revealed only by covert glances, but other people made a bee-line for them, as if they were personally familiar. After dealing with the tenth interruption, Murray decreed that they should move to a corner of one of the lounges. It was a little better there, but it took two or three days and surprisingly patient insistence by Murray before they were left alone in the mornings and the voyage settled into a routine.

After lunch most people took a siesta, and in the late afternoons she was usually claimed to play deck quoits with Lord Barrington or some of the other young men and women. There were tea dances and games and sometimes band concerts, of a much higher standard than those she had endured in Kuching, and although Murray usually escorted her to such events, he sat back taking little part in them himself.

Dinner was a very elegant occasion and afterwards there was always dancing till after midnight. Since there were many more men than women on board, Shuah was never short of a partner, and prominent among them was Lord Barrington. It was he who rushed to find her the first time he sighted porpoises, and she laughed at their clumsy antics as they flopped and thumped around the ship. Together they stood at the rail and watched the flying fish that leapt and darted over the sea like shimmering butterflies, as they steamed through the innumerable islands of Malaysia and out across the Indian Ocean.

As the days passed, she became uncomfortably aware that Peter was becoming very possessive about her, in a way she did not like. He could be quite good company, and often made her laugh, but she was not fully at ease in his company. Certainly he never awakened that warm response in her that Murray had done from the first time she saw him. That feeling was as alive now as it ever had been. Those morning lessons were a solace to her, and she threw her whole heart into them, determined to learn all she could and please her hard taskmaster, and she made such good progress that he often praised her efforts. He was proud of her achievements, but somehow he treated her more like a puppet than a real person. Throughout the rest of the day he would distance himself from her, but though he might join a different group of people or sit alone with a book, she was aware that he was keeping a close watch upon her.

Once or twice Lord Barrington protested, but Murray simply cut him short, saying, 'Shuah has only me to chaperon her on this voyage, and as I explained before, I'd be failing in my duty if I allowed her to ruin her reputation. You must remember that she's very young, barely eighteen, and doesn't fully understand the ways of English society.'

She never really understood this thing called 'reputation' that seemed so important, not only to Murray, but also to most of the English on board. If guarding her reputation meant that she should not spend too much time in Peter's company, she did not mind at all. She tried not to encourage him, but he continually sought her out, and it was impossible to avoid him within the confines of the ship. She wished Murray had not forbidden her to tell anyone that they were married! Sometimes she dared to hope that his attitude showed that he cared about her—perhaps it was only a little, but it was a crumb of comfort.

Like a hawk Murray watched over her, swooping down every evening to command her to retire to her cabin whenever he decreed the time was right. She did not mind. She was always awake and up early in the morning. There was something magical in watching the last faint stars fade from the sky as morning broke over the wide silvery sea, and it was pleasantly cool at sunrise, before most of the passengers stirred. Murray was usually up at that time too, and she cherished the companionship of that hour they would spend together, walking, talking a little, watching the sailors at their work.

On the last evening of the voyage, as they sailed through the Mediterranean towards Marseilles, a specially elaborate and grand ball was organised. Shuah and Murray and many of the other passengers would disembark the next day and shorten the final stage of the long journey by taking the train north across France. There was an excellent dinner, during which they pulled crackers containing souvenir trinkets and paper hats, balloons were hung in nets over the ballroom, and some of the passengers put on a hilarious and much appreciated cabaret.

An air of excitement pervaded the whole ship and Shuah could not help being aware of it, yet she was not really a part of it. All the talk was about how they would soon be home—and to men and women who had been exiled for five or six years, that meant so much! For Shuah, every day increased her uncertainty—what lay ahead for her? Would she—could she—fit in? Her home had always been in the longhouse, deep in the jungle, governed by the rules and traditions of the Ibans. Every day she learned more about England, but she could not yet think of it as 'home'.

Murray had said that until she found her own relations she could stay at his father's house. There was a little consolation in that because she would still be near him, but there was also the issue of Dorothy to be faced. That was unbearable because she knew that he intended to take this other woman fully to wife, and that fired a stubborn anger, deep and brooding in Shuah's sensitive soul. She felt a primitive pagan fury that she found difficult to control. Honesty made her admit to herself that she was jealous of Dorothy even though she had never met her. It took all her will-power to keep that feeling even half smothered, and only her pride had enabled her to push the thought to the back of her mind for so long.

Now, on this last evening on board the great liner, she was determined to pretend she was enjoying the celebrations which went on till well past midnight. She danced with several of the men, and more than once with Lord Barrington, who had promised to keep in touch with her. 'I've got Masterson's address. I'll come and see you, Shuah. Might even be able to help in the search for your family.' The dance had finished, but his hand lingered on the small of her back as they moved towards the edge of the floor.

'Thank you, Peter,' she murmured. 'I don't know what my future will be...'

'I know what I'd like it to be. I want you, Shuah!'

'No, Peter.'

'I shan't give up,' he said.

Then, suddenly, Murray was there, reaching out to catch hold of her hand. 'This dance is mine, I believe,' he said. He had not danced with her since that evening at Raffles Hotel. Now he took her hand and led her to the dance floor. In a moment she was held closely in his arms, waltzing around the ballroom, experiencing again that same tantalising breathlessness as before. It was the last dance, and balloons dropped from overhead, streamers were thrown, tying them together with fragile paper colours. It was all new and exciting to Shuah and she leapt to catch a balloon, only to lose it, but Murray reached up and from his height easily secured one for her. They were both laughing at the nonsense, the light-hearted fun of it all, so that for a moment she forgot her fears for the future.

It was only a momentary oblivion, however, brought on by the sheer pleasure of dancing with Murray and by the joyousness of the occasion. Then the band struck up 'Auld Lang Syne', and everyone joined hands in a huge ragged circle and sang lustily, and cheered and clapped—and the end of the journey was suddenly so near that Shuah could not bear it a moment longer. Tears started into her eyes, and before Murray could see them, or move to stop her, she turned and fled from the ballroom. She did not think where she was going; she wanted only to escape from the rapturous excitement, to be alone so that no one could see those tears that were now streaming uncontrollably down her cheeks.

The liner had anchored just outside the harbour and several people were on deck, gazing across at the lights that twinkled along the coastline of France. Exclamations of excitement buzzed in the clear autumn air.

Shuah walked quickly away from where the bulk of the crowd had gathered, to a quieter place in the shadow of a lifeboat, and leaned back against it. There was beauty in the scene, the shimmering moonlit sea and the glittering lights beyond, but it was blurred by the tears that coursed down her cheeks.

'Shuah!' Her name was spoken softly, in that vibrant voice that sent a shiver down her spine. Murray stood looking down at her, his face in shadow. 'What's the matter, Shuah?'

'I—I'm scared,' she confessed.

'Oh, no! Not that again!' His voice held a note of impatience.

'I can't help it—I've tried. But what is to become of me? You don't really like me...'

'That, Shuah, is absolute nonsense. Haven't I looked after you well?'

'Yes. Thank you,' she said tonelessly.

'I prophesied that you'd be the centre of attention, and you have. Haven't you had a good time?'

'I suppose so.'

'You've had Barrington and half the other young men dancing constant attendance on you.' He spoke with a fiercely angry note.

'What does that mean to me, when I'm your wife, Murray?'

'For God's sake, Shuah, surely you're not still persisting in that nonsense! We're not married; and we never have been. I explained before we went through that ceremony that it would be meaningless under English law. The Raja and everyone else agrees with me, and I wish to heaven I'd never been tempted to undertake it!'

That was the cruellest blow of all. She shrank from him and bowed her head, feeling more alone than ever in her whole life. Murray wanted only to be rid of her— he yearned only for this other woman, this Dorothy whom he had loved for six long, lonely years. All Shuah could do was to accept the fact that despite being Number One wife, she would have to take second place in Murray's life. Yet as she walked slowly and with dignity past him, along the deck and down the companion to her own cabin, she clenched her hands. She might appear submissive, but there was some stubborn fibre within her that even yet would not entirely relinquish hope.

CHAPTER NINE

Two DAYS later Murray and Shuah, having crossed France and the Channel, were transported by cab from Victoria Station, to No. 39 Elveden Crescent, London, W.1. As Murray helped her to alight, she glanced up at the terrace of tall Regency-style houses built of creamy-coloured stone with iron railings enclosing tiny gardens. As soon as their luggage had been placed neatly on the pavement and the cabbie paid, Murray sprang up the eight steps that led to the pilastered doorway. He raised the heavy brass knocker, and clanged it resoundingly while Shuah waited quietly at the foot of the steps.

The door was opened by a lady in her mid-sixties, short and plump, wearing a black gown trimmed with white lace, as was the little cap on her grey hair. The worried expression that had drawn down the lines of her face lifted immediately when she saw Murray, and as he grasped her in his arms and gave her a hug, she smiled and exclaimed with pleasure, 'Murray! Oh, my dear! It's so good to see you!' She turned and called into the house, 'It's Murray! Murray's here!'

Shuah heard quick light footsteps, and a younger lady appeared—it was Dorothy of course! She was quite small, with a neat figure modestly clad in a beige-coloured gown with a cream lace high-necked yoke. Her face was a small perfect oval and her fair hair swept tidily back from a central parting above her smooth brow. Her lips parted in a gentle smile, and it was like a knife twisting in Shuah's heart as she watched every nuance of expression.

'Hello, Dorothy,' Murray said.

'Welcome home, Murray.'

Dorothy's voice was brisk, but it had a pleasant musical modulation. She and Murray gazed at each other for what seemed to Shuah a long, long moment, as if reviving memories, then he took her into his arms and kissed her, and Shuah could bear to watch no longer. She turned and looked away, fighting to control the tears that started into her eyes, blurring the greenery of the park across the street.

'Shuah,' Murray called to her. He skipped nimbly down the steps and caught hold of her arm, turning her round so that she had to look up at those strangers—his people—who were gazing down at her in astonishment. They had now been joined by a man almost as tall as Murray but older and thinner, white-haired, dressed in a high-buttoned dark suit above which a white starched collar stood tall above a small black bow tie. Shuah had no doubt that he was Murray's father, for the facial resemblance was clear, even though his features were pallid and drawn. His nose had that same strong bone structure, and above it his steel-grey eyebrows were thick and prominent.

'Come up and meet my family, Shuah,' Murray said.

He kept hold of her arm, and his firm touch helped to restore her confidence as they mounted the stairs. When they were almost at the top, he announced, 'I should like to introduce Miss Sutherland, who has lived in Sarawak for most of her life. Hers is a long story, and I'll tell you about it later. I've invited her to stay until she finds her own family. Shuah—these good people are Mrs Mortimer, her daughter Dorothy—my fiancée. And my father.'

Mr Masterson was the first to recover from the surprised silence that followed Murray's statement. 'You're very welcome, my dear.' He stepped forward, reached out a hand and Shuah placed hers into its bony grip.

Mrs Mortimer's hands began to flutter in agitation. 'Oh, my goodness! If only I'd known! An extra guest, and I've got nothing prepared...'

'Please don't make anything special for me,' Shuah said. 'I know what a trouble it can be. When Murray and his men came to the longhouse, we had to kill half a dozen chickens and the warriors went out to catch fish—but then there were a dozen extra men to feed.'

Mrs Mortimer managed a bleak uncomprehending smile, shook hands with Shuah, then turned abruptly and hurried inside, saying, 'I must see Cook. I don't know what we've got...'

Dorothy stepped forward; her sharp eyes held a touch of wariness, but she grasped Shuah's hand and shook it vigorously. 'Pleased to meet you, Miss Sutherland. Come in—I'm sure you're dying for a cup of tea.'

She ushered Shuah through a small hall into a finely proportioned room thickly carpeted in rich colours, with heavy furniture of shiny mahogany, and a wealth of ornaments, gilt-framed pictures and plump cushions. A tall vase of pampas grass stood in the fireplace and above it the large black marble mantelshelf was decked with a strip of fringed damask, displaying some silver-framed photographs, among which Murray featured prominently.

'Do sit down, Miss Sutherland. Make yourself at home,' said Dorothy. 'I'll leave Uncle Harry to look after you while I go and reassure mother. She flusters if her routine is upset.'

She left the room, and Shuah noticed that as she passed Murray a smile flashed warmly between them. Then Shuah's attention was caught by Mr Masterson, who lowered himself creakily and carefully into an upright chair close to her. 'Did you have a good journey, my dear?' he asked.

She liked his face immediately because it resembled Murray's, and as they talked she looked for other signs of family likeness. His manners were gentle, his voice held a slight quaver. If he had ever been a man of autocratic command, like his son, there was little sign of it now. Where Murray was a restive, dynamic character, his father had an air of contentment. He seemed old for his years—she judged him to be in his late sixties—and he was obviously well looked after.

A maid entered, carrying a laden teatray. She was middle-aged, with a starched linen cap perched on her grey hair, her eyes bright and smiling, her round face beaming, neat in a black dress covered by a pristine white apron.

'Kirsty, it's good to see you!' exclaimed Murray. 'And not looking a day older, either!'

'Get away with you, Mr Murray!' said Kirsty. But her eyes twinkled with pleasure at his remark. 'I manage, although the old bones are a bit stiffer than they were. It's good to have you back, sir. The old house needs livening up.'

He chuckled, as if with pleasant memories, and Shuah remembered how Chubby had suggested that Murray was the ring-leader in many pranks at school. It seemed as if Kirsty had similar recollections. 'We must have a real chat before long, Kirsty.'

'That's right, Mr Murray. Come and have a cup of tea with old Kirsty in the kitchen later on.'

The maid left, and presently Mrs Mortimer and Dorothy rejoined them. The older lady presided over the teapot while Dorothy handed round cups of tea and delicate morsels of food.

'Is this your first visit to London, Miss Sutherland?' Dorothy enquired, obviously consumed with curiosity which she was endeavouring to hide beneath a ladylike politeness.

'I think so,' Shuah replied. 'But I know very little about my early years. I was only about five when I was found and adopted by the headman of the Iban village where I grew up.'

Mrs Mortimer set her delicately raised cup back into its saucer with an agitated clatter and made a little choking sound. Shuah looked from her to Dorothy and Mr Masterson, and saw that their amazement at her arrival was as nothing compared with the astonishment with which they were regarding her now. She glanced at Murray, who was sitting back with his long legs crossed, looking unconcerned and at ease. His powerful masculinity dominated the fussy over-furnished room, and he brushed a crumb fastidiously from his dark suit. He caught her eyes, inclined his head and gave her a half smile, but even that did little to boost her confidence.

'Now that we're all together, I'll explain,' he began. 'As I said, it's a long and very strange story.'

There was a rapt attention as he recounted how he had discovered Shuah in Bartulu and recognising her as of English blood had taken her back with him to his station. She noticed that he omitted to mention the ceremony of marriage they had entered into. Since all along he had refused to acknowledge it, that did not suprise her, but the empty hurt of his rejection remained. Surely, some time, he would have to tell Dorothy? But perhaps he would do that later, when he was alone with her, when he went to her *bilek*—and that thought brought a jealous resentment welling up in Shuah like a physical pain. She clenched her fists, but made herself overcome her emotions and forced herself to listen as Murray carried on with the story. He was explaining how they had only the name of Shuah's parents to help them in the search for her identity, and how little they knew of Edward Sutherland other than that he had been a botanist.

'My goodness, what a problem!' exclaimed Mrs Mortimer. 'I wouldn't know where to start!'

'I'll go to Kew Gardens tomorrow and institute enquiries,' Murray said. 'I feel sure this botanical link is my best chance of solving the mystery.'

'May I come with you, Murray?' Shuah asked.

'Certainly. Indeed I think you should. You're positive proof of the truth of the story, which I fear they have not taken seriously enough.'

'These botanists get so involved in their special subject that they tend to think nothing else matters,' commented Mr Masterson.

'Well, they'll have to stir themselves and search back through their records. I shan't rest until I've been able to restore Shuah to her own family.'

His lips were compressed with his determination, and a shiver of apprehension ran over Shuah. He was wasting no time in starting his search for her relations; it could even be that he would find them tomorrow—and what then? The last thing she wanted was to be parted from him, especially when they had only just arrived in this alien land.

At about six o'clock they all separated to change for dinner. Shuah already knew of the custom, for it had been part of life on the liner. 'I'll show you to your room, Miss Sutherland,' said Dorothy, who had herself slipped away after tea and prepared the room. 'I hope you'll be comfortable—if there's anything you need, please let me know.'

'It's quite delightful, Miss Mortimer,' Shuah said, thinking how useful it was that Mrs Crossley had instructed her so thoroughly in all the correct phrases for various situations.

Dorothy left. Shuah was not quite sure that she liked her, but she told herself she had to try, for if they were to be married to the same man, it would be better if they could be friends. She must model herself on those three Malay wives she had known in Kuching. Admittedly she had detected a hint of bossiness in Dorothy which might cause a problem, but she was not going to worry about that now, for come what may, Shuah assured herself, she was Murray's Number One wife.

Her room was at the front of the house, and beyond the busy road lay a park with trees and flowerbeds, and gleaming between them she could see a lake. The shimmering water helped to make her feel at home, for despite the unfamiliarity of the European trees it reminded her of the pool below the longhouse. There was a knock on the door, and Kirsty came bustling in, carrying a can.

'Here you are, miss. Hot water—an' that's what I'll be in if I don't get down again quick! It's sent the missus into a right flap, having you here, unexpected-like.'

'I'm sorry—you must be very busy,' Shuah said.

'Oh, I'm used to it. She means very well, but she does like to pretend she's got lots of servants, like she used to have when she was a young woman. You got everything you need?'

'Yes, thank you.'

'Fancy Mr Murray bringing you back with him! He's a card, he is! Never know what he's going to do next!'

'But you like him, don't you?' asked Shuah.

Kirsty grinned. 'As I said, it'll liven the old place up no end, having him here. Miss Dorothy's all right, but she's always out doing her good works. Mustn't stand here chattering, though.'

She left, and Shuah poured the hot water into the bowl that stood with its matching rose-garlanded ewer on the marble-topped washstand. She felt it inadequate compared with the regular bathing to which she had always been accustomed.

The evening meal was excellent, despite Mrs Mortimer's prediction. Between each course she leapt to her feet, excusing herself by saying, 'I must go and see what Cook is doing.' An interval would follow, then Kirsty would bring in fresh dishes, and presently Mrs Mortimer, looking more hot and bothered with every

exit and entry, would take up her position at table again.
Even if Kirsty had not told her she was the only servant,
Shuah would have guessed that Mrs. Mortimer was doing
considerably more than speaking to the Cook, and on
one occasion she volunteered to help, only to be withered
by a look.

'Certainly not!'

They finished the meal and moved back to the sitting-
room, where, after both Dorothy and Mrs Mortimer had
been absent for about ten minutes, Kirsty brought in a
tray of coffee. As darkness fell, Mr Masterson walked
round the room putting a match to the glass-globed gas-
lights, being careful not to touch the delicate mantle and
adjusting each flame until it hissed pleasantly and cast
a golden glow over the room. From the dining-room,
Shuah could hear Kirsty humming to herself as she
cleared the table and carried trays of crockery to the back
of the house.

Everything was so strange that Shuah could not feel
at ease. Once or twice she caught Murray's eye, and he
gave her a smile, but immediately his attention would
be drawn away from her by a quick question from
Dorothy or his father. They all had so much to talk
about, which was only natural after an absence of five
years. It would be different tomorrow, she told herself.
Presently a bottle of whisky was brought out, and the
ladies seemed to take that as a cue for them to retire.

Shuah slept well, and woke up early in the morning
to find the sun streaming in through the window. She
stretched and yawned, leapt from her bed and looked
out. The sun shimmered on the lake invitingly and there
was no one else about. She wondered if Murray had
already taken his morning bathe as she hastily unpacked
her sarong and stepped into it. She remembered that he
always insisted that she should cover her breasts, so she
fastened the gaily patterned cotton under her armpits,

picked up a towel and a cake of soap and made her way out.

Barefooted she ran down the steps. She had to wait for a horse and cart to pass and she smiled at the driver, who stared at her open-mouthed, then she darted across the road and through a little iron gate in the railings that surrounded the park. She relished the feeling of the soft grass beneath her feet, and gazed about in delight at the pretty flowers. She was a little surprised to find no one else was bathing, for the park was surrounded by houses, but pausing only to drop her towel at the edge, she ran straight in to the clear water, so fast that she was up to her thighs before she had time to register its temperature. Then she stopped, almost petrified. She had never been in such cold water in her life! But with determination she went in deeper, ducked under and quickly surfaced, momentarily breathless. She pushed back her thick hair and began to soap herself, her face, hands, arms, and that done she threw the soap over to the bank and, as her body acclimatised to the chilly water, swam and dipped and dived. It was a long time since she had been able to indulge in what she considered a real bathe, and she was enjoying herself enormously.

'Shuah!'

She heard the call as she surfaced, and stood up. Murray was there, and she waved one bare arm gaily towards him. 'Are you coming in?' she called.

'No,' he shouted. 'Come out at once!'

Both his voice and his expression were so sternly disapproving that although she was puzzled, she thought it best to obey. The wet sarong clung to her figure as she waded out of the water, and then she noticed a burly figure in a dark blue uniform lumbering quickly across the park towards them.

'Hello, hello—what's going on here?'

'It's all right, officer. No harm meant.' Murray spoke to the policeman in a decisive, calm voice, but she caught an underlying sense of urgency from him. He held her towel wide, advanced rapidly towards her and almost roughly wrapped it round her.

'Bathing in the lake's not allowed,' the policeman said.

'Oh!' Shuah's eyes opened wide with surprise. 'But why not? It was lovely!'

'The young lady's from abroad,' Murray said. 'She didn't understand. She's used to bathing daily.'

'Bit of a head case, is she, sir?'

'Certainly not!'

The policeman's eyes were riveted to Shuah's bare legs and feet beneath the wet sarong, for the towel covered her only from the shoulders to just below her waist. 'I could charge you with indecent exposure, young lady,' he said.

'Kindly turn your back, officer,' Murray snapped, and he took off his jacket while the policeman instinctively obeyed. Murray flicked the towel from her shoulders and slung the jacket over them. 'Wrap the towel round your legs,' he instructed her. Then he turned to face the officer again. 'All right. Now I'll escort the young lady back to the house.'

'Is the young lady related to you, sir?' the policeman asked.

'I'm his . . .' Shuah began, but the word 'wife' died on her lips.

'I'm her guardian,' Murray interrupted her. 'Name's Masterson. If you want any further information, contact me at No. 39.' He indicated the house with a nod of his head, but his attitude suggested that he did not expect the matter to be pursued. 'Come, Shuah.'

He grasped her hand and stepped away at such a pace that she could scarcely keep up with him, especially as she had to hold the jacket and towel in position. Before they reached the railing that separated the park from the

road the towel slipped and fell, and there was a furious
roar from the policeman who was lumbering along
behind them. Shuah stopped to pick up the towel and
as she straightened, Murray's arms caught hold of her
and he swung her off her feet and strode away out of
the park and across the road, carrying her as easily as
if she had been a child. He dodged between the horses
and carts with such boldness that several of the drivers
called out in a mixture of anger and astonishment.

'What yer fink yer doin', mate?' called one.

'Want an 'and wi' that baggage?' chuckled another.

Murray ignored them and stepped on to the pavement
on the opposite side, but instead of climbing the steps
to the front door, he carried her along a side path towards
the rear of the house. Silently Shuah clung to him, with
her arms twined round his neck, cosy in the warmth of
his jacket which held something of that musky male
aroma that she had come to associate with him, and
which was so appealing. She was all too aware that she
had made a stupid mistake and aroused his anger, and
as she did not understand why, she said nothing, waiting
for his temper to simmer down.

He continued along the path—the narrow-fronted
house went back a long way—and something in the way
he held her suggested that his mood had calmed, and
placatingly she rubbed her cheek up and down against
the unshaven bristliness of his. She hoped to melt the
icy remoteness with which he was treating her, and took
comfort because though he did not respond, at least he
did not draw away from her touch. But was he even aware
of it? There were times when he seemed able to shut
himself off from her, to treat her as if she was not a real
person. He had done that at Raffles Hotel when she had
danced with Peter Barrington, and on the boat too,
several times. Her need to break this mood in him was
now so great that she swallowed her pride. 'Forgive me,
Murray,' she murmured into his ear.

'No need for that,' he said in a curt, gruff voice. 'Get inside,' he ordered, wrenching open the door.

Shuah stepped into the kitchen. Kirsty was kneeling before the black-leaded grate in which she had just lit the fire. She was dressed in an overall, old but clean and neatly patched, with a mob-cap pulled low on her head. At the sound of their sudden entry she turned sharply, her eyes popped open wide and she lifted one sooty hand to her face in astonishment, leaving a black mark on her cheek. Then an indulgent smile creased her lined, rosy-cheeked face.

'Still up to your old larks, is it, Mr Murray, sir?'

'No harm, Kirsty.'

'That's what you allus said. Don't know what the missus'll think!'

'Shuah—er—fell in the lake.'

'Oh?' Her voice expressed doubt. 'All right, I believe you. Thousands wouldn't!'

'I'll tell you about it later.' He gave the maid a conspiratorial wink and placed a silencing finger to his lips. Kirsty shook her head and made noises that sounded like 'tut-tut', but Shuah got the impression that the maid was really neither surprised nor shocked.

'Follow me up the back stairs,' Murray said. 'With luck, you can get back to your own room without Mrs Mortimer seeing you.'

'Would she be angry?' Shuah asked.

'Upset is more the word,' he said. 'She works so hard at keeping up appearances. I'll explain it to you one day.'

Meekly she pattered along behind him, up the stairs and out through a door at the top that led to a landing off which were the main bedrooms. He glanced around, reached back to take hold of her hand, then, making no sound, moving with pantherlike stealth—surprising for such a big man—he led her to the door of her room and thrust her inside.

Following her in, he closed the door gently and leaned back against it. 'When you wish to take a bath,' he said, and the critical frigidity of his tone gave her a crumpled feeling inside, 'ask Dorothy. The bathroom is just across the landing. She'll show you how to light the geyser.'

'What is geyser?'

'It's to heat the water. This is England, Shuah. You'll have to bath indoors here.'

'But why mustn't I swim?'

'There are places where you can, but it's definitely not allowed in the park! You can swim at the seaside, but you must wear a special costume that will cover you much more decorously than a sarong—and you should be out of sight of any men.'

She stared at him in astonishment. 'Even you?'

His expression did not soften. 'Perhaps especially me,' he said, and that puzzled her. Would she ever get used to this strange land with its innumerable incomprehensible customs?

A shiver ran over her, and that reminded her that she was still cocooned in Murray's jacket. She shrugged it from her shoulders and handed it back to him. 'I'm sorry it's wet.'

He did not put it on, but slung it over one shoulder and opened the door. He was about to leave, but hesitated on the threshold, and in a moment she realised why. Dorothy's voice came to her clearly. 'Murray!' she said in a tone of shocked surprise.

'Don't tell your mama,' Murray whispered. 'Shuah went for a bathe in the lake!' There was a chuckle in his voice.

'Good gracious! What ever made her do that?' Her voice was sharp.

Murray said, 'Don't be hard on her, Dorothy. She's still got a lot to learn.' Then he closed the door behind him and Shuah was alone.

She remained immobile; her damp sarong clung chillingly; she felt humiliated, stupidly ashamed. She loosened it and listlessly allowed it to fall at her feet, but all the joy of the morning had faded. Tears pricked behind her eyes, and she dashed them angrily away and kicked the sarong aside. It would do her no good to cry—she had to put as bold a face on the future as possible.

Murray had said they would go to this place called Kew today, and begin the search for her identity, for he was anxious to get on with the least possible delay. No doubt he was right—the sooner they found this family everyone said she was sure to have, the better! Perhaps then she would be able to call on them to assist her. Surely they would help when she explained that she was Murray Masterson's wife? But who were these unknown people with whom she could claim kinship? At the moment they were complete strangers, so would they be willing to help her? Or would they find her ways as strange as Dorothy obviously did?

CHAPTER TEN

THEY SET off together soon after breakfast. Murray walked at a brisk pace so that Shuah was stretched to keep up with him, but she would not ask him to slow down. Instead she gave up trying to walk and fell into the quick jog-trot with which the Ibans moved through the jungle when they were travelling long distances.

'Is it very far to these gardens?' she asked.

Murray glanced at her and slowed his stride. 'Too far to walk. We'll take a train. Not as big as the one across France, though.'

They entered a building where a flight of concrete steps led to platforms bright with electric lights. From under a bridge came a terrifying roar, as if from some enormous wild beast, and in near panic, she caught hold of Murray's arm. 'Whatever is it?'

'The train; it's perfectly safe.' To reassure her, he placed her hand into the crook of his arm, in the way she had noticed that other couples walked. She liked that. It gave her a protected feeling, as if he acknowledged that they belonged together—though she knew it only stemmed from that sense of duty that was so predominant a part of his character. Her hesitation had been only momentary, for if Murray told her it was safe, she believed him implicitly. They boarded the train, and she relaxed as they rattled along, passing streets of newly-built houses to arrive at Kew Gardens station.

'It's ages since I was last here,' Murray said. 'I'll go to the museum and make some enquiries, but first I thought you might like to see the Palm House.'

Inside the huge domed glasshouse she was astonished to see many trees and shrubs with which she was familiar—not the huge forest trees, of course, but coconut, banana, pawpaw, bamboo all growing strongly in the artificial atmosphere.

'I come here when I'm on leave and feel homesick for Sarawak,' Murray said. He was staring up into the thick fronds of a palm, an expression of pleasure softening the craggy profile of his face—she had no need to ask whether he really meant those words. It warmed her heart that he had come to think of Sarawak as 'home', a sentiment she shared and which was reawakened strongly by the varied greenery and the lusciousness of the exotic plants.

She took deep breaths of the steamy atmosphere. 'It smells of the jungle,' she murmured.

'I spent hours here when I was on my first leave. I was so miserable that this place was my only consolation.'

'Did you miss Sarawak so much?' she asked in wonder.

He gave a harsh laugh. 'Not at all. I'd been counting the days till I came back. I thought I was in love—and I was fool enough to believe that she loved me, that she'd wait for me! What a fool I was!'

'Who was she?'

'A girl I met when I was at university.'

'But you still love her?'

'I scarcely remember what she looked like, and I'm sure she'd never have settled happily in Sarawak! Thank goodness I'm able to take a more rational view of life now.'

She would have liked to ask him more, but he stalked away. She followed more slowly, sensing that he wished to be alone.

Suddenly he halted. 'Look!' He was pointing to one of the screw pines, a large-leafed, pineapple type of plant with twisted, sharply pointed, fleshy leaves. He seemed to have completely shrugged off the mood that had caused his unexpected confidence. 'See what the label says?' She hesitated over the long words, and he read them for her. '*Pandanus sutherlandii*: your father's name! I wonder if there's any connection?'

'The Raja said they had plants here with my father's name, but it's a very ordinary plant,' she said with a sense of disappointment. 'I know where lots of those grow, in the swamps by the river.'

'It may seem ordinary to you. I'm sure it was not considered so when the first specimen arrived in this country. No one here would have seen such a plant before; other screw pines, perhaps, but not that particular variety. Come, Shuah, let's go to the office and see if we can find out why it got its name. It must have some connection with your father.'

Murray hurried her out of the Palm House into the bright but cool sunshine of the lawns and gardens and strode off in the direction of the office. Excitement brought a smile to Shuah's face quite naturally—the Ibans were accustomed to expressing their feelings openly, and again she moved in an easy jog-trot to keep pace with him. It was an automatic movement, she could have done it with a load balanced on her head, but it attracted curious looks and half-suppressed smiles from other visitors.

Murray's enquiries led them into the presence of a middle-aged man of medium height, who was introduced to them as Dr Bland. He was delighted to talk about the plant.

'*Pandanus sutherlandii*.' He nodded. 'A most remarkable plant. There are many screw pines, but the one we have here in the Palm House is the only example in Europe of that particular species. What do you wish to know about it?'

'It was the name of the plant that caught my attention. Was it by any chance sent here by a plant-collector called Edward Sutherland?'

Dr Bland's enthusiasm faded—plants interested him more than people. However, he tried to answer. 'He was not one of our own plant-collectors. As far as I know, he had no connection with Kew. Indeed the last gentleman despatched on such a mission from Kew was

Richard Oldham in 1861, and he went to Japan. The plant you mention came from Malaya.'

'Exactly, and I feel sure it must have some connection with Edward Sutherland. He was shipwrecked when travelling to the Dutch East Indies, and his little daughter, the sole survivor, was rescued by some natives and brought up by them in the jungle. Dr Bland, this young lady is that same child!' A flicker of interest brightened the little man's eyes, and he bowed in Shuah's direction. Murray continued, 'I believe the Raja of Sarawak wrote to you asking for information about her father?'

'I certainly recollect receiving that enquiry, but, as I said, this Mr Sutherland was not one of our plant-collectors.'

'Then where, may I ask, did you get the plant labelled as *Pandanus sutherlandii*?'

'From a private collector, a titled gentleman.' He paused and wrinkled his forehead. 'His name escapes me at the moment. If you'll excuse me, I'll have to look it up in our files.'

Dr Bland was away for ten minutes or more, and when he returned he carried a ledger over which he was nodding his head with an expression of satisfaction. 'I have it. Here is the plant you mention, *Pandanus sutherlandii*. A very fine specimen. It has been of interest to botanists all over the world.' Shuah shuffled in her seat, and Dr Bland glanced at her, recollected the real purpose of his search and cleared his throat. 'It came to us from Lord Antingham, an eminent botanist who sponsored several expeditions to various parts of the globe in search of new and rare plants. He gave his name to many species.'

'Fascinating,' Murray agreed smoothly. 'I should very much like to get in touch with Lord Antingham. Do you have his address?'

'Unfortunately, he died about six years ago. He bequeathed his entire collection to the botanical gardens and we transported several very fine specimens to add to our collection.'

'Was there any information with the plants?'

'Lord Antingham was a methodical collector, and all his plants were carefully listed.'

'Then may I ask if any address is given which would help me to trace the family of Edward Sutherland?'

'I asked one of my assistants to look through the documents when I received the letter from the Raja of Sarawak, but he could find none.'

Murray was not prepared to give up the search so easily. 'Would it be possible for us to see these documents?' he asked.

'Certainly. You would, of course, have to do it here, on the premises.'

'Happily,' said Murray. Dr Bland led them to a desk, left them for a few minutes, then returned and placed before them a pile of assorted sheets of paper, some yellowed with age, others almost new.

'I'll be in the next room—if I can be of further help...' Dr Bland's voice trailed away as he left them.

'Can I look at some?' Shuah asked Murray.

He handed her a notebook. 'I suggest that we glance through quickly at first to look for the name Sutherland, or Edward or Malaya—I think those are the most likely clues.'

She was pleased to have some work and proud that he showed such faith in her reading ability. The notebook proved quite difficult to decipher because the writing was in a variety of different styles of handwriting. Methodically she ran her finger down the pages, seeking that elusive name—and suddenly she found it.

Edward Sutherland has been successful in the hybridisation of an orchid Paphiopedilum 'Sweet Suzanne'. It is a beautiful bloom, white-centred, pink flecked with crimson, with flowers on long arching sprays. Mrs Mary Sutherland has made a delightful watercolour study of the flower overleaf.

Shuah read it over again, slowly and carefully, and was filled with a strange choking sense of wonder that those words related to her parents. 'Murray,' she said, forcing her voice to sound calm, 'I've found something.'

He turned towards her immediately, read those lines at which she pointed, then nodded. She turned the page over carefully, almost reverently, lifted a sheet of tissue paper and revealed a delicate water-colour of an orchid in a rich shade of rosy-violet with a white centre. Beneath was its name, 'Sweet Suzanne'. The light touch of the artist emphasised the translucent beauty of the spray of flowers that arched across the page, contrasting with the stiff, fleshy green of the leaves.

'Mary Sutherland.' With a feeling of awe Shuah read the signature. Her voice choked a little as she added, 'Do you think that might be my mother?'

'It would seem likely,' Murray agreed coolly. 'We know she accompanied your father on his expedition. And how useful she would be, having the gift to make such lovely drawings of new plants. What more does it say?'

Murray turned the page and she tried to read, too, but he was faster than she, and she caught only glimpses of the information—mostly academic, botanic, relating to the methods used in cultivation and propagation and naming the parent plants from which Edward Sutherland had produced his new hybrid orchid. Suddenly the forefinger of Murray's well-shaped hand tapped at the bottom of the page.

'There's an address,' he said. 'Mead House, Colethorpe, Surrey. It appears to be part of some correspondence regarding experiments Edward Sutherland was carrying out over the hybridisation of an orchid—probably that very bloom we've just seen in the picture, although at this stage the cultivation is incomplete and it has not been named.'

Shuah did not fully understand, but did not interrupt, for the tone of Murray's voice conveyed a kindling excitement as he weighed up the significance of what he had found. The writing on that particular page was elaborate, every word dressed up with a flourish or a curlicue that she found impossible to decipher. She gave up, and waited.

'I get the impression,' he continued presently, 'that although your father must have been quite a young man at this time—this letter is dated 3rd October 1885—Lord Antingham was extremely impressed by his work. Orchids were evidently a passion with both of them.'

'They are strange plants, and some are very beautiful,' Shuah said. 'There were some in the trees near Bartulu, and they spread over the roof of the longhouse, beautiful white ones that burst into bloom every nine weeks or so—a great mass of them.'

'Pigeon orchids,' Murray said, softly. 'Lovely things. They burst open so quickly and last for just one day, clothing everything miraculously in white, then fade away like snow melting beneath the sun.'

Their mutual pleasure in the reminiscence seemed to bind them together. Their minds had leapt thousands of miles away from the rather stuffy, dark-panelled, book-lined office, halfway round the world to that land of jungle and brilliant tropical sun they both knew so well. His face wore a softened expression, very pleasing to her eyes, and his clear-cut profile was silhouetted against a narrow shaft of light that streamed through the small, high window. Then almost immediately he shook the mood from him, his lips compressed into a firm line, reflecting the cool purpose of their search, and he squared his shoulders as if well satisfied.

'Do you know where this place is?' she asked.

'Colethorpe? No, but it won't be difficult to find.' He copied the address into a notebook. 'I think this may be all we need. It would appear that this was your father's home address, before he married. You may still have relatives there or neighbours who will know of your family. It's the best lead yet, and in any case I think it's as far as we can hope to go today.'

She nodded, not quite trusting herself to speak, feeling rather emotional. Murray stood up. Dr Bland came over and asked whether they had discovered anything.

'An address which may be useful,' Murray told him.

'And some pretty paintings that may have been done by my mother,' said Shuah. She turned back the pages, wanting another look at them, allowing her fingers to linger lightly on the sheet, intensely moved by the thought that, many years before, her mother's hand might have rested on that very same spot.

'Orchid "Sweet Suzanne",' Dr Bland said knowledgeably. 'That was one of the items that came to us from Lord Antingham's collection. You'll find a specimen in the Orchid House.'

'Could we see it?' Shuah asked breathlessly.

'Most certainly.'

A few minutes later she stood staring in delight at the beauty of the blooms, several on one spray, some fully opened and others in bud. She recognised the features that had been captured with delicacy and expertise in Mary Sutherland's paintings, its flowers shading from magenta to a pale pinky mauve, and larger than she had expected.

'It's beautiful!' she exclaimed. 'The most beautiful orchid I've ever seen!'

'It's certainly very lovely. Makes you realise why orchids have long been regarded as among the finest flowers in the world,' Murray agreed. 'And the modern hybrids far outshine even the best of the wild ones.'

For a few moments longer she gazed at the orchid, entranced by its colour and form, but also marvelling that her father, that man of whom she had only the dimmest of recollections, could have been responsible for producing a such a flower. It made his loss seem the more poignant, somehow, and tears pricked behind her eyes as at last she turned away.

Murray took a gold watch from his waistcoat pocket and looked at it. 'If I write a letter immediately we get home, it'll catch today's post. The sooner we get this business cleared up, the better.'

In Shuah's highly emotional state she found it impossible to speak. She moved away silently, her feelings mixed. She wanted to find her identity, to learn more about these very remarkable people, the man and woman who had been her parents, towards whom she felt a bond tightening and who seemed more real with every bit of information they had found—particularly with the paintings done by her mother. But she could not but be aware that every step nearer to solving the mystery was overshadowed by a threat. As soon as he found her relatives, she knew that Murray intended to slip out of her life as dramatically as he had come into it.

Days passed as they waited for a reply to the letter Murray had sent to the address in Colethorpe. Gradually Shuah grew accustomed to the traffic, the constant stream of horse-drawn carriages, carts, buses and the occasional motorcar—it was all so different from life in the jungle, or even in Kuching. She enjoyed listening to the calls of the street traders, the milkman, the watercress girl, the muffin man and sometimes an organ-grinder. Life seemed so easy with goods being delivered by errand-boys instead of being grown or hunted, picked or gathered.

Murray had insisted on giving her a small weekly allowance. Dorothy took her around the shops and instructed her about buying things. 'Rubbish!' she would say of some items, though often Shuah thought them pretty. Or, 'That's quality. That will last.' With a sigh Shuah would accept her advice. Dorothy would get on well with Mrs Crossley, she thought.

Murray continued with her tuition, and sometimes Dorothy sat with them; at those times Shuah found it more difficult to get her words right, because she was nervously aware that Dorothy was so very clever. That was obvious too in her organisation of the household, which, coupled with the loyal hard work of Kirsty, kept everything running like clockwork. Shuah tried to help in various small ways, but there was little for her to do.

At church on Sunday the sunshine lit the rich colours of the stained glass windows to jewel brilliance, and the melodious voice of the Reverend Matthew Percival led the service with impressive resonance. Shuah had attended church regularly in Kuching and on the liner, so was familiar with the responses. She sat next to Murray, while Dorothy was on his right, and when his baritone and her contralto were uplifted to sing the hymns together, Shuah felt a knot tighten in the pit of her stomach—they were so well matched. The accord of those voices seemed to emphasise that she was an outsider—not really English.

Dorothy was a keen churchgoer who listened in total absorption when Mr Percival delivered his sermon. He was aged about forty, with a large head and pleasant features, enhanced by thick fair hair, silvered at the temples. He had a calm but sad air, and Shuah remembered that Dorothy had mentioned he was a widower. She guessed that the two little girls who sat in one of the front pews must be his daughters.

When the service was over and the congregation filed out of church, Mr Percival stood just outside the porch door, exchanging a few words with each member. Dorothy introduced him to Murray, and the two men shook hands with conventional murmurs of pleasure. Then she drew Shuah forward. 'This is Miss Sutherland.'

'Ah, yes. I am very pleased to meet you.' He smiled at her. 'Miss Mortimer told me about you when she was here arranging the flowers the other day. I hope you'll both be able to attend our church bazaar next week.'

Shuah glanced at Dorothy, who answered immediately, 'Most certainly, Mr Percival. I shall carry on with my church work until I leave for Sarawak.'

Dorothy's expression was serious, and Mr Percival's face had a pensive expression as he gazed back. Shuah thought he was going to say something more, but Murray was again addressing him. 'Miss Mortimer and I must call on you soon to discuss the arrangements for our wedding.'

'Of course. Any time—any time at all.' He nodded, but to Shuah it seemed that his voice lacked enthusiasm.

'Perhaps one afternoon next week?' Murray said.

'Certainly.'

Dorothy moved away to catch up with her mother and Mr Masterson, who were sauntering through the graveyard towards the gate. Murray and Shuah hurried after them, and Mr Percival turned to another member of his congregation.

A couple of days later Shuah found Dorothy packing a basket with several items of food: bread, dripping left from the Sunday roast, home-made jam, and some eggs. 'I'm taking this to a poor woman, one of Mr Percival's parishioners. She's just had her seventh baby, and her husband's out of work, as usual!'

'May I come with you?' Shuah asked. Dorothy nodded, and Shuah added, 'I love small babies. She's a lucky woman to have such a big family.'

'I wouldn't say that,' Dorothy replied grimly. 'Her husband's a drunken brute of a man.'

'Too fond of the *tuak*, you mean?'

'Beer. Same thing, I'm sure.'

Dorothy put on her hat and speared it in place with a pearl-headed pin. Shuah did the same. The obsession the English had for hats was something she could not understand, but since it seemed so important, she complied with the custom. They took a tramcar for a short distance.

'When I go back to Bartulu, they'll never believe all the things I've seen and done,' Shuah said.

Dorothy looked at her sharply. 'You expect to go back?'

'But of course! I promised I would!' She remembered that Murray had been doubtful, but she refused even to think of that.

'It may not be possible,' Dorothy said. 'It will depend on finding your grandparents, and whether they can afford it.'

'Murray will take me,' Shuah said.

Dorothy looked startled. 'No,' she said, quite definitely, 'he won't be able to take you back. He'll have a free passage only for himself and his wife; certainly not for you. Your place is in England now, Shuah.'

'But I don't belong here!' Shuah exclaimed.

'You'll settle in better, once you've found your own family,' Dorothy said, rather more kindly. Then a trifle curiously, 'Did you really like it so much in Sarawak?'

'I knew nothing else. I was happy.' Shuah shivered as a cool draught blew fiercely into the tram. 'And it's so cold here.'

'Murray says I may find the heat trying when I go out there,' Dorothy said.

'I'm sure you'll soon get used to it.'

'I hope so. I've got to make the best of it, anyway. Can't let Murray down again. He was engaged to another young lady before he proposed to me—did you know that?'

'He did mention he was in love with a girl he met while he was at university.'

'Infatuation—that's all it was! But he was like a man possessed when she wrote to say she wouldn't marry him. I think her parents put pressure on her, didn't want her to go so far away. I always knew she wasn't the right girl for him.'

'Have you known Murray a long time?'

'We practically grew up together. I know he asked me to marry him on the rebound, but I think the understanding we have is a good basis for marriage. Certainly he knows I'll never let him down, the way she did.' She stood up abruptly, terminating the conversation. 'This is our stop.'

They alighted at a crossroads where tall buildings cast dark shadows. A group of men were gathered at the corner, leaning indolently against the wall or squatting on their hunkers, all wearing dark, shapeless clothes, cloth caps and heavy boots. They stared at the two smartly dressed young women, the one so small and the other rather tall, and although none of the men moved, they looked unfriendly, even menacing. Dorothy marched past without giving them a glance. 'This way, Shuah. Keep close to me.'

Shuah was only too pleased to obey, feeling more scared than she had ever been in the jungle. Rubbish rotted in the wet gutter where children played barefooted, ragged and grubby, shouting, screaming, tumbling in the filth. Children in the longhouse often got dirty, of course, but someone would soon send them to the river and make sure they were properly clean. These children looked as if they had not been washed for days—but if they were not allowed to bathe in the lake, what could they do? They looked thin, too, as if they could do with a really good meal.

She followed Dorothy as she turned into another street and then into a narrow alley that gashed, dark and smelly, between the long rows of tall houses. Presently Dorothy stopped by a low doorway and knocked. A weak voice answered and she walked in, beckoning Shuah to follow. Shuah had to duck her head to enter, and so little light filtered through the tiny window that it was a few moments before her eyes grew accustomed to the gloom.

A small fire burned in a clean black stove, on top of which a kettle steamed. A woman lay on a bed, her face so pale and thin it was impossible to guess her age. Tears streamed down her face. Two young children sat unnaturally still and quiet on the foot of the bed, wideeyed, pale-faced, scared looking. Clasped tightly in the

woman's arms was a tiny bundle which she was rocking
helplessly, moaning as she did so. 'No—no—no...' One
glance was enough to tell them that the new baby was
dead.

'Oh, my dear Mrs Gates! I'm so sorry—so very sorry!'
Dorothy dropped to her knees by the bedside and covered
her face with her hands, praying silently.

Shuah stood by, feeling helpless in the face of so much
grief. She moved towards the children and reached out
a hand, but they cowered away, as if fearing a blow.

After a few minutes Dorothy stood up and took the
food from her basket. 'The children might like some
bread and jam,' she said with crisp practicality.

Shuah spread it and held it out, and they took it
hungrily. The woman turned her stricken face in their
direction. 'I'm not crying for him, poor little mite. What
sort of life is this to bring a child into? He'll be better
off where he's gone. It's just—just... Well, it all seems
so sad, don't it, miss?'

'It is very, very sad,' Dorothy agreed sincerely. She
paused, then said gently, 'You should have something
to eat, Mrs Gates. You've got the other children to think
about, you know.'

'Yes. I shouldn't have allowed myself to give way. I
know it. I just couldn't help it. It's such a comfort to
have you here, miss.'

Dorothy sat holding the woman's hand, talking to her
in soothing tones, while Shuah wondered that life in these
back alleys should be so different from the way it was
at Elveden Street—so different, too, from the life she
had known in the longhouse of Bartulu.

When Dorothy had done all she could to comfort Mrs
Gates and pressed some money into the poor woman's
reluctant hand, she prepared to leave.

'You'll tell the vicar, miss?'

'I will, and I'm sure he'll come to see you very soon,'
Dorothy promised.

'He's a good man.' Mrs Gates murmured, and Dorothy nodded.

When they were again in the street, Shuah asked the question that had been troubling her, 'Why is she alone? Why are the other women of her tribe not there to look after her?'

'She has no close family; she grew up in an orphanage. A neighbour's been going in every morning since she had the baby, but most folks can't be bothered. Losing a baby's not so unusual.'

'I know. It was the same in the longhouse—babies died every year—but surely a woman needs comfort and company at such a time? I wouldn't like to be alone if it happened to me.'

'That's why I call on Mrs Gates at least once a week. Mr Percival often looks in, too, but if her husband's at home, he won't have it. Drives away any help that may be offered.'

'Where is he now?'

'At the pub, I shouldn't wonder,' Dorothy snapped angrily, walking very fast. 'I'll call at the vicarage on the way home. Mr Percival will be able to help her.'

Shuah hoped very much that he would. The sadness remained close to the surface of her mind for the rest of that day.

CHAPTER ELEVEN

IT WAS AN unfortunate coincidence that some acquaintances of Mr Masterson had been invited to dinner. They had moved into the house next door two or three years earlier and had expressed a desire to meet Murray, and their curiosity had been awakened even more when they heard about Shuah, whom they appeared to regard as an extraordinary phenomenon. The evening started pleasantly enough. The meal was delicious and the conversation ranged widely over a variety of subjects before it turned specifically to life in Sarawak.

'What was it like to grow up among savages?' Mrs Saunders asked.

'Savages?' Shuah queried stiffly. 'What do you mean by savages? Kobe and Sabat, who adopted me, were among the kindest people I've ever met.'

'But they're cannibals, aren't they?'

'You're thinking of head-hunters,' Murray said.

'Isn't it the same thing?' Mr Saunders pursued the subject.'

'Not at all,' Murray said. 'In the past, the Ibans and other tribes took heads, but they were not cannibals. It scarcely ever happens nowadays. It's part of my job as Resident Officer to take a tough line on such things, and we all do our best to keep enmity between the tribes at a minimum. The Ibans are some of the most charming and friendly people I've ever met.'

'Really?' said Mrs Saunders, with obvious disbelief. 'It sounds dreadfully uncivilised to me. I can't imagine how a white child could have survived. What sort of life did you lead in the longhouse? Wasn't it dirty?' She shuddered delicately.

'Oh, no!' Shuah exclaimed. 'The Ibans love all children. They'd never allow them to be as dirty and undernourished as yours are here.'

A stunned silence followed her words and Mr and Mrs Saunders stared at her in astonishment. How could this girl, who had grown up among natives, criticise life in their civilised society?

'How dare you suggest that our children are not well cared for!' Mrs Saunders exploded.

'I saw children in the streets today who hadn't been properly washed for weeks—they were thin, too!'

'That's up to their parents. Our two boys are away at a very good boarding school.'

'But surely all the children of the tribe must be important to it?' Shuah asked. 'I saw some today who were in a disgusting state.'

'That's not my concern. If parents are too idle to work and just spend their money in the pub, you can't expect the rest of us to look after their brats.'

'Among the Ibans, a tribe is judged by how well it takes care of its children. In them rests the future of all the tribe—they're its hope for survival,' Shuah tried to explain. 'Only strong healthy children will grow up to be brave warriors and good providers, who in their turn will protect the longhouse and look after the wellbeing of everyone who lives there.'

'And make good head-hunters, you mean?' Mrs Saunders sneered. 'You can't deny it happens sometimes.'

Shuah sighed. Mrs Saunders was determined to stick to her beliefs, however wrong.

'Head-hunting was part of a fertility rite that got out of hand,' Murray proposed. 'It was originally simply a way of showing a young man's valour, and when he wanted to marry he had to present the girl of his choice with at least one head, which it was believed would bring blessings on the whole village.'

Shuah turned and looked earnestly at Murray. 'But it's no longer a necessary part of the marriage ceremony. It was not used when...'

'Certainly not,' he interrupted quickly, frowning at her.

She was thinking back vividly to their own wedding ceremony, but such a cold, closed look came over his face that a shiver ran over her.

He continued to address the rest of the company. 'I assure you, head-hunting has been almost completely stamped out. There's much less of it now than when I first went to Sarawak. But the White Rajas, very wisely in my opinion, allowed the people to keep the heads they already owned because they are an important part of some of their ceremonies and rituals.'

'I've no wish to defend the practice of head-hunting,' Shuah said. 'I don't ever remember a fresh head being brought into the longhouse...' Mrs Saunders uttered a tiny scream, but Shuah finished her sentence with determination. 'What I do know is that I was looked after with loving care, and in many ways I was sad to leave the longhouse.'

'But surely you don't wish to go back there?' asked Mrs Saunders.

Shuah thought hard, and was aware that everyone was waiting for her reply. 'No,' she said slowly. 'I suppose I'd find it difficult to go back to that way of life now.'

'Oh, my dear Dorothy! How can you think of going to such a country?' Mrs Saunders murmured.

A look of exasperation flickered over Murray's face. 'Life in Sarawak is very different from life here, I've explained that.' Then he deliberately turned to face Dorothy directly. 'I still won't force you to come out there with me, my dear. If you feel you couldn't stand it, say so now.'

'No, Murray.' Dorothy reached across the table and laid a hand on his arm. 'I'm prepared to face whatever comes. I gave you my promise six years ago and I shall not break it now.'

'Well said, Dorothy,' Mr Masterson approved warmly. 'My son couldn't wish for a better wife, or I for a better daughter-in-law. Let's drink a toast to their future life together.'

'We'll go tomorrow and arrange the date for the wedding,' Murray said.

Shuah swallowed a lump in her throat as she stood up and raised her glass with the others.

Next day, Murray and Dorothy left the house together after lunch. Shuah knew they were on their way to call upon Mr Percival, which made her feel utterly miserable, so she went to her room. She began to mend a small tear in the seam of one of her dresses, stabbing savagely at the material and cobbling it together in a way she would never have done normally. Suddenly a commotion in the street made her lift up her head to glance out of the window. Below was a motor-car of bright yellow, with brown upholstery; the door was held open by a uniformed chauffeur; a man was climbing from the driver's seat dressed in a full-length coat, with a peaked cap worn back to front, his face half hidden by large goggles. It was not until he removed those that she realised that it was Lord Barrington.

The sight of him was totally unexpected, although he had said he intended to call upon her. It seemed such a long time since they had parted, on their arrival in England, that she had begun to suppose he had forgotten. That had not troubled her at all. But now he was here, and just when she was feeling so low, she was really pleased to see him. She pushed up the sash window and leaned out, waving a hand to attract his attention.

'Shuah!' he exclaimed, looking up. 'The very lady I was hoping to see. May I invite you to come motoring with me?'

'Motoring?'

'I've just bought this car. Well, I've had it a week now, to be accurate. Come down and have a look.'

Shuah needed no second bidding. She ran down the stairs, let herself out of the front door, skipped lightly down the steps to the pavement, and with natural un-affected honesty called out, 'Peter! This is a pleasant surprise!'

'The pleasure is all mine, I assure you, Shuah.' He put out his hands and clasped hers warmly, and his quiff of fair hair fell forward over his youthful brow. 'I've been dreaming of this day when I would meet you again, ever since we parted.'

'You don't expect me to believe that, do you?' She shook her head.

'It's the truth,' he pleaded. 'You'll never believe the troubles I've had. It's much worse running the estate than it was to keep the old rubber plantation going, and not enough ready cash to do the things I want. But I was determined to come and visit you, and we got here with almost no trouble at all—thanks to Gibson,' Peter indicated his chauffeur, who was smartly uniformed with a peaked cap, brass-buttoned jacket and jodhpurs. He clicked the heels of his polished riding-boots to at-tention, and gave a stiff little bow. 'He's a wizard at mending the damned thing when it breaks down,' Peter added.

'Does that happen often?' Shuah asked.

'Hardly ever. Only once on the way here, and Gibson had it going again in no time.' He kept hold of her hands rather too long, and she could not ignore the admiration expressed in his bold blue eyes. 'How are things with you, Shuah? Have you discovered your family yet?'

Her face clouded a little as she shook her head. 'Murray took me to Kew, and we discovered an address in a village called Colethorpe.'

'Colethorpe!' he exclaimed. 'In Surrey?' She nodded, and he added with quick excitement, 'That's not far from my place.'

'Murray wrote to the man he thinks may be my grand-father, but there's been no reply.' Quickly she sketched in the few facts.

'You say it's a couple of weeks since Murray wrote? Then why wait any longer? Let me drive you over—now!'

'I—I don't know...'

'Why not? It's a lovely day. We'd be there in no time at all.'

'I expect Murray will take me in a day or two.'

'I'll save him the trouble.' Murray might indeed be pleased, she thought. Hesitantly she said, 'I don't know if my grandfather's still there.'

'Then let's go and find out. Get a warm coat or a cloak, and a muff. I've got a good rug.'

'But it's not really cold today.'

'It will be when we get going, believe me! But you'll enjoy it, Shuah. Motoring's tremendous fun, really exhilarating.'

Peter's enthusiasm was infectious, and probably he was right when he said that Murray would be glad if he helped her to discover whether this long-lost grand-father really existed. In fact, when she came to think about it, it seemed too good an offer to refuse. Certainly there could be no harm in it.

'You're very kind, Peter,' she said. 'Will you come in while I get ready?'

'I'll stay with the car. Don't be long. Better to get off while the weather's good.'

She ran into the house and looked around for Mrs Mortimer, but as there was no sign of her, she decided she must be lying down in her room. Kirsty was in a chair in the kitchen, fast asleep, and it seemed a pity to wake either of them. She had seen Mr Masterson set out earlier in the direction of the library, so she wrote a note for Murray and left it on the table in hall.

Dear Murray,
Peter Barrington called. He has offered to drive
me to Colethorpe in his motor-car to search for

my grandfather. I shall be back soon.
Shuah

Peter produced a long veil with a celluloid panel to protect her eyes from the dust and wind while allowing her to see where they were going. He wrapped this round over her hat and knotted it beneath her chin. Gallantly he handed her into the passenger seat and tucked a thick rug over her knees before taking his place behind the wheel. The chauffeur swung the starting-handle, and when the engine roared into life, hastily clambered into a seat which protruded from the back. The car back-fired, and Shuah felt quite scared as it jerked forward. Peter pumped the horn to scatter the curious bystanders who had gathered around to admire the beauty of the mahogany woodwork, the deep-buttoned leather upholstery and the shining brass lamps, gear-sticks, and pipes.

For a long time they drove through city streets busy with tramcars, wagons, carts and cabs. It was quieter in the newly-built suburbs, and quite peaceful when they reached the open country. Shuah gazed around in delight at the cottages in their colourful gardens and the wild flowers blooming in the hedgerows and on the commons. Peter occupied the middle of the road, humming happily to himself above the noise of the engine, travelling at just beyond the legal limit of twenty miles an hour. Shuah held on to the seat, and was glad of the warm clothing and rugs as their speed made the wind chilly. Suddenly the engine spluttered and choked, and then with a bang it cut out and the motor rolled to a standstill.

'Gibson'll soon get it going again,' Peter said cheerfully. 'These things happen, but it's a great way to travel, isn't it?'

'I suppose so,' Shuah said, rather doubtfully. 'Do you think it's better than the train?'

'Of course it is. I mean—it's so much more intimate, isn't it? There are always so many people with you on the train.' Now that he was not holding the wheel and concentrating on the road, and Gibson was lying on his back beneath the car, tapping at something or other, Peter stretched his arm along the back of the seat, and brought it to rest on her shoulder.

Shuah sat bolt upright, lifting herself away from that undoubtedly amorous gesture. 'How far is it to Colethorpe?' she asked.

'Not far. Be there in another hour,' he assured her. 'If we don't break down again!'

'And if we do?'

'We can always stay at an inn for the night,' he said lightly. Then, seeing her expression, he pretended to make a joke of it. 'Don't worry. It won't come to that.'

She began to wonder if she had been wise to set out with Peter, remembering how attentive he had been on the voyage from Singapore. It was a relief when at last Gibson slid out from beneath the motor. 'I've mended it, my lord. I'll give it a crank.'

Within a half hour they were at a standstill again, and this time it took Gibson a great deal longer to repair the fault. Peter had shifted so close to her that even by sitting forward she was almost encircled by his arms. She wriggled away, and climbed down from the high open-sided vehicle.

'Perhaps it would be quicker if we walked,' she said icily. 'I shouldn't have accepted your invitation. I had no idea the journey would take so long, or cause so much trouble.'

'Don't act the prim English miss with me,' Peter said, leaping out and hurrying round to where she stood by the side of the stony, dust-covered road. He put a hand on her shoulder and swung her round to face him. 'I'm crazy about you.' He spoke lightly, but with an undertone of passion. 'I'm considered quite a catch, since I've inherited the title. But there's no one excites me like you do!'

Gibson coughed, and they both turned towards him. 'The motor is ready, my lord.'

They travelled on for another half-hour or so, and Shuah kept her eyes on the road ahead. With the rush of the wind in their faces and the noise of the engine, it was impossible to make conversation. Peter had to slow down as they caught up with a line of wagons loaded with sacks of barley, drawn by magnificent shire horses, their harness and brasses gleaming in the late sunshine. They were making for the malthouses beside the common.

'This must be Colethorpe,' Peter told her. He stopped the car, and shouted to a young woman who was hanging out some washing on the village green. 'Can you tell me where Mead House is—Mr Sutherland's place?'

The young woman left her basket of wet linen and moved a few steps nearer, anxious to be helpful to such a good-looking young man, yet nervous of the new-fangled contraption he was riding in. Her directions were clear and precise. 'Keep a-goin' along here, turn down the loke alongside the church an' that'll take you to the master's house.'

Peter turned to Shuah. 'Sounds hopeful! Evidently Mr Sutherland still lives here—and is well known in the village.'

The automobile rumbled along the cobbled street of the village, passing the harness-maker's and cobbler's shops, two inns, the post-office and a grocery store. In those few minutes it took to reach the tall-towered church and turn down the narrow drive beside it, doubts she had never actually faced before crowded into her mind. Was this Mr Sutherland truly her grandfather? And, if so, would he be pleased to see her? He had not answered Murray's letter, so had she been foolish in coming to visit him, uninvited?

She felt increasingly nervous as they drove nearer. Mead House was a handsome mansion in Georgian style, built of red brick. It had a wide, well-proportioned façade and an impressive front door, on either side of which were three large windows, with others symmetrically above and dormers in the roof, half-concealed by a parapet. It was well maintained, a solid, well-built property. The gravel of the drive had been recently raked, its edges were cleanly chiselled, the lawn freshly mown, and the herbaceous borders were bright with colour. Peter brought his motor to a standstill close to the house, and Gibson leapt down from the back to swing open his master's door, then hurried round to help Shuah to alight.

'Looks as if your grandpapa is a man of considerable means,' Peter remarked. In answer to the smart rap he gave on the gleaming brass knocker, the door was opened by a man-servant in a dark suit. His astute eyes made a quick assessment of them, moving from Peter to Shuah, taking in also both the automobile and the chauffeur.

'Is Mr Sutherland in?' Peter asked.

'If you'll step inside, I'll enquire, sir,' said the butler. 'What name shall I say?'

'Barrington.' Peter produced a visiting-card from his pocket, and the butler's attitude became even more deferential. 'Please take a seat, my lord. It's Lord and Lady Barrington, I take it?'

Shuah expected Peter to give her name, but he answered, 'Just say, Lord Barrington and a friend.'

'Very good, my lord.' The butler placed the card on a silver salver and moved away with slow dignity.

Shuah turned accusing eyes on Peter. 'You should have given my name!'

He grinned disarmingly. 'Just thought we'd surprise the old fellow.'

'Were you afraid he might refuse to see me, if he knew who I am?'

'Never entered my head,' Peter denied.

'I wish he'd answered Murray's letter.'

Peter shrugged. 'Maybe he didn't get it. Anyway, the old family seat's only five miles further on. You'll always be welcome there, you know.'

Shuah ignored that suggestion. She was glad when the butler returned. 'Mr Sutherland will see you. This way, if you please, my lord.'

They were ushered into a comfortable study, book-lined and masculine looking, with a large polished table and several deep armchairs upholstered in leather. A white-haired, red-faced man who had been sitting in one of these rose as they entered. He was tall, heavily built, in his sixties and sombrely dressed, every inch the re-spectable Victorian. No smile lightened his face as the butler announced, 'Lord Barrington, sir.' He waited for Peter to approach him.

The two men shook hands. 'I'm pleased to make your acquaintance,' Peter said.

'You must be the new baron. Just back from overseas, aren't you?' said Mr Sutherland.

'I am, sir. And it was on my way back that I made the acquaintance of this young lady.' He paused, and held out a hand to draw Shuah forward.

Mr Sutherland's gaze turned in her direction—his eyes encountered hers, and his entire face and body stiffened, as if with shock. He stared at her for a long, long moment, yet she had the strangest feeling that it was not her that he saw. It seemed that he was fighting against betraying emotion, and as he regained control, she could almost feel the strength of will-power he had to exert.

'Who are you?' he asked hoarsely.

'Your grand-daughter, I believe, sir,' said Peter, easily—almost flippantly.

Then those shrewd grey eyes narrowed. There had been no friendliness in his face, but now it seemed to Shuah that its expression closed against her. He had never seen her before, yet she had no doubt he had recognised something about her. He had been surprised by her ap-pearance, but his response was guarded.

'So. You're the young lady who claims to be Edward's daughter?'

'Do you have any doubts, sir?' Peter said.

'I can see a strong likeness to my late wife,' he said. The words seemed to be wrung out of him. He paused, thoughtfully, looking from one to the other. 'I received a letter from someone who claimed to have discovered a girl he believed to be my grand-daughter.'

'It was from Murray Masterson, who brought me to England,' Shuah said. 'We—we've been waiting for a reply from you, Grandpapa.'

He looked sharply at her, as unwelcoming as ever. 'I renounced my son when he refused to come into the business and married that woman. That being so, I felt no need to meet any of his progeny.'

'I've no wish to cause you any trouble, sir,' Shuah said, hurt by the coldness of her reception and uncertain how to react to it. 'I'll leave immediately, if you wish.'

'Not so fast,' he commanded. 'Tell me—what was your purpose in coming here?'

'I came to meet you, Grandpapa, and to learn more about myself, and my parents.'

'The letter said that your parents had been ship-wrecked, a fact of which I was notified many years ago. I assumed that their child had drowned with them.'

'Naturally you would, sir,' agreed Peter. 'It was only by a miracle that the child was rescued by some Iban tribesman.'

'And I'm expected to believe that you lived with these natives until recently?'

'It's true, Grandpapa. They were kind and loving people,' Shuah said. 'They found me afloat in a small boat and took me in and cared for me.'

'What's your first name?'

'I am called Shuah, but I'm told that is probably not my real name. Perhaps you know what it should be?'

'If you don't have a name, by what right do you claim to be my grand-daughter?'

'Undoubtedly Shuah is the daughter of Edward Sutherland, the botanist, and his wife, Mary,' Peter said. 'So how can you deny that she's your grand-daughter?'

'I am not denying it, Lord Barrington. I'm merely wishing to have it properly confirmed.' Mr Sutherland's gaze rested thoughtfully on Peter, and his attitude appeared to soften a little. 'Sit down and let us discuss this rationally.'

He waited until she and Peter had seated themselves on a large chesterfield and then he turned towards Shuah. 'As far as I am aware, this is the first time I've ever set eyes on you. Edward wrote to my wife when his child was born, but that meant nothing to me. Had it been a boy, I might have offered to adopt it, bring it up here. Edward was always in impecunious circumstances. How could he make a decent living, fiddling about with plants—no money in that!'

'Did my grandmama keep in touch with my parents?'

'She was soft-hearted enough to suggest it, but I couldn't allow that. Edward repudiated us both when he insisted on marrying that girl—the daughter of our own gardener! No, I told my wife very firmly that if she went to London to see them, then that would be her choice and she could stay there. I would not have her back here.'

'Sir, I apologise for intruding upon you. I can see I'm unwelcome,' Shuah said, and would have sprung to her feet, but Peter caught hold of her arm and restrained her.

'I didn't say that, child,' Mr Sutherland protested. His eyes narrowed, and he glanced across to Peter. 'What is your interest in my grand-daughter, sir?'

At last he had admitted their relationship! Shuah relaxed a little, although she was still anxious to leave.

'I'm devoted to her, sir,' Peter replied without hesitation. 'As I said, I met her in Singapore, and we spent a great deal of time together, there and on the ship coming back to England. I assumed you'd be delighted

to make the acquaintance of such a charming young
lady!'

'You must allow me to adjust to this extraordinary
situation in my own way. When I received that letter, I
didn't believe it—the story was too fantastic. But now
that I've seen her, I can no longer doubt. I concede that
it's my duty to look after her.'

'There's no need for you to look after me,' Shuah said
stiffly. 'We're going back to London, aren't we, Peter?'

'I'm afraid that's impossible tonight,' he replied. 'But
you'll be welcome to stay at the Hall.'

She felt as if a trap was closing round her. How foolish
she had been to come here with Peter!

'No need for that.' Mr Sutherland reached for the bell-
pull, and the butler appeared almost immediately.
'Prepare the guest suite for my grand-daughter.'

The butler's mask slipped very slightly. His eyes flew
to Shuah, revealing his astonishment, but it was
smothered almost immediately. 'Very good, sir,' he
murmured. 'And shall I tell Cook that we have company
for dinner?'

Mr Sutherland glanced at Peter. 'Will you dine with
us, Lord Barrington?'

'Alas, I fear I have to return home before it is dark.
I'm motoring, and can't risk the roads at night.'

The butler withdrew, only to return a few minutes
later. 'Sir, a Mr Masterson is here, asking for Miss
Sutherland.'

'Ah! That's the man who wrote to me about you, isn't
it?' Mr Sutherland asked Shuah.

Wide-eyed, she nodded. Her heart leapt, as it always
did at the mention of Murray's name. But her joy was
tempered with alarm, uncertain as to why and in what
mood he had followed her here with such urgency.

'Show him in, Barker,' Mr Sutherland instructed.

CHAPTER TWELVE

MURRAY ENTERED the room with his head high and his intelligent brown eyes coolly taking in the situation. His glance flickered around, then turned on Shuah with a long, hard look.

'Murray! You found my note!' She watched him carefully, her eyes appealing for understanding.

'I did. And I followed on the first possible train.'

He turned away as the butler announced—'Mr Masterson, sir'—and moved forward to greet her grandfather. The two men shook hands with formal politeness, but neither showed any pleasure.

'I wrote to you about Miss Sutherland,' Murray said. 'I trust my letter arrived?'

'It did.'

'I received no reply.' Murray's tone was sharp.

'I didn't write one. My son was dead to me long before he was lost in that shipwreck. Your letter came as a bolt from the blue—and brought me no pleasure. How was I to know the young lady was not an impostor, encouraged by a fortune-hunter?'

Murray's head jerked up in anger, but he replied in a carefully controlled voice, 'Sir, I have come here only to protect Miss Sutherland's interests, and that I shall do, no matter how you insult me.'

Mr Sutherland shrugged his shoulders. 'I've been in business long enough not to trust anyone. I was merely waiting for proof. Now that I've seen my grand-daughter, my doubts of her parentage are—lessened. But I still know nothing of you. May I ask what is your interest in this matter?'

Murray's lips were compressed with anger, but he answered clearly, 'If you mean—have I any financial or other claim upon her?—the answer is none. But I have been acting as her guardian since I discovered her in an Iban village, and I shall not relinquish that charge until I am assured that she is in good hands.'

'But you have no legal right to be her guardian. Now that she has come to me, seeking my protection...'

'It wasn't that,' cried Shuah.

Murray turned to her. 'You should have waited for me to accompany you.'

'Peter offered to bring me, and I thought it would save you trouble, Murray.'

'No need to be alarmed, Masterson,' Peter said. 'Now that Mr Sutherland's seen Shuah, he's quite convinced of her identity. That's what you've always wanted, isn't it?'

'You know I've no wish to leave you, Murray,' Shuah exclaimed. 'I only wanted to find out who I am. I didn't come here to stay.' She turned to Mr Sutherland. 'I've no wish to be a burden upon you, Grandpapa.'

'You are here, and I have no choice,' said Mr Sutherland. 'You're under age, and the law insists that you must have a guardian. Therefore, as your paternal grandfather, that must be my responsibility.' Turning to Murray, he added, 'You may leave Miss Sutherland in my care.'

Murray's eyes flashed with anger. He was not accustomed to being dismissed in this peremptory fashion. Shuah had felt the fury tight-leashed within him the moment he had walked into the room, and that had been inflamed by her grandfather's attitude. But it was to Shuah that he spoke, and his voice was clipped and icy. 'Presumably this is what you and Barrington planned?'

'We didn't plan anything, Murray. You always said that I should find my relatives. We only came for a visit, didn't we, Peter?' She turned appealing eyes to Lord Barrington.

'Didn't have any idea what to expect, but it all seems to have turned out very well. Shuah's been accepted by her grandfather, and now you can safely leave her in his care, Masterson. Leave you free to get on with the preparations for your wedding, what?'

'From now on,' said Mr Sutherland, 'I shall decide what is in my grand-daughter's best interest. I'll see my solicitor tomorrow and have the matter properly settled.'

'But I can't stay! I haven't brought my things...' Shuah protested.

'I'll send the boy to London by train to collect them first thing in the morning,' her grandfather promised.

She could scarcely believe it was happening to her. She had come here only to meet her grandfather, to see him, to talk to him, and now he was taking over as if she was but a chattel, a possession—and not even one that he liked very much! He was treating her as if she had no feelings or mind of her own.

There was a discreet knock at the door, and a plump woman came in. She was about sixty years old, severely dressed in black, with a châtelaine hanging at her waist. 'Sir, Miss Sutherland's rooms have been prepared.'

'Go with my housekeeper, child. I'm sure you'd like to wash and rest before dinner,' Mr Sutherland instructed Shuah. 'And, Mrs Barker, be so good as to find some night-attire for my grand-daughter. Her luggage will be brought here tomorrow.'

'Very good, sir.'

Shuah glanced from her grandfather to Murray, appealing to him with eloquent eyes for guidance. 'I only came to call, not to stay.'

'You should have thought of that before you set out,' Murray said coldly.

'Can't I return to London with you, Murray?'

'I think not, under the circumstances. It seems to me that your grandfather is quite right. He's accepted you into his care, and as he's your next of kin, it is your duty to obey.'

Her heart sank. She felt defeated as she remembered that this was what he had planned for her all along. Now that a relative had been found who was willing, however grudgingly, to accept her, Murray was only too happy to be rid of the responsibility. The craggy lines of his face were hardened and forbidding, his lips tightly compressed. He turned sharply, and performed a perfunctory bow in the direction of Mr Sutherland.

'I've brought Shuah safely from the other side of the world. I've no claim whatsoever upon her, but before I leave her with you, I'd like your assurance that you'll look after her best interests and her happiness.'

'I have already undertaken that, sir,' Mr Sutherland snapped impatiently.

'Then good day to you, sir.' With the briefest of nods to Lord Barrington, he marched for the door—but she could not let him go, just like that!

'Murray,' she called, and running after him, she caught hold of his arm. 'Don't leave me, Murray!'

'You'll be perfectly all right here, Shuah. You'll live in luxury. You'll be better off than you've ever been in your life.'

She brushed that aside. 'When shall I see you again?'

He made no answer, but firmly lifted her hand from his arm and stepped back. He caught the eye of the housekeeper. 'Look after her well, Mrs Barker.'

'That I will, sir.'

Then Murray spun on his heel, and with his lithe, long-legged swinging stride, marched out of the room. Shuah stared at the door long after his broad shoulders had disappeared through it, and knew she would be unbearably lonely without him.

'Will you come this way, Miss Sutherland?' The housekeeper's voice brought reality home to her. Dully she began to follow, and then Peter rushed over and caught hold of her hand.

'It'll work out for the best, Shuah. You'll love it here when you get used to it, and I'll be over to see you every day. We'll have fun together, like we did on the boat.'

He seized her hand in his and raised it to his lips. 'Until tomorrow!'

She followed Mrs Barker across the wide hall, up a gracious flight of stairs, along a landing and into a suite of rooms. Her mind was in such a turmoil that she was scarcely aware of the housekeeper's discreet withdrawal. How could she possibly adjust to being separated from Murray? She had spent so much time in his company since they left Kuching, and her love for him had deepened with almost every day. She was especially miserable remembering his angry abrupt departure. How she wished she had never decided to accept Peter's offer to bring her here! Both he and Murray seemed to think she would enjoy being at Mead House, but she cared nothing for the luxurious surroundings.

Her eyes clouded with tears as she looked around the rooms to which Mrs Barker had led her. Undoubtedly they were beautiful, exquisitely furnished, with windows overlooking the meticulously kept gardens. She had admired the aspect as she arrived but now she scarcely saw it, for her mind was preoccupied with what would happen, and she could foresee little that might be to her liking. Presently a maid brought in a jug of hot water, and asked if there was anything else she required.

'No, thank you.'

The maid bobbed a curtsy and withdrew. She reappeared about an hour later to announce, 'Dinner is about to be served, miss.'

Shuah followed the girl down the stairs, across the hall and into the dining-room. Mr Sutherland stood with his back to the blazing fire, his hands clasped beneath his coat-tails, his portly stomach an imposing mound encased in a black waistcoat and looped with heavy gold watch and fob chains. For a moment she hesitated in the doorway and the two of them surveyed each other, neither certain how their relationship would work out. Then he nodded, and she felt that in his harsh, unfriendly way, he approved. He did not quite smile, but merely said, 'Come and sit down. Mustn't keep good food waiting.'

The long table had been set with two places: the carver chair at the head was obviously for him, and Shuah seated herself in the other, on his right. The rest of the table, that could comfortably have seated a dozen people, stretched away emptily, its highly polished surface reflecting the glow of the lamp-light.

'I've been wondering what to call you, child.'

'Shuah.'

'That's ridiculous! Edward was a fool, but even he wouldn't have christened you that.'

'I know no other name.'

'Hmph! Then I'll just call you "child".'

'I'm not a child.'

'To me, you are.'

The butler came in bearing a tureen of steaming hot oxtail soup. After he had served them and withdrawn, Shuah turned back to her grandpapa.

'The house is so big—do you live here alone?'

'Of course. Apart from the servants. Your grandmother died ten years ago, and I've never remarried.'

'Don't you find it lonely? Have you no other relations to share the house?'

He gave a short bark of a laugh. 'None that I would welcome!'

'You had no other children?'

'No, only the one. And he let me down badly. Always was headstrong, determined to go his own way—fiddling about with plants. What sort of work is that for a man? Should have come into the business with me. I built it up from nothing. I'd have been proud to extend the name of the company to Sutherland and Son, but he turned his back on that. Didn't want to go into brewing, he said. All he wanted was to gaze at those orchids of his! And that girl encouraged him!'

'Do you mean my mother?'

'Who else? I had plans for Edward to marry the daughter of one of the landed gentry, and I could have arranged it, too. I'd got the money and they had the blood. It would have been an excellent match for everybody. But would he agree?' His voice was an outraged growl.

'I suppose he was in love with my mother,' Shuah ventured to suggest.

'Huh! That's what he said—and nothing would suit him except marriage to her. I realised then that if he took over this business he'd only lose it all, everything I'd worked for. He would have frittered it away on some mad scheme, so I cut him off. I thought that would bring him to his senses, but he was stubborn. He ran away with that—trollop!'

Although Shuah had never heard the word before, the very way he said it made it sound derogatory. She had to force herself to restrain her resentment and try to understand. He was her grandfather; by his age alone he had earned respect.

'It must have been very sad—especially for my grandmama.'

Mr Sutherland's face had reddened as the tirade poured from him. Now he turned towards her, and she saw in the taut lines of his face that the anguish, the frustration he had felt at his son's incomprehensible behaviour, was still as real for him as it had been all those years ago.

'It killed her! She loved that boy with all her heart, and he thought only of himself. I'll never forgive him. Never!'

He took no blame on himself for the rift, and instinctively she knew that nothing would change his opinion. In her heart she felt that he had been more wrong than had her father, but undoubtedly all had suffered, Mr Sutherland as much as anyone.

'And my mother's parents—did you know them? Did they feel the same?'

He stared at her, fury making his eyes stand out in the puffy fleshiness of his face. 'Platten was the gardener! That's all he was! I ought to have seen it earlier. He was the one that poisoned the boy's mind when he was only a child, feeding him a load of twaddle about plants and flowers. It's my belief he planned it from the start, threw them together when they were young, encouraged her to inveigle herself into Edward's affections. Don't mention those people to me!'

'Are they still alive?' she asked breathlessly.

'I neither know nor care!' he thundered.

A heavy silence fell between them that was broken only when Mr Barker came in, followed by a maid smartly dressed in a black gown with a frilly-edged white apron and streamers from her jaunty cap flowing down her straight slender back. They brought roast sirloin of beef with horseradish sauce and a selection of vegetables. Mr Sutherland carved, and the servants left, and Shuah tried to turn the conversation to less emotive ground.

'Have you always lived here, Grandpapa?' she asked.

'In this village, yes. My father was innkeeper at the King's Head and had his own brewery at the back. I went into the business with him, but I wasn't content just to jog along as he had done. I put money by and made it work for me—bought my first malthouse a few years later. I worked hard, won some good orders and expanded the business. I've built four new malthouses since then. My assets are considerable, I don't mind telling you, child. That chap who brought you here was quite impressed—I could see that.'

'Murray Masterson...'

'No, not him, Lord Barrington. He's inherited an old estate. I know it well—it's not far from here. I bought three pubs from his uncle only a few months before he died. He needed the money, and I'm always ready to buy. Alehouses are a good investment for a brewer.' He had been eating steadily as he talked, and now paused to regard her shrewdly. 'Fond of each other, are you?'

'I've tried to discourage him...'

'Don't do that, child.' He brushed aside her reply. 'I wouldn't mind being related to the Barringtons. No, I wouldn't mind that at all. It would go a long way to making up for all the disappointments I've had over the years.'

Shuah gazed at him in dismay. Her grandfather had got quite the wrong impression. 'I'm going back to Sarawak with Murray Masterson,' she said.

Her grandfather was in no mood to listen. 'Nonsense! *He*'s no good for you. Barrington's the one you want to marry. He'll propose before long, I'd stake my life on it. I saw him looking around. Nothing shoddy or second-rate in *my* house, I made sure of that! See that cruet in the centre of the table? It's solid silver! The best that money could buy.' He chuckled as he gloated over his treasures. His list of expensive ornaments seemed endless, and he always told her exactly how much each one had cost, until her head seemed to be buzzing with figures that were quite meaningless to her.

It was not the sort of information she wanted to know, but how could she ask more about her father, when the very mention of his name made her grandpapa almost apoplectic with rage? The meal ended with coffee, which was served in the lounge, and as soon as she could Shuah made tiredness an excuse to retire to her room.

'That's right. Get your beauty sleep, child. Lord Barrington said he'd call tomorrow. I told him he'd be welcome at any time.'

With those words reverberating discordantly in her ears, Shuah tossed and turned in the big half-tester bed, its tall ornate head and foot of twisted brass gleaming like gold. How was she to escape from this trap into which she had run? No doubt, by now, Murray had returned to London, was back home with Dorothy. Had he intended it to be goodbye for ever when he left? Tears welled into her eyes, and she felt utterly helpless. She toyed with the idea of leaving Mead House the next day and catching a train back to London, but she had not brought any money and, besides, past experience made her cautious, unsure of what her welcome would be. There seemed to be nothing she could do, except wait and see what happened.

Her grandfather was away all the next day, and when she saw him in the evening for dinner, he announced abruptly, 'Your name's Suzanne. I've been to see my solicitor and he was able to look it up in some documents.'

'Suzanne! Just like the orchid!' she exclaimed.

She told him about the visit to Kew and the beautiful pink-flecked flower, and for once he seemed to listen, though when she had finished, his only comment was a dismissive snort.

'How did the solicitor know my name?' she asked.

'Your grandmama left some money for you. It's been invested over the years and would bring in a annuity of about £400. I've told him to open a bank account in your name. Miss Suzanne Sutherland.'

'Grandmama knew my name! That's wonderful! And how kind of her to leave me some money.'

'She could never bring herself to believe that you had all been lost. She insisted that the money should remain invested for you.'

'Is it really mine—to use in any way I like?'

'Of course. It'll make a useful dress allowance. And, talking of clothes, I'll send Mrs Barker with you to order some new outfits tomorrow. Some things that will fit your status as my grand-daughter.'

'Thank you, Grandpapa,' she replied dutifully.

During the days that followed, being separated from Murray was every bit as unbearable as she had expected. She had little love for the life she was leading at Mead House, but it settled into a routine and she could see no way out of it. Peter called frequently, encouraged by her grandfather, who made no secret of his hope that they would marry. She wished she could tell them both that she was married already, but what would be the use? She knew by now that would simply be discounted. They all said it had never been a real marriage, but that did not change her belief one iota. She had made her vow before Sabat, and even if she never saw Murray again, as far as she was concerned he was her husband for life.

One afternoon, when she had been about two weeks at Mead House, feeling particularly depressed and lonely, she wandered aimlessly around the house, opening doors and looking into rooms that she had not previously explored. A distant murmur of voices and laughter drew her to a door covered with green baize. She opened it and found herself looking into the kitchen. Half a dozen astonished faces stared back from the spacious warmth with its delectable smells of newly-baked breads and cakes. Both Mr and Mrs Barker were there and an older lady, with her sleeves rolled up over plump arms, that Shuah guessed was Cook. She already knew the chambermaid and the parlour-maid and had seen the boy who attended to the fires, and the only other one was a very young scullery-maid. They were all seated round a well-scrubbed table on which stood a three-pint teapot covered with a knitted cosy, teacups and saucers and a plate of biscuits.

'Miss Sutherland!' Mrs Barker stood up hurriedly. 'Is something the matter? Can I get you anything?'

'I just wanted to find someone to talk to,' Shuah smiled. 'May I join you?'

The housekeeper glanced at her husband, then back to Shuah. 'It's not usual for family to come into the kitchen.'

'I'm sorry. You mean, this is your private room. I'm not allowed...?'

'I can't say you're not allowed, miss,' said Mrs Barker stiffly. 'You have every right to go where you wish in the house. It's just—not normally done.'

Shuah was about to turn away, but Cook's voice stopped her. 'Finding it lonely up there, are you?' There was understanding in her tone.

'I am rather,' Shuah admitted.

'Then come and join us, lass. We've just made a pot of tea.'

Cook indicated a chair beside her. 'Thank you,' Shuah said. 'I've always lived in the midst of lots of people—I'm not used to being on my own.' The chambermaid fetched another cup and poured tea for her.

'I'm not surprised. I've often thought myself what a lonely life Mr Sutherland leads, but it's of his own making. Gave up all entertaining when his wife died.'

'You knew my grandmother?' Shuah asked eagerly.

'I certainly did! You remind me of her. When she was young, she had hair just the colour of yours, and that same creamy complexion.'

Shuah was delighted at being so favourably compared with her grandmother.

'She was a society beauty,' Mrs Barker remarked. 'I came here to work for them, just after they got married. Mrs Sutherland used to give grand dinner parties and have visitors for long weekends; the house was always abuzz with people, especially when Edward was little.'

'I don't remember my father,' Shuah said. 'I wish I knew more about him.'

'Mr Edward was a great favourite with everyone. The times I've seen him sneak in that back door!' Cook nodded her head in its direction. 'After one of my buns or tarts. Lemon curd was his favourite, home-made with lemons and eggs and sugar, full of goodness, and he'd glance around and I'd pretend not to notice if he took only one. But if he tried to take another, then I'd chase him out of the kitchen. It was all a sort of game, really.'

'He liked to be in the kitchen with us,' agreed Mrs Barker, with a smile at the pleasurable memory.

'Liked the staff too much, in the end,' said Mr Barker drily. His wife shot him a warning glance, but he ignored it. 'Spent hours with Archie Platten—he was head gardener here at that time. Lived at the gatehouse. Young Mr Edward was always down there. I've heard Archie say he knew a rare lot about plants, understood all that scientific stuff about 'em, could trot out their Latin names and that sort of thing.'

'Did Mr Platten have a daughter called Mary?' Shuah asked breathlessly.

Mr and Mrs Barker exchanged glances with Cook, and there was a short silence before she answered, 'Yes.'

'She was my mother.'

'Ah. We weren't sure if you knew.'

Shuah nodded. 'Then you must have known my other grandparents?'

'Know them well,' said Mrs Barker.

'You mean they're still here—at this cottage?'

'Not here. Good Lord, no!' Mr Barker shook his head. 'Mr Sutherland turned them out double quick after Mr Edward ran away with Mary.'

'Don't see why he blamed her parents any more than he did himself,' muttered Cook.

'Well, you know what he is, begging your pardon, miss. But the master was furious. He'd set his heart on having his son in the business with him—and when Mr Edward refused point blank, and married Archie Platten's daughter into the bargain, that was the last straw.'

'Do you know where Mr and Mrs Platten are now?' Shuah asked.

This time the silence was more portentous. She gazed from Mr Barker to his wife, and then to Cook—none was willing to meet her questioning eyes.

'Better tell her,' said Cook.

'Be more than your job's worth if the master finds out you've been talking,' warned Mr Barker.

Shuah looked around apprehensively. 'Please? I must know. Perhaps I'll be able to do something to help them.'

'They're quite old, you know, and Archie suffers from rheumatics pretty bad. Can't work any more.' Cook paused and took a deep breath. 'They was took into the workhouse a year or so ago.'

She did not understand. She pictured a sort of longhouse, with her grandparents having their own *bilek* and other friendly families around. 'Then I could go and see them there?'

'There's nothing to stop you, I suppose. It's the other side of the village, a couple of miles' walk. But you won't let on to your grandfather that we've told you, will you, miss?'

'No, of course not.' Shuah sensed they were unwilling to impart any further information, so she finished her tea and stood up. 'Thank you for telling me.'

'It's only right you should know,' said Cook, rising heavily to her feet. 'Time we was getting back to work.'

CHAPTER THIRTEEN

ALL THAT evening Shuah pondered on what she had been told, and the more she thought about it, the more determined she was to visit these other grandparents. She avoided any mention of her plans and waited until Mr Sutherland had left the house the following morning—rather later than usual, for some reason. Then she hurried to her room and donned a light jacket, pinned on her hat, picked up her gloves and set off. She told no one where she was going, just walked out of the house and down the drive.

By the road were high wrought-iron gates, kept open during the day but closed at night, and on the left-hand side was the gatehouse. She had passed it many times, but now it held a meaning for her, and she paused. The cottage was single storey, with whitewashed walls and a thatched roof, surrounded by a neat garden bright with flowers. As she gazed, her vivid imagination tried to picture the little girl who had once lived there—Mary Platten, her mother. She knew so little about her, only that she had fallen in love with the boy from the big house and had run away with him. In her mind's eye Shuah saw again those lovely drawings her mother had made of the orchid, and wished that she could remember her.

Small and homely though the place was, it seemed more attractive to Shuah than the mansion she had just left, with its grand, enormous rooms filled with costly possessions, but so lacking in love. A trellis porch wreathed in twining, variegated greenery shielded the black front door. Suddenly it opened. A man walked out—and she gasped with surprise and pleasure. It was

Murray! Impulsively she called his name and rushed to open the little wicket gate.

'Murray—Murray!' She ran towards him, disregarding the man and woman who stood behind him. 'You've come back! You've come back! I thought you'd gone for good. Oh, it's lovely to see you!' She would have flung herself into his arms, but he caught hold of her hands and held her away from him. He was looking down at her in the perceptive way that could be so disconcerting, but she was oblivious of it. She was so eager to share with him her exciting information. 'This is where my mother lived—and her parents are still alive. Did you know that? I can scarcely believe it!'

'It's perfectly true,' he assured her. 'I came back to Colethorpe yesterday because I felt I must make sure you were in good hands with Mr Sutherland, and when I made enquiries in the village, I was told the story of your other grandparents. That's why I've just been to see these good people.' He turned and introduced her to the middle-aged couple. 'This is Miss Sutherland, about whom I've been telling you,' he said, and Shuah held out her hand, and the man bowed his head as he took it and the woman bobbed a curtsy. 'Mr Smith was assistant gardener to Mr Platten, and they moved into the cottage when your grandparents...' Murray broke off, searching her face. 'Do you know what happened?'

She nodded. 'Yes. Grandpapa was furious when my father married my mother. I don't think he's a very kind man.'

'Has he not treated you well, Shuah?' Murray asked.

'He's been very generous,' she replied, conscious that she was wearing expensive clothes that he had insisted on having made for her.

'Good,' Murray nodded. He evidently wanted to believe that all was well with her. 'A hard man, but just, so I have heard.'

Shuah left it at that; she was too eager to find out more about her other grandparents to waste time discussing Mr Sutherland.

'Would the young lady like to come in?' asked Mr Smith.

'Yes, please,' said Shuah.

With a sense of wonder she stepped inside, and her heart was full as she thought of the trouble and sadness that had been felt here. Yet her parents' love for each other must have been real and strong. Each in their own way had sacrificed so much to be together—especially her father, who could have inherited both wealth and position. But her mother also, for she had gone with him to the other side of the world, faced untold dangers, taking her baby daughter with her.

Murray seemed to understand, and stood in silence as her eyes roved over the small low-ceilinged room, sparsely furnished, but spotlessly clean, made comfortable with handmade rag-rugs on the floor, pretty patchwork cushion covers, and plants flowering in pots on the windowsill. 'I think my mother must have had a happy childhood here,' she said.

'I didn't know her when she was right little,' said Mr Smith. 'She'd have been about twelve when I first came to work here. Mr Platten was really good to me, taught me all I know. He was a wise man when it came to gardening—and Mary loved all living things just as much as he did. She was often out there working with the flowers, and sometimes she helped us in the greenhouses. Mr Edward was the same. Mad about those orchids of his—spent hours and hours tending them. He got some good results too. Produced a new hybrid, you know. He was quite famous in the plant world—it was dreadful that they should have been lost like that. Dreadful!'

It warmed Shuah's heart to hear her parents and grandparents spoken of with such admiration and respect, and everything Mr and Mrs Smith said was favourable. They talked on for some time, then Shuah said, 'I'm just longing to meet them. I'm on my way now to this place where they are living.'

'I'll come with you,' Murray said.

His tone was abrupt, but she had no wish to oppose him as he ushered her to the door. She was about to move out into the garden when she heard the explosion of a car back-firing as it slowed to turn through the Mead House gates.

'It's Barrington,' said Murray in a harsh voice.

Shuah drew back so that she was hidden within the cottage. 'I don't want him to see me,' she exclaimed.

Murray also stepped inside again. 'Don't worry,' he said curtly. 'He needn't know you're with me.'

'What I meant was that I don't want to see Peter.'

'You don't have to explain. I can see it would be embarrassing for you. I was well aware of your grand-father's opinion of me, and of his ambitions for you.'

'I didn't think you approved of Peter,' she said.

'I don't. But my opinion no longer matters. I felt re-sponsible for you before, but since you chose to come here with Barrington, that has altered the situation.'

'I only wanted to save you trouble...' She was inter-rupted by Mr Smith, who was hovering anxiously.

'Mr Sutherland's a harsh man, begging your pardon, miss,' he pleaded. 'I wouldn't like to lose my job over this.'

'Oh, no! That mustn't happen,' she cried. He sounded so concerned that she turned her attention to him, and was not really sure whether Murray had accepted her explanation. 'Please don't worry, Mr Smith. I shan't say a word to Grandpapa about having been here.'

'Why don't you leave by the back way?' his wife sug-gested. 'It's a short-cut to the workhouse, along by the river and across the common.'

Shuah glanced at Murray, and he nodded.

The path from the back door was narrow, and Murray had to follow Shuah as they walked through the intensively cultivated vegetable patch. At the end were rows of raspberry canes and gooseberry bushes and beyond that a clipped hawthorn hedge with a gate that opened on to the towpath beside the river. There he fell into step with her.

She was exquisitely aware of his presence; her heart thumped just because he was there beside her. There was so much about him that was pleasing to her: his physique; broad-shouldered, narrow-hipped, straight-backed; the healthy athletic ease of his movements; the way he held his head high; and that air of command that gave her such confidence in him. Other people saw it too, and his least instruction was usually acted upon immediately. Yet he was by no means aloof. There had been friendly informality between him and Mr and Mrs Smith. They had been impressed by him, that had been obvious, and Shuah understood, because she felt exactly the same way. Even if it had been only devotion to duty that had brought him back, she was glad he was here, and instinctively she reached out and caught hold of his hand.

He turned and looked at her. 'Yes?'

She almost said, 'I love you,' but she dared not. Instead, she explained her impetuous action by saying, 'Just think, Murray! My mother must have walked along this very same path with my father, all those years ago!'

He nodded, and there was understanding in the depths of his dark brown eyes. The flood of emotion she felt made her turn her face away, but he kept hold of her hand. They walked on in silence for a short distance towards a clump of alders and willows, some of which leaned over the water, stirred by a light breeze, and she became aware of the gentle gurgle of the slow-flowing river. A coot gave its croaking call, breaking the stillness—it was a place of peace and loneliness, little changed over the centuries.

The pressure of Murray's fingers tightened. He drew her to a standstill beneath the trees. 'Shuah,' he said gently, 'did they tell you where your grandparents are?'

Something in the solemn way with which he was regarding her gave her a sense of foreboding. 'At the workhouse.'

'But do you understand what that means?'

She was reminded of the significant looks that had passed between Cook and the Barkers. 'They said quite a lot of people live there. I suppose it must be a bit like a longhouse.'

'I'm afraid it's not in the least like that,' he said. 'In the longhouse, everybody is more or less equal and the older people are respected and well cared for.'

'Doesn't that happen here?' She questioned him anxiously, for she knew only the Iban way and could not imagine how life could be so very different.

'I don't want to upset you,' Murray said. 'Your grandparents may be perfectly well and happy—but you must be prepared, for they are quite old, possibly infirm, and certainly they are destitute.'

'What does that mean?'

'They have no money and no home of their own. Your mother was probably an only child, so there was no one to look after them. I don't want to worry you, Shuah, but I must warn you that they may not be in happy circumstances.' He was standing facing her, and now grasped her other hand and squeezed her fingers. 'It may not be as bad as I think. At least they're alive, that's the important thing—more than you dared hope, isn't it?'

'Yes. It's wonderful!'

He smiled in a way that warmed her heart. 'I'm sure they'll be overjoyed to find they have such a lovely granddaughter.'

If he thought her lovely, why didn't he show it? Why didn't he take her into his arms?—it would be wonderful to make love with him, here in this beautiful spot!

He walked briskly on, and she jog-trotted along beside him. Presently the riverside path met a road, and about a mile along it they came to the high wall with high iron

gates, beside which was a notice: Colethorpe Union
Workhouse. Master and Matron: Mr and Mrs Blacker.
Shuah looked with awe at the enormous high building
of stark red brick. The gate was unlocked, and led into
a large bare courtyard where two gaunt old woman
shuffled along aimlessly, both clad in dark serge dresses
with grubby cotton aprons and bonnets.

Murray pulled the iron handle by the side of the main
door, which set a bell jangling inside. A few minutes
later, a plump sour-faced woman opened the door. She
looked them over briefly, was obviously impressed by
Murray's handsome well-dressed appearance, and
speedily recomposed her features into a more friendly
disposition.

'I wish to speak to the Master,' Murray said.

'Are you one of the new governors, sir?'

'No, my name's Masterson.'

'I'm Mrs Blacker. Perhaps I can help you? My husband's resting.'

'We wish to see Mr and Mrs Platten.'

Mrs Blacker sniffed. 'It's work-time, you know.'

'Fetch them at once, if you please.' Murray's voice
was so imperious that Mrs Blacker backed away.

'You'd better come into the Master's office, sir. See
what he has to say.'

They followed her into a large white-walled dining-
room with long wooden tables and benches. It was
empty, but the smell of unpalatable meals lingered in
the cool, dank atmosphere. Mrs Blacker led them into
a warm, cosy room to one side, where her male
equivalent was reclining in a sagging armchair.

'Mr Blacker,' she said to her husband. 'This gent and
lady say they want to see Mr and Mrs Platten.'

'And you'd better arrange it at once, or I'll be having
a word with the governors.' Murray's voice was
imperative.

It was effective in stirring Mr Blacker into struggling
to his feet and bowing obsequiously. 'Certainly, cer-

tainly. Take a seat, and my wife'll arrange to have them fetched.'

The waiting seemed interminable to Shuah as she sat stiffly, dismayed by the unfriendly reception, bewildered by the place, its lack of comfort, its unpleasant air. Presently Mrs Blacker returned, followed by a thin pale-faced woman who hobbled in, leaning heavily on a stick. She was dressed in the same uniform as the women in the courtyard, but her apron was clean and white and her bonnet starched and fresh, and beneath it her bright brown eyes were amazingly full of life. Small but sharp, their gaze darted from Mr Blacker, to Murray, and finally came to rest on Shuah and lingered there. Just as Mr Sutherland had undoubtedly recognised the resemblance to his wife, so now Mrs Platten appeared mesmerised.

'Who—who are you?' Her voice held a note of amazement.

'I think Mrs Platten had better sit down,' Murray said.

He carried a chair to where Mrs Platten stood in the middle of the room and gently eased her on to it. Shuah moved over to the old lady, clasped her thin work-worn hands and smiled down at her. For her, there was no longer any doubt as to their relationship.

'Where is Mr Platten?' Murray asked.

'He's being fetched from the men's wing,' said Mrs Blacker.

'You've sent for my husband as well?' A smile broke over Mrs Platten's face.

She turned eagerly as the door opened again to admit an elderly man of middle height, with stooped shoulders and snow-white hair and beard. His eyes went at once to his wife, sitting in the chair, and he hurried towards her as fast as his shuffling gait allowed, oblivious of anyone else.

'Suzanne, are you all right?'

'Of course, my dear.'

Shuah started. She must have been named after her grandmother, just as the orchid had been named after her.

'What's this all about, then?' asked Mr Platten. 'I was afraid something was wrong.'

'We've got visitors, Archie,' Mrs Platten said. She held tightly to her husband's hand, but her gaze turned back immediately to Shuah, and it was to her that she spoke. 'Please, tell me. Who are you?'

'I'm your grand-daughter,' Shuah said gently. 'My parents were Edward and Mary Sutherland.'

Slowly the old lady nodded her head. 'You're the living image of his mother, isn't she, Archie?' She looked up at him, but he was staring open-mouthed, holding on to the back of her chair for support.

'Is that true?' he asked, his voice hoarse with astonishment. 'We were told they were all lost—Edward, Mary and little Suzanne.'

'You've only got to look at her to see it's true,' his wife said. She held open her arms, and Shuah rushed into them and they kissed and hugged. Then the old lady drew back her head and gazed long and hard into her face. 'I can hardly believe it! It's like a miracle!'

'Suzanne,' Murray said, and Shuah remembered that she had forgotten to mention about her name. 'Sweet Suzanne—like the orchid.'

'That's right,' exclaimed Archie. Then Shuah was gathered into his arms, and she was unable to hold back the tears that trickled down her cheeks. A knock at the door reminded them that they were in the Master's room, from which the business of the workhouse was run.

'I'm sorry we have nowhere private we can talk to you, and we can't even offer you a cup of tea,' bemoaned Mrs Platten.

'Let's go outside and find a quiet corner in the grounds,' suggested Murray.

'This place is horrible! It's best to be out among the growing things,' agreed Archie.

He led them to a bench against a south-facing wall beside the vegetable patch, and Shuah sat between her grandparents and held one hand of each of them. There was so much to say that time seemed to stand still. Murray sat quietly, leaving Shuah and her grandparents to get to know each other. They listened enraptured to her story, and told her of their agony when they learned that the boat on which Edward and Mary had been travelling had been lost. Suzanne Platten spoke freely of her daughter's great love for Edward.

When Mr Sutherland had first turned the Plattens out of the gatehouse, they had been able to move to another job, with a cottage attached, in a nearby village called Merston. Mary had returned to her mother when Shuah was born, and Mrs Sutherland had secretly called on them once, determined to see her grandchild. Soon after that, however, Edward and Mary had moved to the house in London, taking their baby daughter with them. They had remained there for just over two years, before setting out on the ill-fated expedition in search of orchids and other rare plants.

The sound of a clanging bell interrupted them. 'It's the dinner bell,' said Archie. 'We'll have to go.'

'It's little enough, only bread and cheese, but if we miss it, we'll go hungry,' explained Mrs Platten.

Slowly they walked back to the huge, grim building. It had two separate entrances, one marked 'men' and the other 'women'. They stopped just outside the courtyard. 'Come and see us again, my dear,' said her grandmother, as Shuah bent to kiss her fondly.

'Of course I will—every day.'

'No, I wouldn't ask that. This is not a happy place for a young lady to visit, and we have work to do.'

The bell clanged imperatively. 'We must get in, or there'll be trouble,' Archie insisted.

Shuah kissed him too. Then he turned and clasped his wife in his arms and kissed her. 'Goodbye, my dearest. We'll have some happy dreams tonight.'

'That we will!'

The old couple walked to their separate entrances, paused to wave a farewell to Shuah and Murray, then hurried into the grim building. Shuah gazed after them, shocked, despite the warning Murray had given her. Surely it was not right for a loving old couple to be separated?

They retraced their steps away from the workhouse and back along the road until it joined the towpath by the river. 'I must help them!' she exclaimed. 'I'm sure they'd be happier if they had a little place of their own.'

'Probably, but they're too infirm to look after themselves alone,' Murray pointed out.

'I've got some money. My grandmama Sutherland left me some, and it's been put in the bank in my name. I'll give that to them!'

She turned to him. They had come to a halt beneath the overhanging willow trees she had noticed earlier. The bright sunshine filtered prettily through the branches and made a mosaic of light on the short grass. 'I don't want to go back to Mead House yet.'

'Let's sit here for a while and talk it over,' Murray suggested. The day was warm, and he took off his jacket and spread it on the ground for her. When she was comfortably settled and he had seated himself beside her, she explained what Mr Sutherland had told her about the legacy.

'Your grandpapa wouldn't approve. He'll expect you to spend the money on yourself,' Murray said, when she had finished.

'But this *will* be for myself, because I'd be so much happier if they had a place of their own instead of living in the workhouse. They put a brave face on it, but I'm sure they're really unhappy. Couldn't I rent a cottage for them, and find someone who would call in and help them every day?'

'I suppose it's possible.'

'I can't do it alone. You must help me, Murray.'

'If you're sure it's what you want, then of course I'll help you, Suzanne.'

'It seems strange to hear you call me that, Murray.'

'It's a pretty name.'

'I'm glad you like it, but I like it better when you call me Shuah.'

'You should try to get used to your English name.'

'I don't feel English.'

'You look absolutely English to me.'

She leaned towards him, looking deeply into his eyes. He smiled at her, and that softening of the lines of his face gave her a warm feeling. She reached towards his cheek and ran her fingers along it in a loving caress.

His eyes roved over her face, upturned towards him, her lips parted invitingly. She held her breath, yearning for his kiss, but he made no movement towards her.

'Murray,' she whispered lovingly.

He drew back sharply and sat up straight and stiff. 'Dorothy and I have made arrangements for our wedding,' he said.

She was not surprised, but it was like a knife twisting in her breast to hear those words. She straightened her body so that she was sitting up, with her head held high and proud, and regarded him in silence.

'It's to be in a little over three weeks,' he continued. 'We have seen Mr Percival, and the banns are to be read in church for the first time this Sunday. We sail for Sarawak soon after.'

'Yes, Murray,' she said. She smiled because she was glad he had told her, so that she could be ready to leave with him as befitted her position as Number One wife. There would be a lot to do before they left England. 'But you'll have time to help me to find a place for my grandparents? We must get something sorted out quickly.'

He nodded. 'I'll have to spend a good deal of time in London, but I'll come here as often as I can.'

She relaxed a little, pleased that he was honouring his promise to her. It was almost as if he was acknowledging that she was indeed his wife. 'When shall I expect you?'

He thought for a moment. 'On Tuesday,' he said. 'Meet me here at about ten o'clock.'

'In the morning?'

He chuckled. 'Of course. Oh, Shuah, have you no sense of decorum?' Then more seriously, 'I sometimes wonder if you're safe alone in this country.'

'Then don't leave me alone,' she pleaded. 'I need you more than Dorothy does.'

The granite-like mask settled on his features again, so that she shrank away from him. 'Nonsense!' he snapped.

He jumped to his feet. She thought for a moment that he was going to leave her there, but he paused and stood for a moment just gazing down at her. She wished she could read his thoughts, but his face told her nothing. He put out his hand, and she sprang up to stand beside him. Even then she cherished a hope that he would kiss her when they parted. But he was striding off in the direction of the station, and she was left alone.

CHAPTER FOURTEEN

SHUAH WAITED in excited anticipation for Tuesday, and when the day dawned at last, she was up early and constantly looking at the clocks in the house, scarcely believing how slowly the hands moved. Long before the appointed hour, she left the house and wandered with apparent idleness through the gardens and along the river path. She lingered, watching a family of swans, their young almost as big as their parents, distinguishable only by their grey colouring. At last she saw him approaching.

'Murray!' she called. She ran to greet him and he opened his arms wide and caught hold of her, and for a few ecstatic moments she was clasped against his chest.

'I thought you'd never get here,' she exclaimed, leaning her head back to look up at him.

'I caught the first train.' He smiled down at her.

She was pleased when he said that, for it seemed as if he, too, had been eagerly awaiting their reunion. And although almost immediately he put her from him and held her at arm's length, and began to speak of the arrangements he had made, that in itself proved he had been thinking about her.

Despite the secrecy of her meetings with Murray, the following two weeks were some of the happiest for Shuah since her arrival in England. As he had promised, he spent a great deal of time in Colethorpe, and being with him and having the exciting project of finding a new home for the Plattens brought her great joy. When he had to return to London, the parting was eased by the knowledge that he would return again in a day or two. He took her to meet the solicitor who handled her legacy, and ascertained that there were no insurmountable problems. The annuity would easily cover the rent for a cottage and give her grandparents an allowance on which they could live quite comfortably.

Finding a cottage was easy enough. Times were hard in agriculture, and several families had left the district to seek work in the towns and cities. Murray discovered an agent who was able to offer three properties for them to inspect, and Shuah quickly decided on a small but comfortable red-brick dwelling called Ivy Cott. It had recently been rethatched, and was situated in the main street of the village only two doors from the general shop and post office. Its back door was south facing and led to a small garden, where her grandfather would be able to potter about among his beloved plants.

Whenever possible Shuah called at the workhouse, and if the weather was fine she sat with Archie and Suzanne on the wooden bench outside, and delighted to hear tales of her mother when she had been small. It took some time for her to persuade them that she really wanted to set them up in the cottage, and that she could afford it, but she was determined.

'I intend to do it, and I'll hear no more arguments about it,' she told them firmly. 'It's no more than my parents would have done if they'd been alive.' To herself she thought too that she would be able to return happily to Sarawak if she knew they were settled into the cottage first. She did not mention that, because no one else seemed to think along the same lines as she did.

She had to see Peter from time to time—more frequently than she would have wished, but that was necessary to prevent her grandpapa Sutherland from discovering what she was planning. She knew he would oppose her strongly, and feared he might even be able to prevent her carrying out her plans. For his part, he had become so obsessed with his scheme to marry her to Lord Barrington that, brushing aside her continual refusal, he convinced himself that it was only a matter of time before he would be able to announce their engagement. He took her to visit the Barrington estates, and evidently he expected her to be impressed by the gracious old house set in acres of parkland, but it meant nothing to her. She waited only for Murray's next visit.

On the day the old couple were to move into the cottage, Murray called for her at Mead House, driving a gig he had hired from the Railway Hotel. Shuah was expecting him, and was dressed and ready to go out. He helped her up into the high seat, took his place beside her, turned the horse and set off down the drive. Mrs Smith was hanging washing on the line at the side of the gatehouse, and Shuah waved gaily to her as they passed.

Murray left Shuah at Ivy Cott and went off on his own to fetch the old couple from the workhouse. Shuah made sure there was a good fire in the black-leaded grate, and the kettle was almost on the boil when they arrived. They walked in and gazed around, and at first they were so overcome they could not speak, but only cling to each other with tears streaming down their faces.

'It's wonderful! I can't believe it!' sobbed Mrs Platten. 'It was like a miracle when you first came to see us, up there. And now you've done this for us! Oh, my dear, how can we ever thank you?'

'You don't have to thank me,' Shuah assured them. 'This has given me more pleasure than anything I've ever done in my life.'

It had all been accomplished in just over two and a half weeks—a busy time, but full of joy for Shuah because Murray had spent so much time with her. He had stayed at the Railway Hotel, and had worked just as hard as she had done to find the cottage, furnish it and get it all ready. At the weekends he had returned to London—to Dorothy. But, day after day, Shuah had been with him, and she had closed her mind to what would happen when the task was completed.

'That was really satisfactory,' he remarked, as he drove her back to Colethorpe after the Plattens had been installed.

'I don't think I've ever seen two happier people,' she agreed.

Murray allowed the horse to walk at a leisurely pace. The road wound between beechwoods, glorious in their autumn colouring of russet and orange. 'How beautiful it is here,' she murmured, dreamily contented.

'This is the sort of scene I yearn for when I'm in Sarawak,' he said, and she understood exactly what he meant.

The clatter of horses' hooves came from behind, from another gig approaching at a spanking pace. Murray drew to the side of the road. Shuah glanced round and drew in her breath.

'It's grandpapa Sutherland!' she exclaimed.

He must have recognised her in that same instant, for as he came alongside, he shouted, 'Stop!' and reined in his own pair of horses that he was driving in tandem.

'What are you doing out here, Suzanne?' he called in his usual bombastic manner.

'We've been for a drive, Grandpapa,' Shuah said. With her eyes she pleaded with Murray to say no more.

'Good afternoon, sir,' Murray said. 'I'm now taking your grand-daughter back to Mead House.'

'Then I'll relieve you of that responsibility and take her home myself,' Mr Sutherland snapped. 'Come here, Suzanne.'

'No, Grandpapa...' Shuah began to protest, for she had no wish to leave Murray. But it was he who interrupted her, and she was dismayed to hear him agree with Mr Sutherland.

'Perhaps it would be a good idea, Suzanne,' he said and his voice was gentle. 'I'm a little late, and still have to return the gig, before catching my train.'

'You're going back to London today?' she asked, breathless with disappointment. 'It's only Wednesday.'

'I've done what I promised,' he said.

'When shall I see you again?' she asked.

'That I cannot say.' His mouth was set in a hard, tight line. She sat close beside him, but as she listened, it was as if he moved a mile away. 'You know that Dorothy and I are to be married on Saturday, and after that we return to Sarawak.'

Of course she knew the wedding was getting nearer with every day that passed, but she had not wanted to think about it, or about the difference it would make to her life.

'Don't sit there dithering, Suzanne!' snapped her grandfather. 'Think of your reputation! Driving about the countryside with a man who's about to be married!'

Shuah could only gaze at Murray in abject misery. 'You'll come back for me, won't you?'

'No, Suzanne. Your place is here.'

'Quite right, Masterson,' Mr Sutherland growled. 'And I'll thank you to remember that and keep away from my grand-daughter in future.'

Murray eyed him coldly. 'Your dislike of me is immaterial, sir. What is important is Suzanne's happiness. I brought her halfway round the world, and I'd like to be sure that you will look after her.'

'What impertinence!' blustered Mr Sutherland, his face reddening. But, fixed with the authoritative expression of Murray Masterson's face, he forced himself to answer, 'Of course I'll look after her well! She can have the best of everything from me. You have my word on it.'

'Good. I know her to be an exceptionally fine young lady and capable of making her own decisions. That gives me confidence that she should be able to make a good life here. As to my keeping away from her, I shall do that only as long as I believe it to be in her best interest.'

Shuah listened, and her emotions churned tumultuously, for even though his words praised her, they also distanced him from her. Mr Sutherland began to splutter, then thought better of it and clamped his mouth shut.

Murray turned to Shuah. He took hold of one of her hands, held it as if it was a precious object and gazed intently into her yes. 'Our fates were sealed long before we met, Shuah. Nothing can alter that. You have youth and beauty and spirit. Believe me, you'll come to find happiness here.'

'How can I, if you leave me?' Her eyes filled with tears, but she fought to hold them back.

His dark brown eyes seemed to burn deep into her soul. 'You must forget me, Shuah. It has to be goodbye.'

She shook her head in sad disbelief. How could she bear it? Did he really mean she would never see his beloved face again? His every feature was already indelibly imprinted on her mind and in her heart; his very being was a part of her.

He lifted her hand to his lips. 'The time has come for us to part. It is best that we do so now.'

She knew there was no way in which she could make him alter that decision. She set her mouth tightly and climbed down from her seat beside him, as dazed as if she had received a knock-out blow. Her grandfather reached down to help her up into his high two-wheeler, and immediately the horses sprang forward, leaving Murray's gig standing. She glanced back and saw that he was staring after her. She felt as if a gossamer thread of enormous strength joined her to him, and when they turned a corner, it was snapped. Murray was lost to her.

'I hope that's the last we'll see of him,' said her grandpapa. 'The sooner he's married and out of the country, the better for you. You'll be married yourself before long.'

'I don't want to marry Lord Barrington,' she said.

'Nonsense, Suzanne. Trust me. I know what's best for you. You've grown up in a foreign land, so you can't understand. It's practically arranged. I've put my cards on the table and given Barrington the full facts of the settlement I am prepared to make upon you. I've been generous. I don't mind telling you, Suzanne, I've set my heart on this marriage. I've no doubt he'll approach you very soon, and when he does, I expect you to give him a favourable response.'

She shook her head in silence. She felt trapped and dispirited. The shrill blast of the train whistle penetrated through the distance as they drove between the open gates of Mead House. She pictured Murray travelling away to London, to prepare for his wedding to Dorothy—and her heart was leaden.

Yet, next day, her spirits lifted slightly. It was not in her nature to give up, and somehow she would see Murray again. As the weather was unusually mild for October, she took her book and wandered out to a seat beside a south-facing wall in the rose garden. There were few blooms now, and the bushes had a desolate air, but it remained her favourite place in the garden. She had started reading *Oliver Twist*, a story that was especially real to her since she had discovered her Platten grandparents in the workhouse.

Suddenly the peace was shattered by a series of explosions, and exhaust-fumes drifted through the sere leaves of the beech hedge that shielded the garden from the front drive. Peter was driving up in his automobile. Her initial instinct was to dive into the jungle of Jerusalem artichokes that rampaged over the far end of the vegetable garden at the other side of the wall, but she stifled it, for that would solve nothing. With a sigh, she rose to her feet and walked calmly to the front of the house.

Peter was divesting himself of his goggles, leather cap and the heavy tweed coat that covered him from high at his neck almost to the ground. Gibson took them from him and produced a clothes-brush, which he flicked over his master to remove the dust of the journey. Peter combed back his ruffled hair, suddenly noticed Shuah watching him, and hurried towards her. 'Suzanne, just the lady I've come to see!'

'I was sitting in the rose-garden,' she said.

'Then let us return there.' He took hold of her elbow and steered her back through the hedge to the seat she had recently vacated. She sat down, keeping her body upright.

Peter remained standing. 'Suzanne, I'm sure you know why I'm here, so I won't beat about the bush. I've come to put my proposal to you formally—to ask you to marry me.' He spoke with aggressive confidence, sure of himself, looking down at her with a proprietorial air.

'Peter, I told you on the boat that I could never marry you. I hoped that you would believe me.'

'But why, Suzanne?' His voice was angry and his face reddened.

'Because I'm already married.'

His mouth dropped open in shock and bewilderment. 'You can't be!'

'I was married before I left Bartulu,' she said.

'Good grief! Does Masterson know about this?'

'Oh yes,' she said. 'He's my husband.'

'He can't be! I mean, he's getting married himself very soon. He's not a great friend of mine, but he's definitely one of the honourable kind. He wouldn't take another wife if he was already married.'

'Murray says that because it was not celebrated in the English way, our marriage doesn't count.'

'Good God!' ejaculated Peter. 'The utter cad! He was always rather "holier than thou" when it came to taking a native mistress. Do you really mean that after going through this wedding, he just abandoned you?'

'He told me before the ceremony that it would be in name only.'

'And has he—er...?'

'He has never come to my bed.' It hurt to admit it, but she had to be honest.

Peter gave a bawdy laugh. 'It won't be like that when you're married to me, Suzanne! And this native ceremony is obviously no real impediment. Masterson's never been your husband—or your lover.'

'According to his beliefs that may be so, but not according to mine. I made my vows in the longhouse, in the tradition of my people, before my adoptive father, who was headman. Those vows are sacred to me. I won't break them.'

'That's ridiculous! It's in the past. You're not an Iban—you're English. Does your grandfather know about this?'

'No. I know he won't accept it. He'll just brush it aside as of no consequence. That's what all the white men do—but it's not like that for me.'

'Your life in Sarawak is over, Suzanne. You're going to marry me. It's all been arranged. You can tell your grandfather I have proposed, and I'll come back for my final answer in a day or two, when you've come to your senses.'

He turned and stamped away out of the garden. A few minutes later she heard the motor start up. She closed her eyes, wearily, shutting out the memory of him standing there. At once it was Murray's face that sprang into her aroused imagination, and with it came the disturbing thought that in two days' time he was to marry Dorothy.

Her mind switched back to the eve of her wedding to him, far away in Bartulu. She recalled the merriment, the excitement, how the men had gone off hunting for monkeys and birds to provide special fare for the feast, and how the girls and the women had made and cooked piles of rice-cakes, and cut up pigs, and plucked and dressed a dozen fowls. How pretty the longhouse had looked after it had been cleaned and freshly decorated with palm leaves and flowers, and the fun and laughter that had accompanied the hard work.

She knew it would not be like that at 39 Elveden Crescent, but they must be making some preparations. She felt excluded, longed to be there, and desire to see Murray sprang sharply into her heart and would not be stifled. The mood was still festering within her when she joined her grandfather for dinner as usual. He was already seated at the table, and Barker was hovering behind his chair poised to serve the rich tomato soup.

'Any news for me?' asked Mr Sutherland, as she took her place.

'Lord Barrington proposed,' she replied.

'Good. I knew he would.' He did not ask what reply she had made. 'You shall have the greatest wedding in the whole country, my dear. I'll spare no expense; you'll be the bride of the year! Ah, it does my heart good to think about it. We'll make it quite soon. Strike while the iron's hot, that's my motto!'

He was so pleased that he neither noticed nor cared that she was rather quiet as they ate their meal. She scarcely listened to what he said, for there was no reality in his words. She had no intention of breaking her vows to Murray by marrying anyone else, and her own thoughts kept straying to London.

As her grandpapa reached for the brandy-bottle, she excused herself, saying she wished to have an early night. Her longing to see Murray again had become too powerful to resist. She ran to her room, but not to get ready for bed. She changed into her outdoor clothes, picked up her handbag, crept out of the house unobserved and hurried along the drive, making for the railway station.

She had a long wait on the station at Colethorpe, for trains were less frequent late at night. It was after one in the morning when she arrived in London, hailed a hansom cab, and instructed the driver to take her to Elveden Crescent. She stopped him at the end of the terrace and paid her fare, and as his horse clip-clopped away she walked slowly and cautiously towards No. 39. Gas-lamps in the street shone on the creamy stone, but no lights showed in any of the windows. That surprised her, for she had supposed, with the preparations for the wedding so soon, that there would have been some activity.

Listening, she could hear no sound from within. She walked to the foot of the steps that led to the elegant front door, but hesitated to knock. She moved a few paces sideways until she was beneath the window of the room she knew to be Murray's. It was half open, and she stood for some time looking up, hoping he would come to it, uncertain, now that she was here, what to do.

Suddenly she made up her mind. A thick-stemmed wistaria grew strongly up that wall, and she kicked off her shoes, rolled down her stockings and put them neatly into the shoes. Then she reached up and caught hold of a branch just above her head. She tested its strength, just as she would have done with a creeper on a tree in the jungle, then swung herself up, using her bare flexible toes to assist her. With nimble speed, making almost no sound, she climbed up to the window and glanced within. She could see a form on the bed, covered with a white counterpane, and knew by the dark hair on the pillow that it was Murray. Quietly she raised the window a few inches more until it was wide enough for her to slide under, and lowered herself to her knees on the floor of the room.

For a few seconds she crouched there, and knew by the soft sound of Murray's breathing that he was asleep. Quietly she stripped off her clothes, then with catlike stealth moved across the room and slipped into bed beside him. The spicy warm aroma of his body sent a delicious thrill though her. In all the months she had been married to Murray, this was the first time she had lain naked beside him, in his bed, in the peace and silence of the night, and the longing she felt for him was exquisite, with such a fragile delicacy that at first she stayed quite still, scarcely daring to breathe.

Time seemed to stand still for Shuah as she lay stretched out beside Murray, drinking in the joyous sensation of being with him, feeling the warmth emanating from him, listening to his gentle breathing. She was vitally aware of his nearness and never had she felt so sensuously attuned to another person. She lay close, yet did not touch him, and being in his bed, naked beneath the sheets, brought a wave of feeling so delicious that it seemed to thrill every inch of her skin, tingling along the whole length of her, from the top of her head high on the pillow to the tips of her toes pushed away to the foot of the bed.

For what seemed quite a long time she remained motionless, her body relaxed, although her mind was racing with wonder. She had no wish to disturb him, for she was not sure how he would react, and she delighted in the sensation of drowning in a deep well of sweet emotion simply because she was beside him.

A shaft of moonlight beamed into the room, as if a cloud had just rolled away, and in its golden light she saw Murray's dark ruffled hair. She raised herself on one elbow to gaze down, deliberating on each small part of him that was not covered by the sheets or buried deep in the pillow. In sleep he seemed more vulnerable, and she felt almost protective, happy to watch over him. A smile played around her lips as she looked at the boyish way his hair spilled over his broad, high forehead. She gazed affectionately at those thick eyebrows raggedly arching above his closed eyelids, with dark lashes sweeping down, almost to that small scar. Her love for him was so possessively tender that she ached to lean over and kiss it.

He stirred—almost as if she had put the thought into action. His mouth moved slightly, so she thought he would call out to her—then smiled fondly at her own absurdity, for he had no idea she was there. She could no longer resist touching him, and reached out to lift a lock of hair that had fallen forward. Her fingers were gentle, her touch too light to disturb him, but even so a slight shudder ran over his muscular shoulders, and he lifted himself a few inches and pushed the bedclothes back. She held her breath as he turned and flung out an arm. His hand dropped over her, hesitated momentarily, then curled round her, and she thrilled to his touch, unconscious though it was. Instinctively and lovingly she flexed her waist, arched her body and snuggled deep into the soft feather-bed, relishing the sensation of being held within his embrace.

Still he did not waken, but she was so close, lying rather higher in the bed than he was, and his breath wafted over her breasts, warm as a sweet summer breeze. Sensuously it caressed her nipples, awakening every primitive womanly instinct imbued within her body. It was almost unbearable to lie there, in her rightful place, at her husband's side, and yet be so fearful of awakening him, of shattering his dream.

Again his lips moved, and his arm drew her closer—and she could keep back from him no longer. She leaned over him and with lips as light as a butterfly's wing, she kissed first his forehead, then his cheek, delicately moving her mouth closer to his until her lips sipped at the nectar that moistened his. His arm tightened its grip. She clung to him and felt his body stiffen, as she lowered herself, bringing some of her weight down upon him. A moan escaped him. She stifled it with another kiss, and joy pulsed through her as unmistakably his lips responded to her. Then his hands started to caress her body, moving slowly, gently, up and down the line of her spine, sweeping over the curve of her buttocks, responding to their softness with a little extra pressure. A gasp escaped her as that exploring hand reached down and stroked the long line of her smooth thigh.

Every movement of his hands increased her pleasure and happiness, and she began to caress him in return, running her fingers from his face, down over his powerful chest. His skin was silken in some places, rougher in others, and her hands played along the full sweep of his body, fondling him, delighting in their exploration as they moved lower through the wiry hair that covered the slim softness of his belly and below into the thick mat of hair where his masculinity was so apparent. She nestled her face against his, and breathed his name.

'Murray! Oh, Murray...' All her longing was in her voice. He stirred, and she thought he must be aware of her.

'Shuah,' he murmured, his voice muffled by sleep.

'Yes, Murray. Oh, yes...'

Again she brought her lips down to his, and as they touched, he grasped her head and held it to him. He was really kissing her now; she was sure he must be fully awake, as the hunger in his mouth matched the desire that was consuming her. There was no denying the frenzied passion that flared between them. He rolled over, his body half-covering hers, and his hands resumed their caressing and exploring, sensually and with an increasing urgency that brooked no denial—even had she wanted to. She was utterly pliant, responding to each touch, clinging to him, gently swaying, wanting him with every fibre of her being.

'Shuah?' He said her name again, and there was a questioning note in his voice.

'Yes, Murray. I'm here.'

'Good God!' He sat up abruptly, pushed her away, and stared at her in utter disbelief. His mouth dropped open, only to be closed with a furious snap a moment later. 'I thought I was dreaming!' he exclaimed. 'How the hell did you get here?'

'I came on the train, Murray. And climbed in through the window.'

'You did what?' She knew perfectly well he had heard her.

'I wanted to be with you, Murray.'

He shook his head. 'Oh, Shuah, what am I to do with you? Don't you know what could have happened? Can't you understand what you do to a man, creeping into his bed in the middle of the night, just as if you were still living in the longhouse.'

His rejection made her so discouraged and angry that she said, 'I wish I was still living in the longhouse.'

'With Dioudi?'

'No, of course not.' She sighed. Why could she never make him understand? And why was he so unbending when it came to sex and love? It was as if he thought it was something unpleasant. She remembered all too clearly that he had been displeased when she had gone to his *bilek* that night in Bartulu. 'I wish you liked me—just a little, Murray,' she murmured.

'Of course I like you, Shuah,' he said, but it was a tight, gruff voice that sounded as if he did not really mean it, and his next words confirmed that belief. 'But by now you should have learned that nice English ladies don't do things like this.'

'Then I'm not nice and I'm not English!' she said, and her voice rose in defiance and frustration. Just a few moments ago, when he had been half-asleep, he had seemed to be about to make love to her, and now all that had changed and he was severely disapproving, as he so often seemed to be. She had been convinced she was pleasing him—but he was just as cross and critical as ever. 'You shouldn't have brought me here. I hate it!'

'It was you who begged me to take you away from Bartulu,' he reminded her coldly.

There was no consolation for her in that. It had not been so much that she wanted to leave the longhouse as that she wanted to be with him. It infuriated her that he had no idea how she felt, even after all this time. She jumped up from the bed and stared miserably down at him, unconcerned by her nakedness, with the window behind her and the moonlight outlining her tall slim figure with a golden glow.

There was a long silence, then he said hoarsely, 'For God's sake cover yourself!' He pulled the counterpane from the bed and thrust it towards her.

She ignored it, too furious to bother. 'I suppose you're worried about my reputation?' she hurled at him.

'Exactly!' he snapped. 'It's high time you learned to act with more propriety.'

'I've tried!' she screamed, with all the frustration that had been bottled inside her for so long. 'I've tried to do all the things you asked of me. I've learned English, I use polite language, I've stayed in Colethorpe for weeks and weeks . . . I almost always wear a hat, and still you're not pleased with me.'

'Poor child!'

'I'm not a child! That's what grandpapa Sutherland calls me, and he treats me as if I'm some sort of jungle creature. That's just what you think too, isn't it?'

'No, Suzanne. I think you've grown into a very lovely young English woman. But I didn't realise you were so unhappy.' He moved across the bed towards her, but she stepped back.

'I'm not Suzanne either,' she shouted. 'I'm Shuah. That's who I was when you found me and I can't keep pretending to be someone different! I don't want to be anyone different . . .'

A knock on the door startled her. It was followed immediately by Mrs Mortimer's voice. 'Who's in there?'

CHAPTER FIFTEEN

STARTLED, SHUAH spun round to face the door, then called out reassuringly, 'It's only me, Mrs Mortimer, I'm just having a chat with Murray.'

She picked up the counterpane and wrapped it sarong-style round herself. Murray leapt up and grabbed a dressing-gown from a chair beside the bed.

'Whatever's going on?' That was Dorothy's voice.

'Murray, are you in there?' Mr Masterson joined them.

'One minute,' Murray called. He was struggling into his dressing-gown.

'Open the door this instant!'

'It's not locked,' Murray said.

Shuah crossed the room and flung it wide. 'Hello,' she smiled. 'I've come back.'

Three startled, bewildered faces stared back at her. Mrs Mortimer's ashen complexion looked lined and drawn, her head festooned with a multitude of curling-papers. Mr Masterson was rubbing his hands through his hair in perplexity, tousling it into a white replica of Murray's. His thin form was hidden beneath a vol-uminous flannelette nightshirt, below which his ankles protruded white and bony, with his feet thrust into carpet slippers. But it was on Dorothy that Shuah's eyes lin-gered, noticing that she had pulled herself up to the fullest extent of her diminutive stature and that her customary serenity was disturbed enough to bring a flush of scarlet to her usually pale face. Her wealth of fair hair cascaded almost to her waist, rippling down her high-necked, long-sleeved nightgown, over which she had thrown a shawl of rich paisley colours.

Tension throbbed from the group; they were all shocked and flustered. Shuah was surprised at their attitude, and hastily began to explain. 'I'm sorry if I've woken you all...'

'Shuah!' Dorothy interrupted in a tight, frigid voice, 'What on earth are you doing in Murray's room?'

'It's perfectly all right, Dorothy,' Shuah assured her. 'I realise you didn't expect me, but I felt I had a right to attend your marriage ceremony. I know it will be different from the way it was when Murray and I were married...'

The mouths of the three people standing in the passage fell open to emit gasps of astonishment. Murray moved to the doorway behind her, and his voice rang out with authoritative clarity. 'It's all a misunderstanding.'

Dorothy looked at him with her eyebrows raised, then turned back immediately to stare at Shuah, her eyes narrowing into hard slits. 'What was that?' she asked with slow deliberation. 'Did you say—you're *married* to Murray?'

'Yes,' Shuah nodded emphatically. 'I was married to Murray the day before we left Bartulu. I'm his Number One wife,' she added proudly.

'Shuah!' Murray's voice barked out. 'You know that's not true.'

Dorothy pulled herself up another inch, remaining remarkably calm, only her heaving breast revealing the strain she was suffering. 'To see you both here, in this state...' Her eyes moved accusingly from Shuah, wrapped in the coverlet, to Murray in his dressing-gown, 'suggests that there must be some truth in the allegation. What was it you called yourself, Shuah?'

'Number One wife.'

Mrs Mortimer uttered a screech of horror. 'Oh, my goodness, it can't be true! What will the neighbours say! Oh, Dorothy—fetch my smelling-salts...'

'Don't fuss, Mother,' Dorothy said sharply. 'I'm trying to understand what this is all about. Now, Shuah, please tell me exactly what you mean.'

'When Murray found me at the longhouse, he thought I should come to England to try and find my relatives. But the tribe were worried about my safety,' Shuah said. 'They felt I should not leave the longhouse with a man I scarcely knew, so Murray agreed to marry me.'

'Is this true?' Dorothy's voice was a bewildered whisper, her face white with shock, as she turned towards Murray.

'No,' he said harshly, 'there's a lot more to it than that. I'll explain it all—but it will take a little time. I suggest we go downstairs, where we can sit comfortably, instead of trying to sort it out here on this draughty landing.'

Mrs Mortimer pointed accusingly at Shuah. 'I don't see how you can possibly explain the presence of this girl in your bedroom—and only the day before your wedding to Dorothy!' she cried, seeming to have forgotten her need for smelling-salts.

'It's all quite simple,' said Murray. He gestured in the direction of the stairs. 'If you'll be so good . . .'

'As you wish,' Dorothy said stiffly, and catching up the long full skirts of her nightgown, and with a haughty rustle of starched linen, she led the way down.

'I hope you have a good explanation, Murray,' said Mr Masterson. 'Because it certainly looks bad.'

Murray did not reply, but indicated that they should follow Dorothy.

Gallantly Mr Masterson offered his arm to Mrs Mortimer. 'Allow me to assist you.'

Mrs Mortimer clung to its frail support, and dabbed at her eyes with a tiny handkerchief, muttering with a bemused air, 'I don't know what the world is coming to, indeed I don't! Things like this didn't happen in my young days.'

Shuah was as bewildered as they were. She hardly knew what she had expected to happen, but she had no wish to upset the whole household as she obviously had, especially since these people had been so good to her.

'Please go down, Shuah.' Murray's face was calm, as if he was in complete control of the situation. He would explain, and all would be well again, she thought. With a wide sweep of his arm, he indicated that she should precede him, and wrapping the counterpane closely round her, she descended ahead of him. In the sitting-room they all seated themselves, with the exception of Murray, who took up a stance with his back to the fire-place, dusty with dead ashes.

'Whatever shall we do?' asked Mrs Mortimer. 'Oh, my poor girl, my poor girl! How could you do this to her, Murray Masterson?'

'I have done nothing dishonourable,' said Murray. 'Nothing that alters my position with regard to Dorothy. It's true that Shuah and I took part in a ceremony of marriage according to the tribal laws of the Ibans, but that doesn't mean we are married under the laws of England. Shuah knows that as well as I do, for I have told her so, many times...'

'I know the vows I made,' Shuah interrupted. 'For me, it was a promise of lifelong fidelity. I am your Number One wife.'

'I suppose it is quite normal for a man to have more than one wife in Bartulu?' Dorothy asked, her voice a little high-pitched, despite the effort she was making to keep her emotions under control.

'Certainly not!' replied Shuah, shocked by the suggestion. 'It's absolutely forbidden among the Ibans to have a second wife, and in my heart I believe that is the way it should be. But I am not a fool. I know that in different countries there are other customs, and that many men do take several wives. In fact, in Kuching, there was a Malay who had three wives, and...'

'Shuah!' Murray interrupted her sharply. 'That has nothing to do with this case.'

'On the contrary, I'm most interested,' said Dorothy, tight-lipped. 'Pray continue, Shuah. I am anxious to know how you expected our lives to—er—intertwine.'

'It seemed to work quite well for Subu and his wives,' Shuah said, for it seemed that Dorothy genuinely wished to know. 'They went everywhere together and they seemed to be quite happy, though of course the Number One wife was the most influential.'

'Indeed?' said Dorothy.

'Subu was not a Christian,' Murray said.

Dorothy ignored him and continued to address Shuah. 'Tell me more. I'm to be Number Two wife, I take it?'

'Well, my marriage to Murray took place several months ago,' Shuah agreed. She was glad that the truth was out at last. She could see that Dorothy was not happy about the situation, but probably she would be able to accept it, given a little more time, just as she herself had done.

'This is nonsense!' Murray exploded.

Mrs Mortimer emitted another small, shrill scream. 'My smelling-salts! I really must have my smelling-salts.'

With an exclamation of exasperated impatience, Dorothy stood up and walked across to the bureau.

Murray shifted his weight from one foot to the other, his lips drawn in a tight line of anger. 'Shuah!' he exploded. 'You're talking utter rubbish! I don't know where you got these extraordinary ideas. Dorothy, sit down and listen to me.'

'Certainly, Murray,' Dorothy said. She handed the green glass bottle to her mother, and resumed her seat. 'You have always told me there were some bizarre customs among the local people, and I must say I'm finding it quite fascinating.'

'Dorothy, I give you my word that nothing has transpired between Shuah and me of which I should be ashamed to tell you.' He threw back his head in a proud gesture, defying anyone to question his honour.

But Dorothy was not satisfied. 'Then why have you never mentioned this marriage before?'

'I decided not to, because I had no wish to cause you even a moment's unease, Dorothy. Since you have not yet lived in the east, I realised you might find it difficult to understand,' he explained slowly and clearly, speaking only to her. 'But I give you my word, as a gentleman, that ceremony was of no real consequence. I have consulted many eminent people, who all agree that an Iban tribal ceremony could not be binding on either of us—even if we wanted it to. And that I most certainly do not!'

Shuah drew in a deep breath. She bit her lip to hold back the tears that suddenly started into her eyes. She had felt rejected before, but never so positively as at that moment.

Deliberately Murray turned from her, walked over to Dorothy and stood before her. He lifted her hands and held them as he continued, 'Shuah and I are both as free as we were on the day we met. But you need not take my word on this, Dorothy. We'll go to your solicitor this morning as soon as his office opens, and put the question to him.'

Shuah could stand no more. Murray's back was towards her, his gaze fixed so intently on Dorothy that he did not not notice as she rose and moved silently to the door. The hurt of Murray's total rejection was so painful that she scarcely knew what she was doing. The one thing she knew for sure was that she should never have come back; she did not belong in this household. She felt ashamed that she had not realised what a burden she had become to Murray. The one certain thing was that she must go—go now, go quickly—and resign herself to never seeing him again. The decision spurred her on, up the stairs and along to his room. Her clothes lay in a heap on the floor where she had dropped them, and hastily she picked them up, threw the coverlet on the bed and dressed herself.

A few minutes later she crept down the stairs again. Voices came to her from the sitting-room, where they were still talking things over. Quietly she opened the front door, walked out into the early morning, hailed a passing cab and began to retrace her journey of the night before, catching an early train back. But she did not go straight to Colethorpe; she alighted at Merston station, for she felt a need for sympathetic company. Even though she had no intention of confiding her troubles to her grandparents, she knew that being with them would bring her some consolation.

'You look pale. Are you all right, Suzanne dear?' her grandmother asked anxiously.

'Perfectly,' she assured her, forcing a smile that seemed to reassure Mrs Platten. Her grandparents' pleasure at seeing her was warm and sincere as always, and it helped to lift her spirits. Soon she was sitting in the snug kitchen, drinking a freshly brewed cup of tea and biting into hot buttered toast. Archie lit his pipe and poked up the fire, and the atmosphere in the little room was one of peaceful contentment—but soon it was shattered.

The sound of horses approaching fast made Shuah look out of the window. She was startled to recognise the gig and its driver—it was grandpapa Sutherland. He reined in by the cottage gate. She guessed he had come to find her, but how did he know where she was?

Anxious that there should be no trouble for Archie or Suzanne, she hurried out of the cottage and over to where Mr Sutherland sat, holding his restive horses in check. 'Good morning, Grandpapa,' she greeted him.

'So, it's true!' he snarled. 'You've moved in with those leeches!' Momentarily stunned, she made no reply. 'I've heard all about it,' he went on. 'They've persuaded you to use your grandmother's money to set them up here. They're only using you for what they can get out of you. I suppose the workhouse wasn't good enough for them?'

'Did you know they were there?' she asked with surprise, for he had told her he neither knew nor cared where they were when she had questioned him earlier.

'I'd no idea. You can't expect me to know all the inmates! But I'm a governor, and this morning when I attended a meeting there was talk about an old couple who had been taken out and set up in a cottage by their grand-daughter. When I heard their name was Platten, it didn't take me long to put two and two together.'

'If you're a governor, you'll know how awful it is in there!'

'What do you expect? Paupers' Palaces, that's what they call the workhouses. Everything provided at the ratepayers' expense! We'd have all the working classes moving in if we made it more luxurious.'

'But they weren't even allowed to be together,' Shuah protested.

'Hmph! Many men are only too keen to get away from their nagging wives! Besides, it'd make extra expense to provide double rooms. Ha! Here they come. A fine fool they've made out of you—but perhaps it'll turn out for the best in the end.'

Shuah glanced over her shoulder and saw Archie coming out of the cottage with his wife leaning on his arm. They had seen and recognised Mr Sutherland and were bravely coming to face him, but Shuah was afraid that such a confrontation would be upsetting.

She turned to them. 'Grandpapa Sutherland has only come to fetch me,' she said, forcing a smile she was far from feeling.

'Quite right,' said Archie. The old couple continued to walk along the garden path in the direction of the gate.

'Good afternoon, Mr Sutherland,' said Mrs Platten.

His face grew so red that it became almost purple, and he spluttered instead of answering.

The old lady continued with determination, 'Now that we have this lovely grand-daughter to share, shouldn't we try to forget the past?'

'I never forget!' snapped Mr Sutherland. 'Just because she's been fool enough to help you—don't think you can wheedle your way through to me.'

Archie and his wife stopped, their faces clouded. 'I told you it wouldn't be no good,' said Archie. To Mr Sutherland he said, 'You don't change, do you?'

'I know what's right, and I stick to it—and I won't have my grand-daughter spending any more nights here.'

'She never has stayed overnight,' Mrs Platten said, then, turning to Shuah and clasping her in her arms, she added, 'But you'd be more than welcome if you wished to. You know that.'

'Yes, I know. I'll come and see you again soon.' She kissed them both.

'Hurry up, Suzanne,' Mr Sutherland called impatiently. 'Can't wait about here all day.'

Shuah walked with dignity out of the gate, and ignoring the hand he offered, stepped up into the gig to take her place beside him. She waved to Archie and Suzanne as they drove off. He whipped the horses into a gallop, and Shuah had to hold on as the gig rocked dangerously along the narrow roads. There was no chance to talk until he reined in as they approached the drive to Mead House, scattering the gravel as he drew the horses to a halt by the front door. A boy ran up to hold the animals' heads and lead them away to the stables.

'Go into my study,' Mr Sutherland ordered. He followed her in, closed the door, and crossed the room to stand behind his desk. At once he began his interrogation. 'If you didn't spend last night with them, where did you go?'

'To London. I wanted to be with Murray Masterson,' she said softly.

'My God! Are you totally devoid of sense, Suzanne? When you're engaged to Lord Barrington!'

'Murray Masterson is my husband, Grandpapa.'

'What!'

'We were married in Bartulu . . .' With a sigh she explained yet again about her wedding to Murray and the reason why, but she had no heart for her story. She knew

he would say the same as everyone else: that it was not
binding.

'Masterson is right. That was no marriage, and the
sooner you get that into your head, the better.'

'Yes, Grandpapa.'

He looked at her sharply. 'I hope you haven't told
Lord Barrington about this?'

'I did mention it.'

'Then you're a bigger fool than I thought! Just like
your parents—no common sense.' He paced across the
room and back. 'I'll arrange a meeting with Barrington
today; take my solicitor along, clear up once and for all
that there's no legal barrier to your marriage.' He paused
briefly. 'Suzanne, you're not to leave the house today,
is that understood?' He came close to her, his chin jutting
forward belligerently, his eyes glaring into hers. 'And
you'd better behave yourself and do as I say, or it'll be
the worse for you, my girl. Any more trouble, and out
you go. And don't think you can run to the Plattens,
either.'

She stood her ground. 'What do you mean,
Grandpapa?'

He spoke with careful deliberation. 'Did you know
that cottage they're living in belongs to the Barrington
estate?'

She was shocked. 'But I rented it from a Mr Barlow...'

'Right. Barlow is Barrington's agent. A word from
me could put an end to that tenancy double quick. So
if you want those old folk to settle in there for the rest
of their lives, you'd better be nice to Lord Barrington.'

He snapped his mouth shut, turned sharply and walked
out. Shuah stared after him. She felt trapped—alone—
there was no one to whom she could turn.

She did not see her grandfather again until dinner that
same evening. A cursory glance told her that he was in
an elated mood—and that boded ill for her.

'I've seen Barrington,' he announced triumphantly.
'He's in total agreement with me, that this native mar-

riage of yours is meaningless. It cost me a bit! Gave him a stronger bargaining position, but I let him know I'm prepared to be generous, and our meeting ended satisfactorily. Very satisfactorily indeed.'

She listened in silence. It seemed that the jaws of the trap were closing even more firmly around her. Murray's words drummed in her ears—he did not want her as his wife. She must be sensible and plan a future for herself without him, especially since the fate of her beloved grandparents hung on her decision.

'It's up to you, Suzanne,' Mr Sutherland said, with the confidence of knowing he held the whip hand. 'Do as I say, and you'll have a fine life ahead of you—just as Masterson predicted. Refuse, and the Plattens will be back in the workhouse within a week.'

Shuah squared her shoulders and lifted her head. She had no option but to agree. 'Very well, Grandpapa,' she said hollowly. 'I shall marry Lord Barrington.'

The next morning she wandered aimlessly around the house, trying to keep her mind from remembering that it was Murray and Dorothy's wedding day. She was not sure at what time it would take place. Perhaps they were making their vows even now, at this very moment! This time he would mean every word he uttered, and that thought tore savagely at her most tender feelings. The following day was no easier. The house seemed unbearable. She walked out into the garden, trying to calm her turbulent emotions and make herself think positively about her future. She wandered down the drive and along the road, ignoring the rumble of the wagons bringing yet more barley to her grandfather's maltings. Everywhere was pervaded by the sickly sweet smell of malt, as if the whole village lay under the deadening grey pall of his ownership.

Then another familiar sound reached her ears—the loud put-put-putter of the engine of Peter's motor, running quite smoothly for once. A moment later the bright yellow automobile rushed round the corner, scattering dust and the hens that had been scratching at the roadside, travelling at his usual mad speed.

He braked to a skidding standstill, and the dust from the road swirled thickly around him. With a broad grin, he leaned towards her. 'Good morning, Suzanne. I was on my way to call on you. Come for a drive.'

He spoke with a proprietorial air already, and she shrugged. 'Very well, Peter,' she agreed.

She climbed up into the open-sided vehicle. Gibson tucked the rug round her, and Peter handed her the veil to protect her from the dust and wind. Out in the country, he braked the car, and pulled it to the side of the road.

'Leave us, Gibson,' he commanded. The chauffeur climbed down from his rear seat, sauntered over to a field gate and stood with his back deliberately turned towards them, staring away into the distance. It occurred to Shuah that this must be something he had done before.

'Mr Sutherland came to see me yesterday,' Peter said.

She nodded, glad that he could not see her face through the veil.

'He says you're agreeable to the match.'

'Yes, Peter,' she replied steadily.

'I always knew I'd get you!' he chortled. 'Take that damned veil off.' When she made no move to obey, he reached across and unfastened it. With a lecherous expression, he pulled her into his arms and began kissing her. His mouth felt wet as it moved over hers possessively. Involuntarily she shrank back, but he only tightened his grip.

'It's no good your acting shy, Suzanne,' he said. 'You're mine now, although I could have had a dozen other girls! A title is a most saleable commodity when it comes to marriage—your grandpapa craved it quite obsessively. You know it's you I want, my beauty, but it didn't do any harm to let the old man think he was hooking me.'

As she suffered Peter's wandering hands, she dared not protest too strongly, for if she did, she had no doubt her grandparents would be condemned to spending the rest of their lives in the workhouse. She could not do that to them, and since Murray's positive rejection, she had little fight left. Yet still she pushed Peter away. 'We're not married yet!' she protested.

'All right, but we'll have the wedding soon. I've waited long enough.'

'Yes, Peter,' she said tonelessly.

He grinned. 'Just continue to be as submissive as that, and we'll get along splendidly.' He called over to the chauffeur. 'Gibson, crank her up.'

She readjusted her veil and Peter drove back to Mead House. He braked sharply, scattering the gravel, and, as if their arrival had been watched for, the house doors were flung open. Mr Sutherland emerged—and close behind him was Murray Masterson.

Shuah's heart turned a somersault, as it always did at the sight of him. Why was he here? What did he want? She tore the veil from her head, her eyes scanning his face anxiously.

Her grandfather was the first to speak 'Ah, Suzanne, my dear.' His voice had an unctuous tone that aroused her suspicions. 'Have you had a nice drive—with your fiancé?'

Shuah ignored him, her whole concentration upon Murray. 'Why have you come?'

'You left in such a hurry that I knew you were upset.' Her heart leapt with the hope that he cared, but that thought was stifled as he continued, 'I had to satisfy myself that all was well with you.' Then she knew it was only his sense of duty that had brought him here. That was why he was so good at his job, an excellent Resident, taking his work seriously.

'No cause for you to worry. She's in good hands, you can see that,' said her grandfather. 'Life's got a lot to offer the future Lady Barrington.'

She heard Murray's sharp intake of breath. His eyes narrowed.

'Suzanne's no longer your responsibility,' Peter said fiercely. 'She's going to marry *me*.'

'Let her speak for herself,' growled Murray.

'Certainly,' said Mr Sutherland. His eyes were fixed on Suzanne's face, making the threat underlying his seemingly open attitude very evident.

Murray strode across to the motor, and stood looking directly at her. She could have reached out a hand and touched his cheek, but clasped her fingers tightly to resist the temptation. He did not care about her. He had only come here to satisfy his sense of duty, so that he could honestly tell the folk back in Sarawak—in Kuching, and in Bartulu—that she was well and happy.

'Is it true that you're going to marry Barrington?' he asked. His voice was cold and expressionless, as if emphasising his indifference.

'Yes, Murray, I'm going to marry Lord Barrington,' she answered quietly.

'We've just been discussing the details of the wedding,' Peter announced, a note of triumph in his voice. 'Suzanne agrees that it should be soon. We'll send you an invitation. Will you still be in England in a month, Masterson?'

Murray ignored him. He stood for a long time, a strange fire smouldering in his eyes. She was mesmerized by his expression, longed to throw herself out of the car and into his arms, to bury her face against his broad chest—but she must not give way. She stiffened, clenched her knuckles until they gleamed white, and forced her features into calmness.

He nodded, as if he had reached some conclusion. 'I shan't attend your wedding, Suzanne,' he said, 'but I wish you every happiness.'

'Does that mean you'll be returning to Sarawak soon?'

He nodded.

'I hope Dorothy is all right. I'm sorry I caused such an upset.'

'Dorothy is well—and happy,' he said. He reached out and covered her hand with his. A shiver ran over her whole body, and she feared she had given her true feelings away, but he gave a wry smile, then gallantly raised her fingers to his lips. 'I must go, Suzanne, and truly this is goodbye. We may never meet again.'

He gave her no time to reply, made no gesture of farewell to the two men, but spun on his heel and marched away down the long drive towards the road. Desolately Shuah watched him go hurrying back to Dorothy, to his wife.

'I shan't be sorry to see the last of that fellow,' declared Lord Barrington.

'Come into the house,' Mr Sutherland invited. 'We'll open a bottle to celebrate.'

Peter flung off his coat and threw it to Gibson.

Shuah stepped down from the car and hurried into the house. She ran up the wide stairway to the privacy of her own room, threw herself on to her bed and wept uncontrollably.

Some time later, a maid came in with a message that her company was requested downstairs. 'Please tell my grandfather that I have a headache. I shall retire early,' she excused herself. Neither of the two men cared enough to enquire further.

She knew her decision to marry Lord Barrington was the right one, but that did not make it any easier to bear. She recalled the high hopes with which she set out from Bartulu with Murray Masterson. Would she have acted differently if she had known then that she would never be truly his wife? She pondered on that for quite a long time, then had to admit that since she loved him so much, she would have had no choice in the matter. She could never wish away the past months; that would be almost like wishing that he had never existed.

Now there was no turning back. She would never again go to Sarawak, for Peter hated the east. She could not keep her promise to return to Bartulu to visit those dear people who had cherished her throughout her childhood. Yet that ache was nothing compared with the agony that squeezed all joy from her—the loss of all contact with Murray. Always, before, she had felt some springing of hope, but now there was nothing but a black void.

It was not until two days later that she managed to pull herself together enough to walk over to Merston and call again at Ivy Cott. The warmth and love with which she was greeted made her all the more certain that she had been right in her decision. It would have been too terrible to snatch their last few years of happiness from these frail grandparents whom she had grown to love and respect.

'I was hoping you would come, Suzanne,' said Mrs Platten, as she poured out cups of tea. 'Archie and me—we've been quite overcome by all the kindness, both from you and Mr Masterson. Did you see him the other day?'

'Yes. He came to the Mead—just to say goodbye,' Suzanne said, and was thankful that she managed to keep her voice level.

'Ay. He promised he'd come and see us when he returned.'

He had not promised even that to her! She said, 'In five years' time.' It might as well be a lifetime.

'If we're spared. But we'll never forget his kindness. We couldn't believe it at first when he said the cottage now belonged to us. Did you know he'd bought the place for us, Suzanne?'

Shuah shook her head, quite bewildered, feeling that she must have heard wrongly. But her grandmama shuffled over to the sideboard, opened a drawer and took out a long envelope. 'These are the deeds,' she said, with pride.

Shuah looked at the document, written in excellent copperplate. It was a conveyance of the freehold of Ivy Cott from the estate of Lord Barrington to Archibald John and Suzanne Platten for the sum of £150, signed and witnessed. As she read, Shuah's mind was racing: if the cottage was theirs, no one could turn them out. Murray had safeguarded their future and they had no further need of her protection. Her head was spinning with the thought: there was now no need for her to marry Peter! It was as if brick walls that had closed around her had crashed apart, revealing the outside world again.

'It's all right, isn't it, Suzanne?' Her grandmama was watching her anxiously.

Shuah realised that she must look stunned, and hastened to assure her, 'It's wonderful! I'm so happy for you. You can live here in peace for the rest of your lives.'

She jumped up and hugged her grandmother, and her longing to see Murray overwhelmed her. She must go to him, tell him how grateful she was. She would take care not to act in such a way as to upset Dorothy, but she must see him just once more. She had to thank him.

Hastily she bade farewell to Suzanne and Archie, clasping each of them tightly in her arms and kissing them warmly. She could not explain the full extent of her joy, because they would be horrified to think that she had been prepared to sacrifice herself for their sakes. She had no time to think about her own future—her only concern was to tell Murray of the joy he had brought to her as well as to her grandparents. She hurried along the village street. There was no need to return to Colethorpe, and she walked to the station at Merston and caught the next train to London. How Murray and Dorothy would react when she turned up on their doorstep, she had no idea. She began to wonder about it when she was on the train, but then it was too late to turn back.

CHAPTER SIXTEEN

ELVEDEN CRESCENT looked just as it had when she had first arrived in England. Shuah hesitated on the top step, then slowly lifted her hand to the bell-pull. The sound jangled from within. She heard shuffling footsteps crossing the hall, and a moment later the door was opened and Kirsty was there.

'Well, I never did! Miss Shuah!' She looked distressed. 'You've just missed them. They set off for Tilbury only half an hour ago.'

'Going back to Sarawak?' Shuah breathed.

'Sailing this afternoon. On the *Ellen Waters*,' said Kirsty.

She was too late! She felt desolate.

Kirsty said, 'If you hurried, you might catch 'em before she sails.'

Hope sprang up again. 'Could I?'

'It's worth a try,' Kirsty encouraged her. She hailed a passing hackney carriage, bundled Shuah inside, and told the driver, 'Quick as you can! The young lady's got a boat to catch.'

The cabby took her to within a short distance of the dock where the *Ellen Waters* was berthed, bustling with dockers and crewmen, passengers and their friends. Shuah gazed around, but could not see Murray or Dorothy or their respective parents. Probably they were already on board. She walked up the gangway and stood on the deck, feeling lost and alone. If only she could go back to Sarawak! She hugged her tweed cape closely round her shoulders, shivering in the cold wind, and the longing became unbearable.

'Visitors ashore!' came the call.

Suddenly she caught sight of Mr Masterson's white head among the crowd, and there was Murray beside him, and Mrs Mortimer dabbing her eyes. She must be sad at parting from her daughter for so long.

'Going ashore, miss?' asked a member of the crew.

'No, I'm sailing,' Shuah said boldly.

He passed on, but his question had scared her. She had no ticket, no right to be there, but she was determined to remain on board. Passengers crowded the rails and at the dockside, shouting farewells to family and friends. Shuah walked to the other side of the ship, where it was quiet, seeking somewhere to hide. She examined one of the lifeboats that hung above the deck—with her agility, it would not be difficult to get into it. Making sure she was unobserved, she removed her shoes and stockings and pushed them up into the boat. She waited as a couple of crewmen sauntered by, and smiled at them innocently when they nodded in her direction. As soon as they had moved on, she tucked up her skirts, leapt up and caught hold of the boat. In seconds she had scrambled up and slipped beneath the tarpaulin covering.

She heard cheers as the ship slid away from the dock. The chugging of the engines increased, the siren boomed. Shuah breathed a sigh, and curled up in the bottom of the lifeboat. She was on her way back to Sarawak!

When she awoke, it was dark. She peeped from beneath the tarpaulin, to see the deck fitfully lit by electric lights. It seemed to be deserted; probably the passengers were at dinner. She wondered wistfully if that was where Murray and Dorothy were, and then pushed that thought aside because she needed to wash and tidy herself. She slid from beneath the cover, but as she dropped lightly to the deck, she heard a startled exclamation.

'Hey, what are you up to?'

A sailor was running towards her. It was the same man who had questioned her suspiciously before they sailed. Shuah picked up her skirts, and fled.

'Stop!' the man shouted.

Shuah ran on, for she must not be caught. They would send her back to England—put her in prison—she would never see Murray again! The sailor was catching up on her. Terrified thoughts charged through her brain. People were coming up the companionway, and she dodged round them. The sailor chasing her had to slow down— she gained a little ground.

He shouted, 'Stop! Stop—stowaway!'

Another group of passengers were coming along the deck, and she darted to the rail and looked down at the cold dark waves. The thought flashed into her highly-strung mind that the Ibans had saved her from the sea. If there was no other way, she would give herself back to the waters. Perhaps that should have been her fate. She was beginning to clamber up the rail when suddenly she was seized in a vice-like clamp by a pair of strong arms.

'Let me go!' she screamed, and kicked.

'No, Shuah.'

It was a vibrant voice that she knew well! 'Murray!' she murmured and immediately relaxed. She released her hold and allowed him to pull her back on to the deck.

'She's a stowaway, sir,' said the sailor who had chased her. 'I'll take her.'

'No,' said Murray. 'I know this lady. You may leave her with me.'

'Can't do that, sir. I'll have to report her to the Captain.'

'You may tell the Captain I'll take full responsibility for her.' The voices were unreal, they sounded distant.

'I'm not sure...' The sailor objected.

'But I am. Masterson's the name, and you have my word that the young lady will cause no harm.'

Impressed by the authority in that voice, the sailor saluted sharply. 'Very good, sir.' He marched away immediately.

Murray swung her round to face him. 'Now, for God's sake, Shuah,' he barked, 'what's this about your being a stowaway?'

'I want to go back to Sarawak, Murray,' she pleaded. 'I can't bear to stay in England alone!'

'But you wouldn't be alone—you're going to marry Barrington. You told me so yourself.'

'I know. I didn't know what else to do. Grandpapa Sutherland said he'd have the Plattens thrown out of Ivy Cott, and sent back to the workhouse if I refused.'

'The brute! I feared he might try and put pressure on you. That was why I negotiated anonymously to buy the place. But I never expected he'd be so ruthless!'

'Oh, Murray, it was so wonderful of you! When they told me the wonderful thing you'd done, I rushed to London to thank you. Then Kirsty said you were sailing, and she pushed me into a cab.' The words tumbled out because Shuah wanted so desperately for him to understand. 'I know now that Dorothy will never accept me, and that you don't want me as a wife, but I promise I won't be any trouble to you.'

'So you really are a stowaway! Oh, Shuah! What shall I do with you?'

But suddenly she saw that laughter lines crinkled the corners of his brown eyes, and there was such a warmth of expression in them that her heart nearly stopped beating. 'I've been hiding in a lifeboat,' she confessed. 'I'm so sorry. I didn't intend to upset things for you and Dorothy.'

'Dorothy's not here.'

She stared at him, unable to believe what she had heard. 'Why? Where is she?'

'She broke off our engagement.' He gave a wry laugh. 'Finding you in my room that night was the last straw. We talked and talked after you left, and I realised that Dorothy was marrying me only because she felt she couldn't let me down.'

A wicked gleam of hope sprang into her heart, and it refused to be extinguished even though she scolded herself for it, because she feared that he might still be sad for his loss.

'She was determined to keep her word to me,' Murray continued. 'Just as I was to her—even though, while I'd been away, she had fallen in love with Matthew Percival. They are to be married next month. That was what I came to Colethorpe to tell you.'

'Just that?' she questioned breathlessly.

'No—I hoped...' he broke off. 'I felt desperate when you said you were going to marry Barrington. I wouldn't have believed it if you hadn't told me yourself!'

'I never wanted to. You must believe that, Murray.'

'You sounded very convincing. I decided to cut my leave short and go out east again immediately. Oh, Shuah!'

His arms had been round her while they talked, and now he tightened their grip, and with joy springing into her heart she reached up and clung to him. 'So—now you're free,' she murmured. 'Could you try to love me—just a little?'

His clasp tightened. 'Try? Oh my darling—if you only knew how hard it's been for me to keep away from you! Shuah!'

He called her name as if it was wrenched from deep inside his heart, and his lips sought and found hers and closed over them in a kiss that was wondrously tender. And when he drew back to allow his eyes to rove over her face, she gazed into them to read an expression of delight that matched her own.

'Murray, my love,' she whispered.

Then all that gentlemanly courteousness was abandoned as passion flared. His mouth closed over hers eagerly, possessively demanding, ruthlessly pillaging. In joyous submission she clung to him. A couple of passengers passed close to them, coughed and laughed, intruding on their togetherness. Murray raised his head, and smiled, still holding her close, without taking his eyes from her. 'You can't believe how happy I am!' he exclaimed.

She looked earnestly into his face. 'And you really mean you're willing to accept me as your Number One wife?'

'No, Shuah.' His tone was solemn. Her face clouded. Then he whispered with his lips against her ear, 'My one and only wife—for ever and ever!'

She gave a little moan of pleasure. He kept his arm round her waist, as if he dared not let her go, as he escorted her down the companion and along to his cabin. The moment they were inside, he swung her round to face him. With mirrored movements they drew together, their arms closing round each other, clinging together. Their kisses linked them, enflaming passions long suppressed.

'My dearest—sweetest—I love you so much,' he murmured. 'My whole world died when you said you were going to marry Barrington. I couldn't bear it—I thought I'd never see you again!'

'I thought that too,' she smiled. 'It's a miracle we found each other.'

'I love you so much. I've kept you at arm's length too long...' He broke off, his sounded voice husky.

'Far too long,' she agreed with flagrant immodesty, pressing her body close to his, and twining her fingers through his dark hair.

'Tomorrow I'll see the Captain about you,' he murmured, with his lips close to hers. 'But it's too late to do that now.'

'Much too late!' she said firmly, reaching up to kiss him again.

He began to unbutton her blouse, and his fingers trembled, just as they had done that very first night after their wedding in Bartulu, when he had unfastened the rattan corselet round her waist.

This time he did not retire to the far corner of the cabin, but continued to unfasten and remove all her clothes until she was lying quite naked on his bunk, and unashamedly she delighted in the caresses his eyes poured over her.

'How beautiful you are!' he murmured throatily.

She smiled with tender pleasure, delighted to please him. He dropped to his knees beside the bunk and kissed her again, his lips lingering on hers, awakening in her a wondrous flowing sensation. Then deliberately, taking his time, lingering over each movement, he allowed his mouth to rove down her throat to her breasts, awakening in her such an infinity of loving that she felt she must drown in its depth. The sensations he aroused were so intense that she was scarcely aware that, without lifting his face from her body, he had thrown off his own clothes. Then, as naked as she, he raised himself on to the bed. She had thought him magnificent when she first saw him. Nothing that had happened in the intervening months had changed that opinion—now the cabin became the most beautiful place in all the world, because of their shared loving.

She woke once or twice in the night, scarcely able to believe that she was lying in his arms, with the glow of their lovemaking still so exquisitely real that it brought a smile to her lips. The throb of the engines and the slight roll of the ship confirmed with absolute certainty that she was not dreaming. Truly she was here, and they were travelling together—slowly, back to Sarawak.

Daylight penetrated the porthole, and she propped herself up on one elbow and leaned over to gaze at his sleeping face, for he was so pleasing to her that she could never have enough of looking at him. As if he sensed that he was being watched, his eyes flickered open. He smiled, and her contentment deepened. He stretched with panther-like strength, raising his arms above his head, then reached out to pull her down, and with love fresh and new between them, the lightest touch of their naked bodies was enough to rekindle the flame of desire.

Much later, as he lay back, relaxed and smiling, she rolled on to her side and ran a possessive finger down his face. She touched the scar beside his eye.

'How did you get that?' she asked.

'From a parang wielded by a Dayak pirate,' he murmured drowsily.

'You could have lost your sight.' She bent her head to kiss the blemish.

'I could have lost more than that! That fellow had designs on my head as a decoration for his longhouse, but I thought it looked better where it was, on my neck.'

A shudder ran over her. She placed a finger on his lips. 'Don't joke—I can't bear to think of it!'

'It was a long time ago, Shuah. Soon after I arrived. I was pretty green, but alert enough to see him in time. I side-stepped, and dodged the worst of the blow. The Resident cobbled it together and it healed pretty quickly. I was lucky.'

'Was it in Simgga?'

'Yes. One of the chiefs had stirred up several villages with false information that we were about to destroy their settlements. They thought we planned to clear the ground to extend the rubber plantations. Not surprisingly, that made them so angry that they attacked the Fort. We'd been warned by one of the loyal *tuai rumahs*, so we were ready for them. It was a near thing, but we managed to overpower them, and what was more important, convince them that the rubber plantations were not to be anywhere near the villages.' He leapt up from the bed. 'But enough of my lurid past; we've got the present to think about. Breakfast, and then I'm going to see the Captain. I've still got to explain your presence, and ask him to marry us, in the Anglican way.'

'If that's what you want, Murray,' she said. For her, another ceremony would be quite superfluous, but she was happy to comply if it pleased him and made him feel she was more positively his wife. She picked up her blouse from the floor, where she had flung it aside, and tried to shake out the creases. 'I didn't bring any spare clothes,' she wailed.

'You'll never look more lovely than you did last night,' Murray declared, pulling her into his arms. 'We'll buy you a whole new wardrobe at the first port we put into.'

He had no difficulty in persuading the Captain to marry them that afternoon, with a couple of the passengers acting as witnesses. Murray slipped his signet ring on the third finger of her left hand as the Captain pronounced them man and wife. Shuah thought it rather a plain ceremony compared with the noisy communal festivities of their first wedding in Bartulu, but she did not complain.

Inevitably the news quickly spread around the ship, and once again they found themselves the centre of attention. Shuah's story had fascinated people before, and now it was coupled to the romance of her marriage to the charming and handsome Resident Officer who had found her and taken her to England. The Captain had them moved into a larger cabin, and every day of the six-week voyage was a joy, beginning with a walk round the deck in the silver dawn. The days grew ever warmer, and with dancing in the evenings, and nights lying in her husband's arms, Shuah felt her happiness was complete.

In the bustle of Singapore, her senses were stirred by the familiar aromas of the east, of spices and heat and dust, where the blazing sun made an oven of every alley. Again they stayed at Raffles Hotel, ate in the tiffin-room, met other men and their memsahibs and danced in the marble-floored ballroom. In the humidity of night, after making love, they lay together beneath the mosquito netting and allowed the breath from the fans to cool their bodies.

It was exciting when, after four days on the Straits steamship, they crossed the bar and entered the Sarawak

River, and Shuah saw again the banks lined with nipa palms and casuarina trees, and the little brown children played in the water, with their sarong-sheathed mothers keeping careful watch. Then the chop-houses and godowns came in sight as they sailed into Kuching.

'Look,' Shuah pointed. 'There's the Astana. And people—someone's waving!'

'It's the Raja—and the Crossleys—and Mrs Bell and her husband!' Murray said as he recognised them.

'I was so nervous when you first took me up that path to meet them,' Shuah recalled with a light laugh.

Murray put his arm round her shoulders and hugged her. 'You'll never know how hard it was for me to leave you there!' he confessed. 'I longed to claim you as my wife, and I thought I'd never have that right.' He looked at her seriously. 'I've never been so happy in all my life, Shuah. I'd kiss you—only everyone's watching!'

'You're kissing me with your eyes,' she teased him. 'So everyone will know how you feel, anyway.'

'I don't mind about that—I'm willing to proclaim my love from the mountain-tops!' he said. 'But the real meaning of my feelings for you can be expressed only when we're alone.'

'You have certainly left me in no doubt about it.' Shuah smiled contentedly.

They stepped into the proa and were paddled ashore. As they walked up the low green hill amid the sweet perfume of exotic flowers, Mrs Crossley and Mrs Bell began to run excitedly towards them. The ladies held their sola topis on with one hand and lifted the skirts of their long white gowns with the other, and called out, 'Welcome to Kuching, Shuah! Welcome back!'

How had she ever thought there was anything forbidding about them? They each hugged and kissed her, and with their arms round her waist escorted her up to the bungalow. The Raja stood on the veranda, pulling at his white moustache, his glass eye glittering wickedly, but he too put his arms round Shuah and kissed her.

'Ha! So you persuaded that fool to make you his wife, after all? Don't know why you couldn't have accepted your fate much earlier, Masterson. It would have saved a deal of trouble!'

'It certainly would,' agreed Murray with a broad grin.

For four happy days they stayed in Kuching, and Shuah spent most of them talking to Mrs Crossley and Mrs Bell, who were avid for every scrap of news from England. The Raja lent them his yacht for the final stage of their long journey to Simgga.

'It's wonderful to have you back!' Harry Lumsden greeted her, with his usual broad grin. 'I wasn't really looking forward to having a strange memsahib around here—never know how a white woman'll fit in. But it's all familiar to you, isn't it?'

'Yes,' Shuah agreed. 'And I'm lucky to have old friends to welcome me.'

Murray shook hands with his two officers. 'Any problems?' he asked.

'No more than usual,' Harry grinned.

'Have you heard any news from Bartulu?' Shuah asked.

'All's quiet up there, as far as I know,' George told her.

'Will you be visiting the village soon, Murray?' she asked.

'Probably next month. I suppose you'd like to come with me?'

'Oh, yes!'

They went in the Resident's proa up-river from Simgga, and stayed overnight in other longhouses, making détours for Murray to meet several Iban chiefs. News of their coming was carried through the jungle ahead of them and everywhere there was a warm welcome, but none so enthusiastic as when they stepped on to the planked landing-stage at Bartulu.

Sabat was there, his brown tattooed arms held out, and she rushed into his embrace. 'You look well—and happy, Shuah,' he said, standing back and surveying with shrewd eyes, taking in her European dress. 'I've thought about you very often. I was not sure how things would work out for you in that distant land. But now I see you, I'm content.'

'I'm very happy, Father,' she assured him.

Uteh, her grandmother, stood just behind Sabat and now stepped forward. She ran experienced eyes over Shuah, and nodded with satisfaction.

'You're with child, I see. That's good, my dear!'

Shuah nodded. It was so early in her pregnancy that she had not been absolutely sure herself, but Uteh's words dispelled all doubt. She glanced at Murray, who lifted his dark shaggy eyebrows, and a smile broke over his face. Then she was surrounded by laughing black-haired girls, tattooed warriors in gaily patterned loin-cloths, and children whose lithe dark-skinned bodies gleamed as they splashed happily in and out of the river. Only one familiar face was missing.

'Where's Dioudi?' asked Shuah.

'He left us,' said Sabat. 'He married a daughter of an up-river longhouse and has gone to live with them. Here is Banu, who has taken his place as our witch-doctor.' He drew forward a young man wearing the hornbill headgear of his office, with a necklace of animal teeth, and a wealth of bracelets and armlets. Shuah reached out and touched his fingertips with her own, and then they all went into the longhouse, which had been freshly decorated in honour of their coming and where delicious smells of cooking wafted up from the fires beneath. There would be a magnificent feast that night—but first they would eat a little food and drink *tuak*, then bathe in the pool.

Shuah sat cross-legged on the rattan mat between Murray and Sabat, and told him about the wonderful things in England, making him laugh with a colourful account of all the hats she had worn.

'Oh, it's good to see you again, Daughter,' Sabat said.

'And good for me to be here, Father,' she agreed readily. Then, more seriously she asked, 'Where did I get my name? Why did you call me Shuah?'

'It was what you called yourself,' said Sabat in some surprise.

'But my name is Suzanne,' she said.

Sabat shook his head. 'I've never heard that before.'

'Perhaps you called yourself Suzie,' said Murray.

Sabat nodded vigorously. 'That's right—"Shuah". That was what you said.' He beamed. 'Is it not the same?'

'Near enough,' she agreed, laughing. Then she stood up. 'How about that bathe?'

In the *bilek* that had been prepared for them, she changed into one of her sarongs, tying it in the native way round her waist, leaving her breasts bare. She glanced at Murray. 'It's all right while we're here, isn't it?'

He gazed at her, and desire sprang into his eyes. 'Oh, Shuah, how beautiful you are! Yes, stay like that while we're here. I knew when I took you away from this life that it would change you.'

'I'm not changed underneath,' she murmured. 'There's a part of me that's still primitive—that thrills to see you look at me like that. That is how I was when I first saw you, when I fell in love with you...'

'And this is how I'll always remember you, Shuah,' he whispered, with his lips brushing her cheek.

'We must go for our bathe,' she laughed, twisting teasingly away from his arms, then catching hold of his hands, pulled him after her towards the door.

'Wait until I get you in our *bilek* tonight!' he threatened.

And her delighted anticipation matched his.

Hello!

As a reader, you may not have thought about writing a book yourself, but if you have, and you have a particular interest in history, then now is your chance.

We are specifically looking for new writers to join our established team of authors who write Masquerade Historical Romances. Guidelines are available for this list, and we would be happy to send a copy to you.

Please mark the outside of your envelope 'Masquerade' to help speed our response, and we would be most grateful if you could include a stamped self-addressed envelope, size approximately $9\frac{1}{4}'' \times 4\frac{3}{4}''$, sent to the address below

We look forward to hearing from you.

Editorial Department
Mills & Boon Limited
Eton House,
18-24 Paradise Road,
Richmond, Surrey,
TW9 1SR.

THE POWER, THE PASSION, AND THE PAIN.

EMPIRE – *Elaine Bissell* _____ £2.95
Sweeping from the 1920s to modern day, this is the unforgettable saga of Nan Mead. By building an empire of wealth and power she had triumphed in a man's world – yet to win the man she loves, she would sacrifice it all.

FOR RICHER OR POORER – *Ruth Alana Smith* _____ £2.50
Another compelling, witty novel by the best-selling author of 'After Midnight'. Dazzling socialite, Britt Hutton is drawn to wealthy oil tycoon, Clay Cole. Appearances, though, are not what they seem.

SOUTHERN NIGHTS – *Barbara Kaye* _____ £2.25
A tender romance of the Deep South, spanning the wider horizons of New York City. Shannon Parelli tragically loses her husband but when she finds a new lover, the path of true love does not run smooth.

These three new titles will be out in bookshops from December 1988.

W❂RLDWIDE

Available from Boots, Martins, John Menzies, WH Smith, Woolworths and other paperback stockists.